Patsy Pridgen

Ms. Dee Ann
MEETS MURDER

Ms. Dee Ann

MEETS MURDER

A Novel By

PATSY PRIDGEN

Columbus, Ohio

This is a work of fiction. Narrow Creek and its inhabitants exist only in the author's imagination (and maybe yours), and any resemblance to actual persons, living or dead, is entirely coincidental and beyond the intent of the author.

Ms. Dee Ann Meets Murder

Published by Gatekeeper Press
2167 Stringtown Rd, Suite 109
Columbus, OH 43123-2989
www.GatekeeperPress.com

ISBN (hardcover): 9781642378238
ISBN (paperback): 9781642376890
eISBN: 9781642378245

For my husband, Al Pridgen Jr., who's an
even better man than Joe Bulluck

Who can find a virtuous woman?
For her price is far above rubies.
The heart of her husband doth safely trust in
her, so that he shall have no need of spoil.
She will do him good and not evil all the days of her life.

—Proverbs 31: 10-12

"I have yet to hear a man ask for advice on
how to combine marriage and a career."

—Gloria Steinem

Chapter 1

I stared out the passenger window of my father-in-law's brand new 1979 Chevrolet pick-up to avoid talking to Joe. Behind me, I could hear the edges of nylon tarp flapping in the wind. Underneath that tarp was a good portion of what we owned, piled high in the truck bed, stacked precariously with a small trough left in the middle so Joe could see out the rearview mirror.

Occasionally, I turned my head to peek at Heather in her infant seat between Joe and me, lulled to sleep by the engine's drone, her delicate mouth puckered, faintly nursing. Having this baby had turned my world upside down, but I felt a surge of love each time I glimpsed her wispy blonde hair and pink chubby cheeks.

Joe was looking straight ahead at the road with his hands on the steering wheel at ten o'clock and two o'clock, just like we were taught way back in driver's education in high school. He wasn't paying me the least bit of attention.

"Do you want to stop at the 7-Eleven up ahead for a Dr. Pepper, Dee Ann?"

Maybe he had been thinking about me, a little bit anyway.

"No, I'm fine. Aren't we almost there?" I sounded small and shaky, not like my usual confident self at all.

"Not much longer. I just thought you might be thirsty."

We'd been on the road a good two hours according to my wristwatch. During that time, I'd noticed the homes getting farther and farther apart. Small brick ranches with sagging carports and aging farmhouses with peeling paint. Mobile homes, single-wide and double-wide. We'd been through a couple of one-stoplight towns, sad little places, each with a run-down five and dime and an old Colonial Store.

Oh, I was feeling a lot of things, but thirsty wasn't one of them. Why had I ever agreed to move?

I thought about the cardboard boxes of linens, dishes, and clothes that Joe and his dad had heaved onto the back of the truck early that morning. "Why in the world did Dee Ann get such big boxes and then pack them so full?" I'd heard Joe's dad complain. "They're so doggone heavy I can hardly pick them up."

Somehow I felt better knowing that Joe and his dad had to strain to lift those boxes. Being miserable myself, I wanted somebody else to be miserable too. I admit I can be mean like that.

Nope, I didn't care how heavy those boxes were. I wasn't going to lift a thing. After all, I had Heather to tend to. Besides that, I carried only one hundred and ten pounds on my five-foot, six-inch frame, even three months after having a baby, and a skinny girl like me couldn't be expected to pick up heavy stuff.

Those boxes would soon join some hand-me-down furniture and an old Toyota Corolla that Joe and his dad had moved earlier in the week. We'd been married only sixteen months, since December 14, 1977, so Joe and I were newlywed poor. There's no disgrace in that. Everybody starts out that way, at least everybody I've ever known, even people with college educations like Joe and me.

Joe's mother says it's good to be poor when you first get married. She says it makes you stronger as a couple. I don't know how worrying about paying the rent makes for a happier marriage, but I didn't tell her that. It would've been disrespectful to openly disagree.

We were young-people poor, though, no doubt about it. I hadn't worked since college, there being an oversupply of high school English teachers when I finished my Master's in Education. But Joe found a job at a finance company after graduation, so we got married anyway. And then, surprise, surprise! Before I could land anything full-time, I was expecting a baby and learned nobody wants to hire a woman who's soon going on maternity leave.

So making a living had fallen entirely on Joe, but our parents said he was the man of the house after all and should take care of earning the money. When he heard about an opening for a collector at Narrow Creek Community Bank, a position that paid slightly more than he was making, he applied. His dad put in a good word with somebody who knew somebody at the bank, so Joe probably had an advantage in the interview.

Of course, Joe's a good hire for anybody. He has a cheerful personality and an easy way with people. He's nice looking too, if I do say so myself, and it never hurts to be an attractive person when you're dealing with the public. I'd say his blue eyes and ruddy complexion are his best features. And his sunny smile.

Joe's position at the bank was entry-level so our money worries were far from over, but Joe said there was more opportunity in being a banker. I think he liked the idea of wearing a dark suit and sitting behind a big mahogany desk.

When I told him that, though, he just laughed. "I won't be sitting behind that desk when I have to go out and call on people past due on their payments. But I'll sure look good in my suit when I put up and take down the American flag in front of the bank every day. That's also part of my job as the new man." I decided Joe wouldn't be getting too proud on me any time soon. Despite our college degrees, I wanted us to stay humble and not give our families a chance to say we'd gotten above our raising.

There was certainly no way anyone could accuse Joe and me of being uppity by moving to Narrow Creek, North Carolina. Joe and I had grown up near Greenville, a university town of thirty thousand people. Narrow Creek had five thousand souls. I'd heard there wasn't even a K-Mart there.

Whenever I'd questioned moving to such a small town in an isolated part of the state, Joe had given me the same little pep talk in his unruffled manner of speaking: "Narrow Creek's not so bad, Dee Ann. I'm sure you'll find something to do there. I bet you'll meet a lot of friendly people, and before long it'll feel like home."

Home, indeed! I suspected Joe just liked the hunting and fishing opportunities provided by all that rural area surrounding the town, and I'd told him so.

"I don't deny that I'm excited about the outdoor life there," he'd admitted. "Do you know we'll be only a few miles from two state parks? I've been told there's a lot of duck hunting in the area too. I've never been duck hunting."

Evidently Joe Bulluck didn't mind leaving our hometown one bit if doing so gave him a chance to shoot a duck. It didn't seem to faze him that I'd have nothing to do in a sleepy little town like Narrow Creek while he was out pretending to be the Great White Hunter.

To win me over, he'd promised we wouldn't have to live there forever. "Probably just a couple of years," he kept saying, "and then I'll get a promotion and be transferred, maybe to a larger town closer to home."

"For whither thou goest, I will go; and where thou lodgest, I will lodge," I finally told myself, quoting Ruth from the Old Testament. Ruth, a young widow, stays with her mother-in-law Naomi, but that verse can also apply to wives who are asked to follow husbands who move for job promotions. Especially wives who are new mothers and don't have jobs themselves.

But I admit that I'm a lot more self-centered than Ruth. I don't think Ruth found fault with her new home, and she probably didn't cry about it either. It has always been my observation that it's hard for real people to be as good as the role models in the Bible.

I cranked down my window a bit to let in some of the pleasant April air, thinking a whiff of spring would cheer me up. No sooner had my hand left the window handle than I heard an awful thud. I whipped my head around, peered out the back window of the truck, and was shocked by what I saw: Heather's white bassinet on its side in the middle of the road.

"Stop, Joe! The baby's bed fell off!"

Joe's eyes widened as if I had startled him out of a daydream about last year's hunting season. He immediately slammed on the brakes and swerved to the side of the road. Between my yelling and his skidding, Heather woke up with her signature earsplitting wail.

Joe yanked the gear shift into reverse and quickly backed up to where the bassinet had landed. He jumped out of the cab and ran the last few steps as I opened my door and scooped up Heather. Joe was muttering to himself as I came up behind him.

"Hell's bells. Dee Ann's gonna have a hissy fit."

He was right. "Joe Bulluck, how in the world did this happen? My grandmother slept in this bassinet. My father slept in this bassinet. What would my mother say if she knew our family's antique bassinet went flying out of the back of the truck to land smack dab in the middle of the road like some old candy bar wrapper?"

"It doesn't look that bad," Joe said as Heather's squalling reached an even higher pitch. "Just one wheel a little out of whack. The basket is fine."

I don't know how Joe could call black skid marks where white paint used to be "fine," but at least the bassinet was still in one piece. Now, though, the tears I had worked so hard to hold back all morning started rolling down my face.

"Get back in the truck, Dee Ann," Joe said in a harsh voice. Although a lot of men are reduced to mush when women cry, Joe often reacts by getting a little ugly, which was the main reason I'd been trying not to tear up.

"I'm doing the best I can moving all this stuff by myself," he went on. "I know you're going through a lot leaving home, but you don't have to get hysterical. Today's not easy for me either, but you don't see me crying on the side of the road."

A small voice inside my head told me maybe, just maybe, Joe had a point. Moving was hard for everybody, and perhaps I was being a tad difficult. But I couldn't seem to help myself. I needed to have the last word.

"I'll cry on the side of the road if I want to," I shot back. "Who's going to see me? Look around you, Joe. We're the only people out here."

We stared at each other for a second, and then I saw Joe look beyond me to a newly plowed field. The smell of freshly tilled soil was in the air, along with the scent of something sweet—maybe that wild purple wisteria that blooms in the early spring. Across the road, thick woods, mostly pine trees, crept to the edge of the ditch.

I opened my mouth to let him have it again, but then he softened and used that line he loves: "Everything will be all right."

Did I mention that Joe is a positive thinker? Unlike me, he doesn't seem to worry about a whole lot in life. He says things will usually turn out fine if you just have the right attitude.

I do enough worrying for both of us. Joe calls me high strung. He says I'm just looking for trouble.

I stumbled back to the truck with Heather, whose wailing had turned into a steady crying jag, a pattern I recognized only too well. A dusty maroon car coming from the opposite direction slowed down, and a skinny old white man in a John Deere cap stared at Joe and the bassinet before easing around the scene of the accident. He didn't even roll down his window to ask if he could help.

I climbed into the cab of the truck, which wasn't easy between holding Heather and being somewhat blinded by tears. I was still fuming. A banged-up bassinet. And not just some bassinet out of the Sears, Roebuck catalog. Oh no, my family's heirloom bassinet.

Heather and I were both still crying when Joe got in the truck.

Chapter 2

It was almost noon when we finally pulled in the paved driveway of our new home in a neighborhood of five-acre lots on the outskirts of Narrow Creek. Heather had sobbed herself back to sleep, and I'd dried my eyes and reapplied my lipstick. Pearly Pink by Maybelline. A fresh coat of lipstick always makes me feel better.

Our landlords, Floyd and Josephine Powell, lived in the grand house on the right side of the driveway. Joe had told me their names, even though he hadn't met them since the bank had taken care of the rental details. I was quite impressed by their stately red-brick, colonial-style home, complete with third-floor dormers. Eight multi-paned windows framed by pewter-grey shutters punctuated the front of the house on both the first and second stories. I've always loved anything Williamsburg.

A matching version of the house stood maybe a hundred feet or so behind the Powells' residence. This version didn't have any dormers or shutters, though, and it was a good deal smaller. Also, where the Powells' house featured a massive double-entrance door and a big brick porch with Chippendale rail, the bottom floor of this building had one ordinary front door and a tiny, unadorned stoop. Simple four-pane windows—two on the second floor aligned over two on the first—reflected the bright

April sunshine. It was nothing fancy, but at least our new home didn't appear to be a dump. Joe had informed me we'd be living on the second floor since the Powells used the ground floor for storage.

The Powells' stately house and the detached apartment building cheered me up, but their front yard had the opposite effect. The pink and white azaleas and dogwood trees in bloom reminded me of my mother's yard back home. Behind the house was a small garden patch tucked into a far corner, just like my mother's kitchen garden. I felt a wave of homesickness wash over me as I wondered if the Powells grew tomatoes, cucumbers, bell peppers, and squash like Mama did.

I'd been a little upset with Joe for signing a whole year's lease for an apartment sight unseen by me. But Joe had explained that nice, inexpensive places to rent in Narrow Creek weren't easy to find. He'd said Floyd Powell considered himself doing a special favor for the bank by agreeing to let us rent the apartment for eighty dollars a month.

It did have two bedrooms, a bathroom, a combination kitchen/dining and living room area, and a window air-conditioning unit. At least that's what Joe had described from his one tour of the place. I was hoping he'd remembered correctly. Men don't always pay as much attention to floor plans and amenities as women do.

Joe stopped at the end of the driveway in front of the apartment. Stepping out of the truck with Heather, I noticed an older man peeping at us from behind the sliding glass door at the back of the Powells' house. When he saw me looking at him, he eased the door open and ambled outside.

"How're ya doing, young fellow?" he bellowed as he shook hands with Joe. "You must be my new renter. I'm Floyd Powell. Yes sir, the bank wanted you to come work for them pretty bad. You're getting a good deal on this apartment, but I'm getting a sweet rate on my certificates of deposit."

He threw back his head of thick white hair and laughed, exposing a set of shiny even teeth that I suspected were dentures. Joe had told me Floyd Powell was a semi-retired landowner who rented out farmland and drove hard bargains at the bank.

"Course it's hard to get young folks to move to Narrow Creek. Nothing to do in a small town. That's what our children say. I built this place back here in case any of them needed somewhere to live to get started, kinda like you and your little family. But wouldn't you know it: they all up and moved away once they finished college and got married. All three of 'em. Gone to Charlotte and Raleigh.

"I told Josie it won't smart to build an apartment behind the house anyway. A storage building is fine—I can keep some of my farm supplies in there. But an apartment that your own children don't want to live in? That's just plain foolish."

Good grief, that man could talk. Joe hadn't been able to get in a word, not even to say hello and introduce me.

A woman I presumed to be Mrs. Powell stepped off the back porch and walked our way. Her short grey hair was teased into a bouffant, and she was dressed in sensible beige polyester pants and a matching tunic. On her feet she sported a pair of baby blue Grasshoppers that I wouldn't have minded owning myself. "What's foolish except an old man who keeps gabbing on and on to a young couple who are bound to be tired and ready to get moved in?" she demanded. "For goodness' sake, Floyd, go find Willie to help Mr. Bulluck unload his truck."

She turned to Joe and me. "I'm Josephine Powell." She offered first me and then Joe her hand, just the proper etiquette I learned back in ninth grade home economics class when we did the unit on poise. "Please call me Josie."

"Joe Bulluck, ma'am. And this is my wife Dee Ann and our baby girl Heather. It's a pleasure to meet you, Miss Josie." Joe has nice manners too. He knew to precede "Josie" with a "Miss" since this lady was almost old enough to be his grandmother.

"I'm happy to meet you both. Floyd didn't tell me what a handsome couple you are. Now let me see this darling baby." Miss Josie leaned over Heather's infant seat. "Floyd said it was a little girl, and I can tell anyway with that sweet pink outfit she has on. Oh, isn't she the cutest thing, Floyd? I declare she looks just like the Gerber baby." Gushing over Heather, she seemed to have forgotten Mr. Powell had been sent to find somebody named Willie.

"How old is she?"

"Three months," I said, sounding proud. I couldn't help believing Heather was the prettiest child in the world. In fact, I thought she bore a strong resemblance to the Gerber baby myself. Of course, my grandma used to say every crow thinks her baby's the blackest. My grandma was big on not being too proud.

"Three months! Oh my!" Miss Josie sighed. "Heather. What a precious name for such a precious baby." Suddenly she straightened up from leaning over Heather, and her expression, which had been all soft and sweet when she was cooing, soured.

"Where is Willie? I declare, that colored man gets lost every time I turn my back."

Both Joe and I flinched a little. Who in the world said "colored" anymore?

"It's Floyd's idea to keep him around the house all day to do odd jobs. But of course all he ever does is eat me out of house and home. Floyd ought to be the one taking out the trash and working in the yard. 'But no,' he says. 'I got to have my free time.' He goes to eat breakfast at Ernie's Grill every morning with a bunch of his cronies and then sits there and gabs away half the day. I tell everybody we don't need Jimmy Carter in Washington when we got Floyd and his crowd in the corner booth at Ernie's solving the country's problems. But while Floyd's putting in his two cents' worth about inflation, I'm left here trying to think up work for Willie."

Mr. Powell ambled around the far corner of the big house, followed by an old, arthritic black man wearing starched overalls and an Atlanta Braves ball cap.

"Willie, this is Mr. Joe Bulluck," Miss Josie said. "And this is his wife, Mrs. Dee Ann Bulluck, and their baby girl, little Miss Heather. They're going to be our new tenants in the upstairs apartment. Take these boxes off the truck and carry them up for them."

"Yessum," Willie said, giving Miss Josie a curt nod. He lifted the first box he could get to off the truck and staggered toward the left side of the apartment building, heading to a side door I hadn't noticed. Mr. Powell retreated to his own house, probably afraid Miss Josie was going to put him to work too.

"Now don't you pay him anything for helping you," Miss Josie told Joe once Willie had disappeared through the door. "I give him a weekly wage for doing next to nothing around here as it is." She turned back to me as Joe picked up a box and followed Willie. "Do you want me to watch the baby while you unpack today?" she asked, using her sweet voice again.

"Thank you for the offer, but she's a bit cranky from the trip. I'll just try to get her settled once we get upstairs," I answered, surprised. Miss Josie seemed nice enough, but did she really think I was the type of mother who would leave her child with someone she had known a total of five minutes? I wasn't like Tennessee Williams' Blanche DuBois, who always depended on the kindness of strangers, especially where my baby was concerned.

The back door of the Powells' house slid open again, this time giving a quick whoosh, and a young man with dark, curly hair and a lean, tanned body stepped out on the porch and sauntered to a red Corvette parked behind the house. Opening the driver's door, he leaned in and popped out the car's lighter, which he held to a cigarette clamped between his teeth. Through the open car door, I saw a pair of miniature pink Playboy Bunny ears dangling from the rearview mirror. After a couple of deep drags, the young man moved our way.

"Sorry to interrupt, Miss Josie, but Mr. Powell said to ask you about the color of grout you want in your tile." A half-smile played across his face as he addressed Miss Josie while looking at me.

"I'll be inside in just a minute, Gary." Hooking his thumbs in the front belt loops of a pair of tight jean shorts, the young man made no reply and also made no move to leave. I couldn't help noticing his handsome, chiseled features and laughing brown eyes. I had him pegged right away: a lady's man.

Evidently noting that his continued presence required an introduction, Miss Josie quickly took care of the social obligation. "Dee Ann, this is Gary Whitt, our contractor. He's remodeling a downstairs bathroom."

She introduced me as her new tenant, emphasizing that my husband was in the apartment unloading boxes.

"Narrow Creek just got a lot better-looking today," Gary said in a husky voice. I held Heather in front of me like a shield and didn't return his seductive smile.

"She and her husband are both quite attractive," Miss Josie said in a no-nonsense voice. "Let's go look at that grout." Taking Gary by the arm, she steered him toward the house. "I'm just out your door if you need me, Dee Ann." Miss Josie departed with a little wave. Gary Whitt left with a teasing backwards glance.

I turned around just as Joe, followed by Willie, stepped out the side door of the apartment building. "Who's that?" Joe asked, glimpsing the retreating Gary Whitt.

"Miss Josie's contractor—and a big flirt," I huffed. "You should have seen the way he was eying me."

"Men like to look at pretty girls," Joe said nonchalantly. "I'm sure you were well chaperoned with Miss Josie between you." Joe doesn't have a jealous bone in his body, which can be a little insulting sometimes.

I followed Joe upstairs and got my first look at the inside of the apartment. It was laid out as Joe had described it with two bedrooms, a bathroom, and an open kitchen/dining and living room. The walls were brown paneling, which made the apartment a little on the dark side, but at least they were clean and wouldn't need painting.

The same yellow linoleum had been used for the kitchen and bathroom floors, and sturdy green and brown flecked, commercial grade carpet covered the rest of the apartment. Neither the linoleum nor the carpet was anything pretty, but both would stand up to wear and tear.

The best feature, one Joe hadn't mentioned and I wasn't expecting, was a fireplace. I envisioned myself sitting by flickering flames on cold winter nights.

Joe and Willie worked hard for a while unloading the truck and lugging all our stuff upstairs. Then Willie stayed to help me unpack the kitchen boxes after I got Heather down for a nap. I think he liked having something to do.

Before he left, Joe gave him a crisp five-dollar bill. "Miss Josie doesn't have to know about this week's bonus," Joe said with a wink.

"You got that right," Willie replied. A slow grin spread across his face as he raised his head and looked Joe straight in the eye. "She don't need to know everything. This can be our business."

Chapter 3

I'd worked at unpacking all weekend when I had a chance, but there I was on Monday, surveying all the things that still needed to be put away. Moving is hard work, especially with a baby who needs constant attention. And a husband whose idea of setting up house is getting the television plugged in and the couch arranged so he can lie down on it and watch sports.

Honestly, Willie had been more help than Joe Bulluck. But I guess Joe did need to rest up some on the weekend for his first week at work. He doesn't have the high energy level that I have. I wonder if that's why I'm skinny, and Joe is a little pudgy, especially around his middle. No doubt lying on the couch and eating Little Debbie snack cakes can add a few extra pounds to a person.

But Joe had looked very handsome that morning in his navy pinstripe suit, his dark hair carefully combed, and his blue eyes shining with excitement. I was proud of him for following his dream to be a banker, even if it meant I was now all alone in a new town in a disorganized house. Of course, I wasn't completely by myself. Heather had been cranky since breakfast, but, thank goodness, I'd finally gotten her down for a morning nap.

I gazed out the window while pondering which pile of clutter to tackle first. Suddenly I saw movement from the back of the Powells' house. Miss Josie was stepping through the sliding glass door carrying what looked like a Tupperware cake carrier. She's coming to pay a welcome-to-Narrow Creek visit, I realized, suddenly flustered.

My eyes swept across the apartment. I could've sworn Joe and I didn't own very much, but what we'd brought on the back of that pick-up truck seemed to have multiplied once it was unpacked. Clothes, books, toys, and linens were everywhere. Empty boxes Joe had promised to take out to the trash were stacked against one wall.

I glanced at the furniture Joe and his dad had moved on a separate trip. Joe's grandparents had given us their old living room couch and two matching club chairs. I don't mean to sound ungrateful, but it was pretty pitiful stuff. It was sturdy, all right, bought from the best furniture store in town—in 1946. The burgundy fabric was worn and faded, and to be frank, the furniture looked a little ratty.

Our television, the seventeen-inch, black-and-white model I'd owned in college, sat on a cheap aluminum stand. We had no end tables, and one hand-me-down wrought-iron floor lamp lit the room at night.

I grabbed a pile of winter clothes that for some unknown reason had ended up behind the television. Hearing a firm knock on the door, I dumped sweaters and coats into the small hall closet.

Hoping I didn't have spit-up on my shoulder, I opened the door to a smiling Josephine Powell dressed in a blue polyester pant suit.

"Hello dear, may I come in?" Miss Josie said as she stepped right past me into the cluttered apartment. "I hope I'm not bothering you, but I want to say welcome with a little something I baked. This is my specialty, Mabel's Pineapple Cake. Mabel was my mother. She's been gone twenty years now, bless her soul, but she left me her recipe, which I've perfected over time, not to be bragging." Miss Josie set the cake carrier on the kitchen counter and beamed at me.

"Why, thank you." I beamed back. "Joe and I both love pineapple cake." It was true, at least in my case. Carrot cake is Joe's favorite.

"Still settling in?" Miss Josie cast a critical eye around the place. "I know it's a job to move, especially with a new baby. I would've come over sooner, but I'm sure you and your husband want your privacy. That's exactly what I told Floyd. I said, 'Floyd, I want to be friendly and a good neighbor, but they're a young couple and they need their privacy.'"

I opened my mouth to say the gracious but untrue Southern thing about how she was always welcome to visit at any time, but I didn't get the first word out.

"And I've been so upset ever since I heard the disturbing news about my contractor. Gary Whitt was killed Saturday night." Miss Josie paused dramatically. "Murdered, no less."

I forgot all about my messy house. "The man I met in your yard three days ago?" I sputtered.

"The very one. I heard the news at church yesterday morning. Seems a friend went looking for him late Saturday night after he didn't show up at some bar—I think it's called The Rodeo—where he usually hangs out on the weekends. He found Gary at his apartment, dead as a doornail. Shot several times. Evidently whoever did it wanted to be sure Gary was dead."

"How awful!" I pictured Gary Whitt's flirtatious smile and laughing eyes. "Are there any suspects?"

"Lots of speculation. Clara Joyner said she heard he was involved in drugs, although I never saw any sign of that when he was working for me. Clara said drug people will kill each other over marijuana deals.

"June Hill thinks it was a robbery gone bad. We've got some mean coloreds living in the projects not too far from where Gary stayed. Someone might've thought Gary wouldn't be home on a Saturday night, broke in to steal his television set and whatnot, and found him there. Then the robber had to kill Gary so that Gary couldn't identify him."

There was that word "colored" again. "I'm sure there are some mean white people in Narrow Creek too," I ventured.

Miss Josie gave me a sharp look. "Why yes, there's a lot of evil in this world, but in Narrow Creek, it's rare for a white person to be murdered. The coloreds are always stabbing and shooting each other though. I just hope some of that violence hasn't seeped into the white community."

I gave up on a rational discussion of suspects. Miss Josie was a product of her time. She came from a generation of white Southerners who had never gone to integrated schools and held unfavorable stereotypes of black people. "Does Gary have any family in town?"

"Just his grandmother and a bachelor uncle. His parents were killed in a car accident when Gary was a little fellow. His grandmother on his mama's side took him in and raised him. She thought the sun rose and set on that boy. I'm sure she's devastated." Miss Josie observed a moment of silence before continuing.

"My Sunday School class has already passed around a sign-up sheet for the bereavement meal. More ladies voted to serve the warm weather menu than the cool weather one, although personally I think April funeral food could go either way." Miss Josie's voice took on a note of irritation. "That means I have to make a marinated vegetable salad, which takes more time than that green bean casserole with the can of mushroom soup.

"And to top it all off, I've got to find another contractor to finish my bathroom. The commode is sitting in the bathtub, and none of the sink faucets have been replaced. Gary has sure left me in a bind."

As I stood there absorbing both the shocking news of the murder as well as Miss Josie's self-centered view of the tragedy, my new landlady suddenly exclaimed, "Why, look what you've done to the place!" She was slowly turning in a complete circle. "I always knew this apartment could be a nice little home for young folks just starting out. That's exactly what I told Floyd when I encouraged him to build this second floor over his fancy storage building. I said, 'Floyd, why don't you add an upstairs apartment? It won't cost much more money, and it would make a nice little home for some young couple.'"

Miss Josie suddenly pursed her lips and wrinkled her forehead. "Honey, don't you think your couch would look better against this wall rather than stuck out in the middle of the floor?" She swept an arm toward the back wall of the living room.

It was finally my turn to talk. "Actually I put it where it is to function as a room divider. See how it defines the living space, setting it off from the kitchen and dining area?" I was proud of this idea that I had seen in a recent issue of *Southern Living*. I also enjoyed using all those decorator terms on Miss Josie.

Miss Josie eyed the card table and two folding metal chairs I'd described as the dining area. "I just had a thought," she said brightly. "You could get a flat double sheet and make an inexpensive tablecloth to go over that brown card table. Just find something pretty, maybe checkered or with flowers, lay it over your table, and cut it off at floor level with some pinking shears. I have a pair you can borrow any time."

I didn't think this was Miss Josie's "thought." I was willing to bet she read *Southern Living* too. I was fairly sure that if I checked some back issues the next time I went to Joe's mother's house, I'd find this idea, complete with a color picture of a cute little table with a floor-length patterned tablecloth made from a bedsheet.

I'd had enough of this woman's bossiness. I felt something mean come over me, something stubborn and contrary. "I plan to use placemats," I said, even though I hadn't thought very much about the card table up to that point. "The kind you can wipe off after a meal. Plastic." The thought of cheap plastic placemats didn't appeal to me at all, but as I said, I was possessed by something hateful.

"Honey, you can certainly put your placemats down on top of a tablecloth. You'd have some color and elegance with the tablecloth and an easy cleanup with the placemats." Miss Josie nodded her head as if a decorating dilemma had just been solved to everyone's satisfaction.

Heather chose that moment to let out a piercing scream. "Excuse me," I said, and raced around the corner to the front bedroom. There lay poor little Heather in her banged-up bassinet, her face scrunched up and red with rage, caterwauling at the top of her lungs. I quickly picked her up, turned around, and nearly plowed into my visitor.

"My goodness, what happened to this baby's bassinet?" Miss Josie frowned at the crooked wheel and black skid marks.

"It fell off the back of the truck when we were moving," I managed to reply over Heather's crying.

"I'll send Willie over to fix it for you." She leaned in close to Heather's face. "We can't have this sweetie pie sleeping in a rickety old bassinet now, can we?" she added in a sing-song voice.

Before I could tell her no thank-you, that Joe was perfectly capable of wheel tightening and bassinet painting, Miss Josie reached for Heather.

"Let me hold her a minute, Dee Ann." A wailing Heather was transferred from one set of arms to another.

"What's the matter, honey cakes?" Miss Josie cooed. "Does her tummy hurt? Has her got the colic?"

I wanted to tell Miss Josie that I didn't use baby talk with Heather. I'd read in several parenting books that speaking standard English to a baby is better for helping a child develop good verbal skills at an early age. But I let the baby talk issue go and said instead, "Breast-fed babies don't get colic. That's one of the advantages of nursing."

"No bottles?" Miss Josie raised an eyebrow. "Maybe that's the problem. This poor baby may not be getting enough to eat.

"Are you hungry, precious?" Miss Josie rocked Heather in her arms, and a little to my dismay, the child stopped crying, and with her big blue eyes, studied Miss Josie's face intently. I felt betrayed somehow.

"I can run out and get her some formula. I used to work on the maternity ward at the hospital, and believe me, I know a hungry cry when I hear one."

Just a minute before, Miss Josie had diagnosed colic, not starvation. I felt myself grow hot.

"She's not hungry. I know what I'm doing, and she's getting plenty of nourishment." My voice sounded high and nervous. "I don't know how recently you worked on the maternity ward, but today, it's considered better to breastfeed than use formula. I'll take her now," I added, practically snatching Heather.

Miss Josie had a hurt look on her face, and I felt a little ashamed of myself for such an outburst. But breastfeeding wasn't easy, and I couldn't let myself be discouraged by someone who was a maternity ward nurse back when everybody stuck a bottle in a newborn's mouth.

"I can see you're busy, so I won't stay any longer," Miss Josie said rather stiffly. "I hope you and Joe enjoy the pineapple cake." She marched to the door and then turned to look at me for a long moment. "I didn't mean to upset you, Dee Ann. I thought we were having a pleasant visit. I didn't think about how stressful it must be for you as a first-time mother to move to a new town."

And with that, Miss Josie opened the apartment door, talking to herself as she went down the stairs. Something about "plenty of nourishment, my foot," and "what that baby needs is some formula." Just before the downstairs door closed, there was "and what that apartment needs is a tablecloth."

Hearing her, I didn't feel so bad about my ungracious behavior. I slammed the apartment door and locked it to keep out both a murderer on the loose and Miss Josie. Joe would be returning that Tupperware cake carrier.

Chapter 4

Although money was tight, one of the few extras I indulged in was a subscription to the twice-weekly *Narrow Creek News and Views*. I needed to get to know my new hometown, and I definitely wanted to learn about any new developments in the Gary Whitt murder.

The newspaper didn't disappoint. In almost every Wednesday and Sunday edition, there was something about the case. Roger McSwain, the Chief of Police, was quoted as saying, "At this point in time, we are examining all the evidence and interviewing quite a list of Gary Whitt's friends, relatives, and acquaintances. We have no suspects, but many persons of interest. If anyone knows anything about the murder, I am asking that person to contact law enforcement."

Soon after this article, there was another concerning a reward of ten thousand dollars, offered by Mrs. Arthur Adams, grandmother of the victim, for information leading to any arrests in the Gary Whitt murder.

Ten thousand dollars! Apparently Gary Whitt's grandmother was well-heeled. Ten thousand dollars was more money than Joe would clear in a year at the bank. I sure wished I had information that could lead to an arrest. I'd turn in my best friend for that amount of cash.

Then there were the letters to the editor. Scores of people wrote in to say how awful it was that big city crime seemed to have invaded Narrow Creek. "I would expect such a heinous act if I lived in New York City," one woman wrote, "but our fair town has always felt so safe that I didn't bother to lock the doors when I went to the Winn-Dixie. Not any more. I've even had my husband install dead bolts."

As to why Gary Whitt had been murdered, some complained about causes as diverse as the influence of television, the hippie culture, lax parenting, and the government being soft on crime.

Thank goodness the paper didn't print anything anybody wrote about the "coloreds" committing the crime. Having heard Miss Josie, I didn't doubt there were others who shared her suspicions, as well as her language.

After devouring all the *News and Views* had to say about the murder, I often found myself turning to a column called "What's Happening Around Town."

Here I read about Special Events such as Girl Scout Troop #313 hosting a Dine Out Night to help fund "educational trips and opportunities for the girls." The Narrow Creek Senior Center was accepting donations for its annual Food Box Drive. First Baptist Church was having a fried fish plate dinner along with an indoor yard sale. Although I wasn't part of any of these functions, reading about them somehow made me feel a little less lonesome.

The "Social Notes" feature, on the other hand, depressed me. I'd see items like "Mrs. Paul (Anita) Smith recently hosted her former Peace College roommate and her husband, Mr. and Mrs. Harvey (Julia) Brooks, along with their children Stephanie and Nicholas from Roanoke, Virginia," or "Mrs. James (Mary) Johnson entertained the Queen of Hearts Bridge Club on Thursday of last week at her home on Avon Street."

I wished I had a house large enough to entertain an old college roommate and her family or even a bridge club, although playing cards has never been one of my interests.

Reading the *News and Views*, I realized there were people all around me who were out and about, enjoying their lives in a small town. Even a small town with a murderer on the lam.

*****

Joe's bank closed each day at noon for an hour for lunch, and Joe came home to eat pimento cheese sandwiches or leftovers from what I'd cooked for supper the night before. I loved that hour of the day. For a few blessed minutes, Joe entertained Heather, and I could run the vacuum or clean the bathroom in peace. Sometimes, if Heather had been especially difficult that morning, I'd finally get my bath.

I know I could have left Heather in the bassinet to scream it out while I got in the shower or did my household chores, but I didn't have it in me to let my baby girl cry if I could help it. My grandma would've said Heather was spoiled by being held too much. Maybe so, but nobody could accuse me of neglecting my child.

Joe's lunch break also gave me somebody to chat with. I'd quiz him on anything he'd heard about the murder from anyone down at the bank. "I've been told Roger McSwain and his two officers aren't sharp enough to handle a murder investigation," Joe had confided. "It seems about all the police ever have to do is write parking tickets and help folks get in their cars when they've locked the keys inside."

"Really? Miss Josie told me there was a lot of crime in the colored community." I'd made air quotes around the word "colored" while rolling my eyes. "If that's true, wouldn't the Narrow Creek police be busy handling that?"

"Sad to say, I'm not sure black-on-black crime would get much attention in Narrow Creek. It was that way back home too. The police were never too concerned about what happened in the black community."

Joe had a point. When I thought about it, I couldn't remember ever hearing about any investigation involving a black victim. "Why hasn't the State Bureau of Investigation been called in to help if the local police are so inept?" I'd asked. Joe had just shrugged, although I was trying to keep him talking. I truly was interested in the Gary Whitt case, especially since there was that big reward money.

I also needed adult conversation. Other than a couple of cashiers at the Winn-Dixie, the only person I'd talked to since Miss Josie was Willie, who'd showed up a day after her visit, taken Heather's bassinet downstairs, and fixed the wheel and touched up the paint in less than an hour. While Willie was certainly helpful to have around, he wasn't much of a conversationalist. "Yessum" was about all I could get out of him.

"Joe," I often complained during those first few weeks of living in Narrow Creek, "my life is nothing but changing diapers day after day. I think my brain is shriveling to nothing." Or I'd hit him with "Living in this town is like being in prison. Except I don't get visitors."

"I've got enough on my mind trying to keep everybody happy at work. I can't worry about you here at home too," Joe would say. "You're just going to have to be content in Narrow Creek for a couple of years."

Easier said than done.

I was feeling sorry for myself one particular Friday at lunch since Joe and I didn't have any plans for the weekend. With no free babysitter, we were stuck at home. Joe didn't seem to mind; for him, there was always a game on television. For me, it was two more days of baby duty. My one bright spot would be watching the Ewing family on *Dallas* Sunday night after Joe had gone to bed.

We were eating reheated hamburger casserole when Joe said, "I almost forgot to tell you. Bill's wife, Cynthia, would like to invite you to attend a meeting of the Narrow Creek Ladies' Society." Bill Ford was Joe's boss at work. Well, his direct boss. Joe had a lot of bosses.

"She wants to introduce you to some of the young women in town. The next meeting is this coming Tuesday night at seven. Cynthia told Bill to tell me to tell you that she'd pick you up if you want to go. I can babysit Heather."

Although I felt a spark of excitement about the invitation, Joe's choice of words annoyed me in more than one way. "Why do men call it babysitting when they're keeping their own children?" I huffed. "I don't call it babysitting when I'm here with Heather. And why doesn't Bill's wife invite me herself instead of telling her husband to tell you to ask me?"

Joe frowned. "Don't go getting on your women's lib high horse. I know Heather is my responsibility too. And I guess Cynthia just wanted to see if you were interested before she wasted her time calling you."

Wasted her time calling me?

Only a man could see that as a valid reason for not extending the courtesy of a personal phone call to issue an invitation. I saw it as a slight: I wasn't important enough to warrant a call. After all, I was the wife of the peon at the bank. But I didn't want to dwell on this snub with Joe. He didn't need me to point out that he had a tall corporate ladder to climb.

"What do you want me to tell Bill? Up for a night out with the girls?"

I looked at Joe's good-natured face and decided for once to be as positive as he was. "Sure. It's nice of Cynthia to invite me," I forced myself to say.

I didn't remind Joe of my brief, not-so-successful membership in the Jaycettes back home when he and I were first married. I must be missing the civic work chromosome. Fundraisers and volunteer projects bore me silly. But I knew that being involved with the community was part of the role of a banker's wife, even a lowly banker. I needed to accept Cynthia's invitation, even as roundabout as it had come.

Besides, new town, new club. Here I'd been moping because I didn't have any friends, and now I had an opportunity to meet some other young women. I loved Heather, but to be truthful, staying home with her all the time was not the blissful experience I'd imagined it would be. I missed adults. I was desperate enough to attend a meeting of a women's civic club.

Joe was beaming. "All right!" he said. "Mama's ready for a night out with the girls." He winked. "I'll pass the word that you would be absolutely delighted to attend the next meeting of the Narrow Creek Ladies' Society." He delivered this last line in a snooty English butler voice.

"Very funny," I deadpanned. I couldn't help smiling, though, both at Joe's foolishness and the prospect of making some new friends.

Chapter 5

Clothes lay scattered across the bed. What in the world did one wear to a meeting of the Narrow Creek Ladies' Society? I'd pulled one garment after another from the tiny closet Joe and I shared, examined it, and then thrown it on the heap. The discard pile was getting pretty high.

I'd worn jeans and a nice cotton shirt to my Jaycettes' meetings back home and I'd fit right in. But I suspected the women in the Narrow Creek Ladies' Society might dress up. I remembered the Ladies' Society crowd at home as a more socially elite group than the down-home Jaycettes. Members of the Ladies' Society were mostly stay-at-home doctors' and lawyers' wives, with the occasional single but financially successful career woman mixed in. The Jaycettes, on the other hand, were teachers, nurses, and secretaries, mainly working married women who, truth be told, really didn't have time to be in a club.

What was I thinking when I agreed to go to this meeting, I asked myself for the tenth time. And why had I not realized I had nothing to wear? My wardrobe told the story of my life for the previous three years: jeans, tee shirts, and flannel shirts I'd worn as a student in grad school; corduroy or polyester pants and knit tops for the days I dressed up to teach my two classes of freshman English at the university. And I still had my now useless—thank goodness—maternity clothes. I loved Heather, but I hadn't loved being pregnant.

I considered a couple of party dresses that I'd worn to dances in high school, but of course these were too fancy for a ladies' club meeting. Besides, they were out of style and probably too small. I pictured myself making my first appearance in a too tight, too short, too fancy dress. I could wear heavy makeup, tease my hair, and use a thick country accent. "Hey y'all. I was a waitress in the lounge at the Ramada Inn in Memphis before I married little ol' Joe and moved to little ol' Narrow Creek."

Heather began stirring in her crib. Nap time was ending.

I picked a pair of brown corduroy pants from the pile, hoping they would fit my post-baby body. Although I'd gotten back to my pre-pregnancy weight, my waist and hips were somehow larger. I was a half size larger in shoes too. No one had told me to expect this expansion of certain body parts after having a baby. I'd always been a little vain about having a tiny waist, fairly small hips, and a dainty foot. Pride really does go before a fall.

The matching paisley shirt still hung in the closet. I snatched it off the hanger as a wave of defiance swept over me. Eyeing my two diplomas on the bedroom wall, I reminded myself that I might not be the best-dressed woman at this meeting tonight, but I was no backwoods redneck. With a Master's in Education and a Bachelor's in English, I vowed not to be intimidated by a bunch of ladies who lunched!

*****

Joe had taken Heather with him to pick up his double cheeseburger and fries at Hardee's as I waited for Cynthia, she-of-the-roundabout invitation. Joe had told me not to worry about cooking supper. "It's your night off," he'd said at lunch. Of course, he didn't come home in time to get a burger for me as well, so my supper had consisted of a last-minute peanut butter sandwich. Still, I didn't have to cook, and Joe would be bathing Heather and putting her to bed.

Cynthia was thirty years old, the same age as her husband Bill, and an accountant with some firm in town. Joe had found out that much for me, but he had no idea what the woman looked like. I took it as a good sign that she had an occupation, although who was I to consider a woman who worked "outside the home" more interesting since I had no job myself? But I planned to have a career one day—as soon as Heather started kindergarten.

I heard a loud, firm knock. I grabbed my purse and opened the door. Before I could even say hello, a Farrah Fawcett lookalike crashed into the apartment on a wave of perfume. Her eyes, carefully made up with the right amount of eyeliner and mascara, narrowed as she appraised the combined kitchen/dining and living room area of the apartment with its multicolored commercial carpet and hand-me-down furniture. "How nice," she said in a shrill voice. I knew a false compliment when I heard it. A big fake smile was planted on her picture-perfect face.

"Dee Ann, is it? I'm Cynthia Ford." She stuck out her hand as if she were greeting a client. Her grasp was cool and firm. My hand was hot and sweaty.

"You look so cute in your little corduroy outfit." At this moment, *little* seemed the most condescending adjective in the world. Cynthia wore a tailored black suit with low-heeled pumps. Her long, feather-cut hair was carefully curled back from her face, and a pair of diamond stud earrings winked when she tossed her frosted tresses.

I peeped at my own scuffed Topsiders and wished I had done something with my hair other than put it in its usual ponytail. If the ladies in this club all dress like Cynthia, I'll be mistaken for the mother of the underprivileged child they're sponsoring for summer camp.

I remembered a line from Shakespeare's Lady Macbeth: "Screw your courage to the sticking-place, and we'll not fail." She was encouraging her ambitious husband to kill the king of Scotland. Though I wasn't planning on knocking off anyone that night, thinking of those words still helped. I stiffened my spine, ready for battle.

"Let's go," Cynthia said in her annoying, high-pitched voice. "We don't want to be late."

No, we certainly don't want to miss a minute, I wanted to retort sarcastically. Instead, mindful that I was with the wife of Joe's boss, I held my tongue and followed Cynthia out the door.

*****

"The Ladies' Society meets the third Tuesday of every month in the Fellowship Hall and Family Life Center of First Baptist Church. Several of our members attend First Baptist, but we also make an annual contribution to the church to show our appreciation."

Cynthia was briefing me as we got out of her silver Mercedes on Church Street in front of the imposing sanctuary. Large sconces illuminated the façade, where several enormous columns flanked a massive set of steps leading to the front door. I wondered how many wedding parties had been carefully arranged and photographed on these steps over the years. Joe and I got married in the small Baptist church I'd attended all my life. Our photographs were taken in the chapel after the ceremony was over.

Another large brick building stood to the left of the church. A lighted sign in front read First Baptist Church

Fellowship Hall and Family Life Center. Muted voices and soft laughter floated from women filing in through double doors.

I trotted along behind Cynthia on a slightly curving flagstone walkway, feeling like a lamb being led to the slaughter. She turned as we got to the door and flashed me a plastic smile. "I'd love to sit with you tonight, but this year I'm serving as club treasurer, so I'll need to be up front with the other officers."

"Of course," I said, trying not to sound the way I felt— snubbed. I already wasn't a Cynthia fan but at least she was someone I knew, however briefly. Now she was telling me I had to sit by myself with absolute strangers.

As we entered the fellowship hall, I soon realized that of the twenty or so women in attendance, I was the only one in corduroy pants. I'd never seen such a chic group of young women. An unwritten code must have declared that an outfit had to look as though it'd just been bought from some elegant ladies' boutique, and only a trendy hairstyle was acceptable. I was so embarrassed that I think my vision blurred; for a moment, everyone looked like a Cynthia clone. I took a deep breath so I could see again, and confirmed that not a dowdy person was in sight. Except me. The ugly duckling among Cynthia swans.

As if to fulfill her sponsor duties as quickly as possible, Cynthia led me straight to the club's president. "Barbara, this is Dee Ann Bulluck. Her husband is the new collector in Bill's department at the bank."

He hangs out the flag every morning and chases down past-due customers, Cynthia might as well have said. "New collector at the bank" was code language for low man on the totem pole.

"Oh, Dee Ann, I'm so glad to meet you," gushed a woman in a smart linen skirt with a matching spring sweater. "I'm Barbara Highland, the lady in charge of this crowd. Welcome to our club." Her appraising eyes slid over my paisley knit top and corduroy pants.

"Thank you," I managed to say. "I'm happy to be here," I lied.

Poise: the ability to be at ease in social situations. Over my many years of school, I'd memorized lots of definitions. Now in my hour of need, this word and its meaning resurfaced. Holding my head up high, I could feel my neck stretching. I have a long, graceful neck, if I do say so myself. It's one of my better features.

Evidently my elegant neck didn't impress Barbara Highland. She'd already turned away to chat with an attractive brunette in a navy wrap dress accessorized with heavy gold jewelry. Apparently she'd sized me up as someone of no importance.

I began to feel faint with embarrassment. Fortunately, the women were starting to sit down, so I filed into the second row of chairs and took a seat beside a petite woman with jet black hair. The chair on the other side of me remained vacant. I tried hard not to take it personally. Joe says I'm always imagining insults.

Barbara Highland presided from behind a long, narrow folding table facing the rows of chairs. She was flanked by a woman on either side: the secretary, who was called upon to read the minutes of the last meeting, and Cynthia, who reported that the club had eight hundred ninety-three dollars and eleven cents or some such amount in its checking account at the Narrow Creek Community Bank.

The old business of the meeting was one big long discussion of the Spring Arts and Crafts Bazaar to be held right there in the Fellowship Hall. I tried to pay attention as one subcommittee after another reported on ticket sales; vendors; the arrangement of booths, illustrated by a diagram on poster board; and the club members' work schedules for the day.

Blah, blah, blah. Suddenly I realized the last report was over, and Barbara was again speaking and looking right at me. "Tonight, ladies, we have a visitor and potential member among us." My hands went clammy.

"That pretty new face you see in the second row is Mrs. Dee Ann Bulluck, sponsored by Mrs. Cynthia Ford. Dee Ann, could you stand and tell us a little bit about yourself?"

Twenty pairs of eyes were trained on me. Now, I was used to public speaking. Heck, I'd given lots of reports in college, and I'd taught freshman English when I was a grad student. I'd never experienced any type of stage fright.

Until that moment. My mouth was as dry as my palms were wet. But I was trapped. Unless I fainted or ran out of the room, I had to get up and say something. Everything I'd learned about courage from Lady Macbeth vanished.

Both my voice and legs were shaking. "My name is Dee Ann Bulluck, and I moved to Narrow Creek recently with my husband Joe and our baby daughter Heather. Although I'm currently not working, I have an undergraduate degree in English and a Master's in Education."

The ladies stared at me as if I'd come from another planet. I tried again. "My daughter is almost four months old, and my husband works at Narrow Creek Community Bank. I look forward to getting to know all of you and becoming involved in the community." The women now smiled and nodded at me. I sat down quickly, before my knees buckled.

"Thank you, Dee Ann, for that most interesting introduction," Barbara said. "I'm sure I speak for everyone here when I say we'd certainly be delighted to have you join our group. Our club always needs new blood, since we all age out at thirty-nine. And we definitely could use another worker at the Arts and Crafts Bazaar." The ladies all politely tittered.

What was so funny about working at the bazaar? I realized I should've paid more attention during the discussion of the work schedule for that doggone fundraiser.

"The membership chairwoman, Mrs. Gloria Smith, will be calling you to explain the first-year probationary period," Barbara added. "Gloria, raise your hand, please, so Dee Ann will know who you are. Dee Ann, be sure to give Gloria your phone number."

Somehow I felt there'd been a test during my introductory speech, and I'd passed—barely.

Barbara rapped the gavel, and the meeting was officially adjourned. The Social Committee served cake and coffee. That nice moist piece of pound cake was the highlight of my night. The coffee was good too, although I knew I needed to avoid caffeine because I was nursing Heather. But since I'd just been through a traumatic experience, I decided to treat myself to a cup.

Gloria, a strawberry blonde in an emerald green pant suit, wandered over as I was picking up cake crumbs off my plate with the back of my fork. "Dee Ann, I'll give you a ring soon to discuss membership requirements during the probation period."

Oh goody, can't wait. My year of probation. Sounds like prison. If I said that to Joe, he'd tell me I was being negative.

"I'll let you know then about the time slot you'll need to work at the bazaar," she added. "Basically, you'll be in charge of a booth, which means you'll sell whatever is on the table. It's a fairly easy job if you know how to make change."

Gloria leaned closer. "You'd be surprised at the math skills of some of these women. I don't know how they manage their household budgets. You look like someone who knows how to add and subtract, though."

"Since the first grade," I answered, thinking maybe this Gloria person was a kindred spirit. But she just smiled and walked away.

After polishing off my cake crumbs and turning in my plate, I didn't know what else to do with myself. Cynthia was chatting with someone who appeared to be her best friend. I sidled up to a group of women in deep discussion. What could be so important? Maybe they're talking about the Gary Whitt murder.

"I heard it's forty-five hundred square feet with an unfinished third floor," said the petite woman with jet-black hair I'd sat next to during the meeting.

"I guess that inheritance is burning a hole in their pocket," chimed in a lady with sharp, birdlike features. "Wade's mother is hardly cold in her grave. Some people will spend every dime they have and then some."

The group all nodded in agreement. "And to be building on that lot right across the street from his old girlfriend and her husband!" Miss Black Hair added, pursing her lips. "I can't believe Judy doesn't see a problem with that."

"Judy has always put up with more from Wade than she should," said a thin woman in a bright pink sweater. "But I guess she's so thrilled to be getting herself such a nice new house that she doesn't care how many of Wade's old flings live in the neighborhood.

"She can't say but so much anyway, since she was a bit of a wild child herself back in high school," the woman continued, arching her eyebrows. "Y'all remember how Judy and that skirt-chaser Gary Whitt used to run around together drinking and driving."

My ears pricked up at the mention of the murdered man.

"I think Judy really cared about him," she went on, lowering her voice and glancing around, "but he was never anything but a playboy—not to speak ill of the dead. Judy was just one in a long line of girls that boy used and threw away. From what I've heard, he never changed his ways. In fact, I've wondered whether it was some jilted woman who went over to Gary's apartment and shot him."

There was a lull in the conversation as everyone considered this theory. "You may be right, Patricia," Miss Black Hair finally said to the woman who'd trashed poor Judy and then put forth her theory of the Whitt murder. "By the way, where is Judy tonight?"

"Baby Jonathan has an ear infection. She called this afternoon to tell me she couldn't come," Patricia said breezily. "She hated to miss the meeting and she said to tell y'all hey. I'll be sure to let her know everything we discussed tonight."

Everything except this little conversation, I thought.

Chapter 6

"How'd your meeting go?" Joe asked the next morning at breakfast. He'd been snoring on the couch with the television blaring when I got home. I'd switched off a baseball game only to have him sit up, rub his eyes, and swear he'd been watching the fool thing.

Honestly, you'd think he'd know better than to have the TV blasting so loud with Heather asleep. I spent my days creeping around when she was napping so as not to wake her, and there her daddy was, blowing off the roof while she slept right through it. Babies must behave better for their fathers.

After I turned off his ball game, Joe had gone to bed without even inquiring about my evening. I think he did say good night, but he left me sitting up wide awake after that cup of coffee I'd drunk.

"To tell you the truth, I'm not sure how it went," I answered. "Nobody was particularly friendly, but then again, a woman named Gloria is supposed to call me about membership requirements. Evidently there's a trial period, like being a sorority pledge, I have to go through before I become a full-fledged member."

"Hmm," Joe said. He was reading the headlines on the front page of the Wednesday edition of the *News and Views*. I looked over his shoulder to see if there were any stories about the Gary Whitt murder. "Local Farmers Attend Ag Convention," "Utility Rates May Go Up," "Contractor Hired to Remodel High School." Nothing on the front page, anyway.

At seven-thirty, Joe was already dressed for work in a crisp white shirt and creased navy slacks. I used heavy-duty spray starch when I ironed to make his clothes look like they'd been sent to the cleaners. We couldn't afford to use the dry cleaners to have Joe's shirts and slacks washed and starched. We just occasionally sent his suits.

His blue tie matched his eyes, and his recently-trimmed dark hair was neatly parted on the side. Joe looked good.

I, on the other hand, had just rolled out of bed to cook breakfast. I stood at the stove in a wrinkled cotton gown, bare feet, uncombed hair, and unbrushed teeth. Getting up in the middle of the night to nurse Heather had taken its toll on my appearance. "I'm not sure I fit in with these women," I said, thinking again about the meeting. "I wore a pair of corduroy pants and felt like somebody's poor relative."

"Un huh," Joe mumbled. His mouth was full of food, and his eyes were on the sports page.

"I definitely have to buy some new clothes to wear to the meetings. And do something about my hair."

"Right," Joe said, reaching for his orange juice.

"Joe Bulluck, are you even listening to me? You asked me how my meeting went, and then when I tell you, you ignore me."

"I've heard every word you've said. You need to buy some new clothes and do something about your hair." Joe calmly turned the page and folded the paper in half.

"Yes, I do." I slammed down a plate of toast. Luckily it was a paper plate, so nothing broke. Still Joe's toast went flying across the table, much to my satisfaction. "I need a makeover, but I don't have any money."

Joe finally put down the newspaper and looked at me. "Spend what it takes to make you feel good about yourself, Dee Ann. Put it on the credit card if you have to. You deserve new clothes and a trip to the beauty shop if that's what you want. We both decided when we had Heather that you'd stay home with her for a while. Money's tight, but that doesn't mean you can't spend some on yourself once in a while."

Now Joe knew when he was giving this sweet little speech that I wasn't about to go out and charge up a bunch of stuff that we couldn't pay for. No sirree, he knew it wasn't in me to spend money we didn't have. I'd been raised better than that. I come from a long line of folks who believed in frugal living. Back home, my family is known for being modest about what we have and not showing off.

As my grandma often said, "You don't put everything you own on your back." I'm sure she wouldn't have approved of my strutting around in clothes bought on credit.

Joe understood all this about me and my family. So while he was telling me to spend money on myself, he knew he was safe from any crazy shopping sprees on my part.

"I'll see what I can find on sale at Belk-Tyler's," I allowed. "Maybe I can look in the Yellow Pages under beauticians and call around to find someone who will cut my hair for a reasonable price."

I was thinking out loud, but Joe laughed. "That's the Bargain Annie I know."

"Of course, if I could find out who killed Gary Whitt and supply the police with that information, then I'd be ten thousand dollars richer and wouldn't have to worry about finding a cheap beautician and buying clothes on sale," I declared, miffed by the Bargain Annie label.

Joe quit laughing. "What in the world are you talking about, Dee Ann?"

"The reward money. Didn't you read that article in the paper? There's a ten thousand dollar reward 'for information leading to any arrests in the Gary Whitt murder,'" I said, quoting the words verbatim.

"Just how in the world do you expect to figure out who murdered Gary Whitt?" Joe was looking at me as if I'd grown another head.

"By reading about the case in the newspaper. And listening." I sounded sure of this strategy even though I'd just thought it up.

"Everybody in Narrow Creek is reading about the Whitt murder in the paper. And I'm sure there are a lot of details the police aren't releasing to the media. For example, remember when you asked me about the State Bureau of Investigation being called in to help with the case? I now know for a fact that a couple of SBI agents are in town working with Chief McSwain, and I've not read that in the *News and Views*."

"Oh, really?" I paused a moment to digest that piece of information. "It's not crazy to think I could solve this murder," I added. Growing up, I'd read a ton of Nancy Drew books and always figured out the mystery before little Miss Nancy Drew herself. Maybe I had a knack for solving crimes.

"Hmm, the SBI is on the case," I repeated. "See what I just learned from you by listening? And guess what I found out last night at my meeting? I overheard a lady say Gary Whitt had jilted a lot of girls over the years, and she wouldn't be surprised if one of them shot him."

"That's a theory I haven't heard," Joe admitted. "Read and listen all you want to about the case, but don't go poking into other people's business and getting caught up in situations where you don't need to be."

"I don't know how that would ever happen with my being stuck in this apartment with Heather all the time," I replied. "The Narrow Creek Police or the State Bureau of Investigation will probably have this case figured out long before I get out enough to investigate." I could hear the whine in my voice. Reality had reared its sensible head.

"I certainly hope so," said Joe. "Ten thousand dollars would be nice, but I'm not sure I want to see the mother of my child become Dee Ann Bulluck, Private Eye." Joe was laughing again.

Given the fact that I knew few people in my new hometown and had little opportunity to go anywhere to investigate anything, he was probably right not to take me seriously.

I decided to concentrate on something I knew I could accomplish. "Heather and I are going shopping today," I announced, full of resolve. "It's time for a Dee Ann Bulluck makeover. Out with the old college girl look, in with the new banker's wife style." I pictured myself in a women's magazine with before and after shots.

"Out with the old cotton nightgown, in with combing your hair before breakfast?" Joe teased.

"Watch it, mister. Who had to get up at four o'clock with Heather?"

"Okay, point taken. You plan your shopping trip." Joe paused and gave me a patronizing look. "And leave the crime-solving to the professionals."

*****

That afternoon, right after Heather's nap when she was fresh and in a good mood, I strapped her in the infant carrier and put her beside me in the front seat of the old Toyota for the trip to downtown Narrow Creek. I'd already loaded her up once to drive Joe back to work after lunch so I could have the car for the afternoon. I'd have to buckle her in yet again to go get Joe a little after five o'clock, but inconvenience is what happens in a one-car family.

My sole option for shopping was Belk-Tyler's, the only department store in town, since I couldn't afford anything from Three Sisters, the upscale ladies' boutique. Narrow Creek had a Sears catalog store, but I prefer to see a garment and try it on rather than go by a picture and hope an item fits after I get it in the mail. Returning things ordered out of a catalog is aggravating, too, even though the people at Sears are usually just as nice about it as they can be as long as I have the receipt.

Unfortunately, Belk-Tyler's wasn't having any kind of sale, and I make it a rule never to pay retail for clothes. So I moved on to a fabric store next door and found the cutest Simplicity dress patterns. One was for a sun dress with a halter top and a flared skirt accented by a sash around the waist. The other pattern was for a simple scoop-neck A-line dress. A classic A-line garment flatters about every body type there is, and I also knew this is the easiest dress in the world to sew. It was a buy one, get one free day, so I got both patterns for sixty cents, the price of one.

Fabric was on sale too, so I bought two yards of a red floral cotton for the sun dress and one and a half yards each of a solid kelly green poplin and a navy linen to make two A-line dresses. Even with zippers and thread, I spent less money for the fabric and notions to make three dresses than I would've spent to buy only one off the rack at Belk-Tyler's. As much as I disliked hearing Joe say it, I was a Bargain Annie. My grandma would have been proud of me.

The rest of that week, I sewed every chance I got, which was whenever Heather was asleep and I wasn't. As I stitched up the A-line dresses, I decided I would pick one to wear when I worked at the Arts and Crafts Bazaar. I planned to accessorize my choice by wearing my real pearl earrings Mama and Daddy had given me for my high school graduation. It's a known fashion fact that pearls never go out of style.

Chapter 7

Completing the second part of my makeover, a new hairdo, proved to be more difficult. Finding a beautician was a bit of a project. Five were listed in the Narrow Creek phone book under hairdressers. All five wanted at least fifteen dollars for a perm, which is what I'd decided I needed for my limp head of hair. I finally got Joe to ask the tellers at work where they had their hair done, and bingo, I got a lead! Somebody's cousin, a lady named Veronica, had a little shop behind her house out in the country. She charged only eight dollars for a perm, and when I called her, she said she didn't mind if I brought Heather with me.

I was slightly late for my ten a.m. appointment at the Kut and Kurl. I hadn't realized Veronica's shop was as far out of town as it turned out to be. But the Toyota was good on gas, and Heather had been happy during the ride. She was propped up in her infant carrier and seemed to be looking out the window during the whole trip. It probably did her some good to get out of the apartment for a while and see the world. I know it cheered me up.

One other car, a nice Volvo station wagon, was parked behind the Kut and Kurl, a single-wide trailer in the backyard of a small brick ranch. I went inside, where a very pretty woman who looked to be about my age glanced up from the beautician's chair where she was writing a check.

"Hello," she said in a soft voice. Her shoulder-length black hair had that slightly tousled look that was so popular, and she had the loveliest green eyes. She gave me a warm smile. "Vee, you have a customer."

"Must be Dee Ann." A tall, skinny woman with teased red hair turned around from the sink and dried her hands on a towel. "You're my next appointment, ain't you, honey?"

"Yes, that's me."

"I'm Veronica," she said, batting eyelids caked in bright blue eyeshadow. "This is Scarlett Hood." Veronica nodded her head in the direction of the lady in the chair. "Scarlett, meet Dee Ann—what's your last name again, honey?"

"Bulluck," I said. "Dee Ann Bulluck. It's nice to meet you both."

"Dee Ann is new around here," the beautician said. "I think that's what Cousin Sherry at the bank told me." Veronica glanced at me for confirmation.

"That's right. I moved to Narrow Creek with my husband and baby girl a little over a month ago."

"Cute baby," Scarlett said, glancing at Heather in her infant carrier. "Welcome to town. I hope you're safe in Narrow Creek. And I'm not referring to the recent murder. You should know the natives bite." This time her smile was full of mischief.

She handed her check to Veronica. "I'll see you in six weeks, Vee," she said. "It was a pleasure to meet you, Dee Ann. Maybe I'll bump into you again somewhere soon. After all, it's a very small world around here."

I heard Scarlett's car wheels on the gravel driveway as I situated Heather's carrier on the floor where my baby could see me.

"I don't care what nobody says; she's a nice lady, even if she does wear her clothes a little too tight and speaks her mind a little more than she should sometimes. It's a shame folks talk so bad about her. I guess that's what she meant about people biting. You know what I think? I think those women in town put her down out of pure-T jealousy, what with her bein' so attractive and all."

Veronica delivered her opinion while she swept up hair around the one chair in her shop. "Just give me a minute, honey, to clean up this floor a little bit, and then we'll git started on you."

I'd noticed Scarlett's somewhat buxom figure straining against the buttons of her blouse. What do people say about this woman? I wanted to know, but Veronica had already moved on.

"You don't mind if I have a cigarette, do you? Oh, wait, I done forgot about the baby. They say on the television now that folks don't need to be breathin' other people's cigarette smoke. I'll just have a piece of gum instead until I git you under the dryer, and then I'll step outside for a minute."

Veronica dumped a dustpan full of hair in a small metal trashcan and snapped open her black beautician's cape. "Okey, dokey, climb on up in this big ol' chair in front of the mirror here. Let's us see now. You've got a nice shade of natural blonde, but your hair is right fine, ain't it? A permanent will give it some body. I'll trim it up some for you too. We'll git you lookin' good, honey."

"Whatever you think," I squeaked as she wrapped the plastic cape around me and tied it behind my neck. For some reason, I've always been intimidated by hairdressers. I find it hard to express how I want my hair styled. I've even told beauticians I liked a haircut that I hated. I guess I just don't want to hurt anyone's feelings. Besides, after someone has already whacked off my hair, there's no point complaining then.

"I got me this shop after Jerry come back from Vietnam in '69," Veronica rattled on. "Jerry is my husband. He's disabled from the war. Can't work because of his nerves. He don't talk about it none, but I think he seen some real awful things over there. But he watches the young'uns when they're out of school while I work back here in the shop. I go up to the house to check on all of 'em when I git a chance. Roy, that's my boy, he's eight, so he don't need much watchin' anyway, and Lisa Marie is seven and a good little helper around the house."

"You certainly have your hands full," was all I could think of to say. This was a prime example of my not knowing the burdens that others carry. Suddenly I felt ashamed of myself for all my petty complaining about the move to Narrow Creek.

"Oh, it's not so bad, honey. We git along all right. There's plenty that's worse off than us. Lord knows. There's men who didn't come back from Vietnam or came home missin' arms and legs. Jerry goes to the Veteran's Hospital when he can, and he's got better over the years."

Veronica had been combing and pinning my hair into little sections while she talked. "Now how tight do you want these curls?"

"Veronica," I said, for once finding some courage in a hairdresser's chair, "I want to look like Olivia Newton-John in the final scene of *Grease*."

Veronica grinned and nodded her head. "Honey, I seen that movie and I know that hairdo. I think we can do it. You know, you kinda look like her in the face. 'Cept I think your eyes are even purtier than hers. What color are they? Blue or green? This is gonna be fun."

As Veronica rolled my hair on tiny pink curlers, I had an idea. Who knew more gossip than a beautician? "The Gary Whitt case is a real mystery, isn't it?" I fished.

Veronica took the bait. "Oh, I don't think it should be all that hard to solve. It's all about drugs. Gary Whitt was the biggest dope dealer in Narrow Creek. Folks don't like to think there's drug use around here, but we ain't no different from the rest of the country. Gary was the top dog of selling all the marijuana and that new drug, cocaine, that comes in here off the interstate."

"Really?" I sputtered. "My landlady called him her contractor. He was renovating a bathroom for her when he was shot." I remembered Miss Josie mentioning drugs as a motive, but I also recalled her saying she never saw any evidence of such while Gary was working for her.

"Oh, that was his cover," Veronica said dismissively. "He was good at building, I'll give him that, but he didn't do much of it. He'd take a job here and there just so it'd look like he was your average workin' man, but his main business was runnin' drugs."

I wanted to ask Veronica how she knew all of this very interesting information, but I was afraid to interrupt the flow of juicy details. As it turned out, I didn't have to.

"He came around the house one time a year or so ago with some of his dope-smokin' buddies. Bunch of low life in my book. Said they wanted to see Jerry. Back in high school, they was all friends.

"I happened to go up to the house to check on things, and there they all sat, drinking Pabst Blue Ribbon and smokin' weed at two in the afternoon. Jerry won't though. I reckon he knew he's on enough drugs from the doctor that he didn't need no more.

"I ain't ashamed to say I put a tongue lashing on 'em. Told that sorry-ass Gary Whitt, pardon my French, not to ever show his face around my house again. 'Git out of here,' I said, 'and don't let the door hit you on the way out.' I had to open the windows—and it was January—to air the house out before the young'uns got home from school."

I glanced at Heather, who'd fallen asleep, oblivious to all this sordid business of the adult world.

"Even though he won't smokin' nothing, I gave Jerry what for too. 'Why'd you let that crowd use drugs in our house?' I asked him. 'What if there'd been a raid? You put your whole family at risk.' I might've been exaggerating a little. It won't likely the Narrow Creek police would've picked that day to come all the way out here to bust Gary Whitt when he carried on his business in town right under their noses all the time."

Veronica paused to reach for a plastic cap to tie over my tightly rolled head.

"Do you know what Jerry told me?" she continued. "He said he was too afraid of Gary Whitt and those guys with him to say anything. He said Gary carried a gun on him, and they were all laughin' and carryin' on about how they shot somebody up in Virginia over a drug deal gone bad.

"That's when I knew for sure Gary Whitt was the real thing when it came to dealin'. Jerry was a little scared they'd all come back and shoot me for kickin' 'em out of our house that day, but since I'm still here, I guess they got over it. I probably won't worth messin' with."

As she fiddled with the dial on the hooded hair dryer, Veronica added one final statement. "No, ma'am, it didn't surprise me none to hear he got shot hisself. Drug folks are mean."

My eyes were as big as saucers by the time Veronica sat me under the hot air blowing out of the hair dryer and went outside to smoke her cigarette. I couldn't wait to run this scoop past Joe. But then I remembered his condescending tone when he told me to leave the crime solving to the professionals. I decided I would keep whatever I learned about Gary Whitt's murder to myself.

Then wouldn't Joe be surprised if I figured it all out and got that big fat ten thousand dollar check? My coming up with a name that could lead to an arrest was a long shot—it would be a surprise to me too—but I could certainly give it a try.

I don't know if it was the fumes from the perm or the steady hum of the hairdryer, but Heather slept for the rest of the visit. Before I left that day, I thought about the valuable information Veronica had given me, and I insisted she take a two-dollar tip. I told her it was because I was so pleased with my new hairdo. Which I really was.

Chapter 8

The Saturday of the Arts and Crafts Bazaar arrived, and again I worried about what to wear. At least this time I wasn't pulling clothes out of the closet and throwing them on the bed. I just couldn't decide between the two A-line dresses I'd made.

Dangling each on a hanger, I decided to get Joe's opinion. "Which dress should I wear to the bazaar this morning?" Joe was eating scrambled eggs and toast at the table with Heather on his lap. I caught him slipping her a tiny bit of egg.

"Don't give Heather that," I fussed. "You know she's not ready for solid food yet. How's she supposed to chew with no teeth? I hope you know the Heimlich maneuver, Joe Bulluck."

"The green one," Joe said, ignoring my scolding. Heather was drooling flecks of egg.

"Don't you like the navy dress? What's wrong with the navy dress?"

"Nothing's wrong with the navy dress. You asked me to pick one, so I picked the green one. Geez Louise. It's no big deal. I'm sure either one is fine."

"It's a big deal to me. I don't want to show up looking shabby again."

"You never look shabby to me, Dee Ann."

Joe meant well, but there's only so much a husband knows about how women judge one another's clothes. I don't know why I even bothered seeking his advice. Still, I decided to go with the kelly green dress. It was a sunny May morning, and that lively green seemed more in the spirit of the day than navy blue.

"Remember Heather's schedule for the rest of the morning. Put her in the baby swing for a few minutes when she gets fussy, and don't let her sleep too long at ten or she won't go down for her afternoon nap. Don't forget she's had a little bit of a cold this week, so it's important she gets her rest." I grabbed a Kleenex from a box on the kitchen counter and gently wiped her runny nose. "The bazaar is over at twelve-thirty, so I should be home shortly after, since I'm not on the clean-up committee, thank goodness."

"Under control," Joe said, saluting me and giving Heather an exaggerated wink. I wondered what kind of mischief he had planned for the morning. Joe didn't follow the rules of handling a baby the way I did. He didn't worry as much about schedules. Then again, he wasn't there all that often with Heather, especially by himself, so he hadn't had to deal with a cranky baby who'd gotten out of whack with her naps.

Oh well, I told myself, I won't be gone that long. Surely Joe can manage for a few hours. I should leave the two of them alone together more often, I decided. The more Joe had to assume full responsibility for taking care of Heather, the better he'd get at it.

I went back to the bathroom, where I'd left my electric rollers heating up. I intended to wow the ladies with my new curly perm. And my kelly green A-line dress accessorized with my pearl earrings.

*****

I'd offered to give Cynthia a ride to the bazaar to pay her back for taking me to my first club meeting. It's always important to keep the books even and not owe anybody. My grandma used to quote something from Thessalonians that warned against being beholden to people. I don't know the verse, but I do remember that word "beholden" as something you didn't want to be.

But Cynthia said she had to run a couple of early morning errands before going to the bazaar and she'd see me there. I couldn't imagine what kind of errands somebody needed to do before eight o'clock on a Saturday morning. I hoped she wasn't giving me some lame excuse because she didn't want to be seen riding with me in my Toyota.

So I was by myself when I opened the door to the fellowship hall and saw that every single woman there was dressed in slacks. Nice slacks, mind you, with matching blouses or lightweight summer sweaters. But not a dress in sight. I would've turned around right then and there and slunk back home, except for the fact that I'd already been spotted.

"Dee Ann," Cynthia exclaimed in her shrill voice. "Come on in. My goodness, you certainly have dressed up for us this morning. You didn't have to get all gussied up for a Saturday morning craft fair. Maybe we can find you an apron in the kitchen so you don't get your Sunday dress dirty." She snickered behind her hand. "I guess when you're home with a baby all the time, you're dying to put on something pretty when you go anywhere."

I was dying, all right; I was dying a thousand embarrassing deaths while Cynthia went on and on about my unfortunate choice of clothing. Why hadn't I figured out these women would see their day at the bazaar as a casual occasion perfect for a cute pair of slacks?

Cynthia suddenly focused on my head. "What an interesting hairstyle. Very curly. Where in the world did you get that done in Narrow Creek?"

"I have a hairdresser out of town," I stammered. I wasn't about to say she lived out in the sticks a few miles from Narrow Creek. Maybe Cynthia would think I'd gone to Raleigh to get my hair styled.

Fortunately, I was spared further interrogation as Barbara Highland swooped in to give me my assignment. "Dee Ann, I need you to handle the ceramics table. We've got some absolutely wonderful handmade items donated by some very generous ladies in our community. Most of these gals used to be club members before they aged out. Come with me, and I'll show you the ropes. Love your hair, by the way. You look like Olivia Newton-John in *Grease*." My self-confidence, which had certainly taken a beating, rose a notch after this compliment.

Barbara led me to a table loaded with ceramic bowls, plates, and vases. I had to admit most of them were quite pretty. Many had been hand-painted with flowers, birds, butterflies, ducks, or deer.

"The prices are on the items and are non-negotiable," Barbara said in a clipped voice. "Watch how people handle these. They look sturdy but can break if dropped. Ceramic stuff can also chip in a New York minute." Gone was her ladylike Southern drawl. This was businesswoman Barbara.

"Put this sign in that small easel at the front of the table where people can see it." She handed me a piece of ivory mat on which was written in a careful script: "You break it; you buy it."

I placed the framed sign in the easel just as the front door opened, and the first customers of the day rushed into the fellowship hall. I had a fleeting thought of Jesus throwing the moneychangers out of the temple. We're not in the sanctuary, only the fellowship hall, I told myself, and the money we're raising is for a good cause. At least I thought it was. I wasn't exactly sure what the profit would go for, but I felt certain we'd be contributing to some worthy charity. The ladies had probably talked about it at the meeting during one of the times I'd been daydreaming.

Business was brisk, and I found I enjoyed peddling ceramics. I even thought about taking a class in how to make the stuff and starting a little enterprise, casting vases and plates and then selling them for a tidy profit. I didn't know how much the supplies cost, but I could see that ladies were willing to spend what I considered to be good money to buy a vase with a grapevine painted on it or a plate decorated with a flock of geese flying around the rim. Then I remembered I'm not the least bit artistically inclined. I'd have to hire someone to do all the painting. So much for profits.

Midway through my shift, Barbara Highland came by the table to relieve me. "We have some Krispy Kreme donuts in the kitchen if they haven't all been eaten by now, and the bathroom is just down the hall. Be back in ten minutes, so I can move on to the next table and give someone else a break."

I've never been one to turn down a Krispy Kreme, so I rushed to the kitchen at the back of the fellowship hall, hoping I wasn't too late. An open box sat on a long high counter. I picked out a sugar-glazed doughnut and polished it off in three very unladylike bites.

"Now where are the napkins?" I mumbled to myself, noting sugar residue on my hands and suspecting the same around my mouth. I'd stooped down to look in the cabinets built underneath the counter when I suddenly heard angry voices.

"Have you lost your mind, wanting to talk to me about Gary Whitt here of all places in front of everyone I know?" There was no mistaking the shrillness of Cynthia Ford.

"Would you rather I come by your house when your husband's home? I don't think so," retorted a voice I didn't recognize. "Gary's dead, and I think you're responsible." I froze. No way was I revealing my presence.

"You're even crazier than I thought," I heard Cynthia screech. "Why would I have any reason to kill him?"

"Hell hath no fury like a woman scorned," was the response. "You couldn't stand that Gary left you for me. I know how you called him all the time. You couldn't move on, could you? Couldn't stand to see him find happiness with me."

"Gary and I parted as friends. We got tired of each other, if you want to know the truth. And you'll find out too, it's not easy having an affair in this town. It got to the point where trying to meet him without anyone seeing us was more trouble than it was worth. I guess you could say the thrill was gone." Cynthia sounded almost bored.

"I don't believe you for one minute. What about all those phone calls? I was with him several times late at night when you called. Gary told me you wouldn't leave him alone, that you wanted him back."

"I don't know if he was trying to make you jealous or what game he was playing," Cynthia said in a cold voice, "but Gary told you a big fat stinking lie. Lots of people called Gary late at night. Didn't you realize he was a drug dealer? I bought a little weed off him now and then."

There was a moment of silence. I wondered how much of my ten minutes was left. I certainly hoped Barbara Highland wouldn't come looking for me. "He told me he was through with all that," the mystery woman said tearfully. "Gary was ready to devote himself full-time to his contractor business and settle down. He loved me and wanted to marry me. I was close to asking Gregory for a divorce."

"Spare me." Cynthia gave a high, false laugh. "Gary Whitt wasn't about to marry anybody. He was the biggest two-timing flirt in Narrow Creek. Maybe you already know that, though. Maybe you're just pretending to be naïve.

Who's to say you didn't kill him when you finally realized what a worthless playboy he was?"

I heard a gasp, and then Cynthia continued. "That would make as much sense as your accusing me. I was through with him; you weren't. Did he tell you he was moving on? Or did he just quit taking your phone calls?

"Let me give you some advice, Lisa," Cynthia hissed. "Pretend you never knew the man if you want to stay married to that goody two-shoes associate minister husband of yours and not wind up a murder suspect."

I heard a sob, footsteps, and then silence. Peeking around the corner of the bar, I saw the room was now empty. I waited one more minute before easing out the door myself, walking back to my table in a daze from all I'd heard.

Cynthia, an adulteress? A drug user? Possibly a killer? And who was this Lisa, married to an associate minister? Did she really think Gary Whitt was going to marry her, or had she realized what a cad he was and pulled the trigger as Cynthia said?

I blame my distracted state of mind for the accident that occurred during my last hour of duty. Reaching across the table to give a woman her change, just as I had done with plenty of other customers all morning, I brushed against a tall yellow vase. Although it seemed that I saw what happened next in slow motion, I was unable to grab the vase in time, and it crashed into a plate, chipping both. At the sound of ceramics shattering, the entire fellowship hall grew quiet. My customer gasped and jumped back. Every shopper there stared in my direction and began murmuring sympathetically.

"She knocked something over on the ceramics table, poor thing."

"Bless her heart; I'm glad I didn't do that."

"Something broke, all right, from the way it sounded."

I was mute with mortification. Barbara Highland scurried over, saw the damage, and to her credit, immediately said, "Don't worry about it, Dee Ann. Accidents happen. The club will absorb the cost."

But I'm a person who believes in cleaning up her own messes and paying for her own mistakes. After all, I was the one who'd posted the "you break it; you buy it" sign.

"Oh, no, I intend to pay for these items," I said. "I wouldn't want the club to lose any profit because of me." Of all the people in the world, I didn't want to be *beholden* to the Narrow Creek Ladies' Society.

"Well, if you're sure." Barbara eyed the damaged merchandise. "We'll mark them down due to their unfortunate condition."

Cynthia picked this moment to dash over from her booth across the room. "Goodness, Dee Ann. What a mess. And I just remembered I was supposed to get you an apron from the kitchen to wear over that pretty new dress. I don't suppose you cut yourself or anyone else, did you? There's no blood that I can see." She sounded disappointed.

Honestly, you'd think I'd pulled out a knife and tried to attack someone instead of knocking over a vase. For a moment—just a moment, mind you—I envisioned chasing Cynthia around the fellowship hall with a machete. Or at least tying her to a chair with that blasted apron she kept talking about and leaving her in the kitchen for the rest of the weekend to think about how demeaning her comments to me always were. Only the fact that Joe's boss was her husband kept me from exposing that dope-smoking, two-timing wench.

I left with a three-dollar chipped plate and a five-dollar cracked vase. I'd done the right thing when I insisted on buying the damaged items, but all the way home I fumed about these unintended purchases as I flushed with embarrassment over making such a spectacle of myself.

Thinking about the confrontation I'd overheard in the kitchen, though, I realized I'd picked up some valuable information. Information that could possibly lead to a ten thousand dollar reward. I decided to view eight dollars spent on damaged ceramics as an investigative expense.

Chapter 9

Summer arrived in Narrow Creek, and my word, it was hot! The window air conditioning unit in our living room hummed constantly. I could picture our meter spinning like crazy, but I decided that Joe and I would just have to spend our last dime to keep Heather cool and comfortable. Not that I like to sweat either. It's one thing to be hot on a beach or beside a pool somewhere. That's a fun kind of hot. Being stuck in a house without air conditioning in the summer is another kind of hot that's definitely not fun.

I sat in my cool apartment and examined what I'd learned about the Gary Whitt murder. The encounter between a couple of Gary's paramours that I'd by chance been privy to in the kitchen of First Baptist Church had raised questions that needed further investigation. I wasn't as shocked by learning that Cynthia Ford was an adulteress as I was by hearing her say she used marijuana. A fashion-plate, status-conscious career woman wasn't my idea of a dope smoker. I wondered whether Cynthia was telling the truth when she claimed her phone calls to Gary were about buying marijuana. Maybe she was still under his spell and trying to get him back as that poor Lisa woman had claimed.

After an initial month or so of heavy coverage, the *Narrow Creek News and Views* had dried up as a source of information. As summer began, the only mention of the crime was a continuous advertisement concerning the ten thousand dollar reward for "information leading to any arrests in the Gary Whitt murder." I wondered whether the newspaper was being censored by the police department or if there simply wasn't anything new to report.

I'd been tempted to tell Joe what I'd overheard in the church kitchen, but each time I came close to repeating the scandalous details, I'd remember his admonishing me to stay out of situations where I didn't need to be. Even though I hadn't intended to be part of the kitchen confrontation, I was sure this would be just the type of "situation" he meant.

I also hadn't told him Veronica's story of Gary Whitt's drug activities. Best to let Joe think I'd given up any plan to solve the murder. What a surprise it would be when I supplied the name or names of the perpetrator or perpetrators and collected that ten thousand dollar check. I could just imagine Joe's stunned expression.

A drug deal gone bad or a jilted woman out for revenge? And then there was still the robber-caught-in-the-act theory. I gazed out the window at the lush June landscape of Miss Josie's backyard.

Brilliant zinnias, marigolds, and petunias caught my eye along with Miss Josie's flourishing vegetable garden. Willie was busy all day, every day—except Sunday, of course—weeding and watering. Not to mention all the grass cutting he did in the Powells' big yard, including around our apartment. Joe had offered to mow some, but Miss Josie told him it was good for Willie to have enough to do for a change.

From the kitchen window I could see Willie sweating away as he often did in the garden. Sometimes, I'd notice Miss Josie coming out of the house wearing a pretty, long-sleeved blouse and a wide-brimmed straw hat and helping him pick cucumbers or squash, her gloved hands moving quickly among the vines. I tried not to get homesick watching Miss Josie and thinking about my mother back home, picking the same vegetables but without a hired man to do all the hard work.

One thing was for sure: I never saw Floyd Powell near the garden. Maybe he felt like Joe did about growing vegetables. When I'd suggested asking the Powells for a plot behind the apartment to plant a few hills of cucumbers, green peppers, and tomatoes, Joe had stared at me like I was crazy.

"That's why you have the Winn-Dixie, Dee Ann," he said. "Do you really want to get outside in the heat and hoe a garden?"

Growing up, Joe had to string up butter beans and chop the weeds out of his parents' garden so much that he'd turned on growing anything himself. I'd helped in a family garden also but had a couple of older brothers who did most of the work. Joe was an only child. Maybe Mr. Powell had been an only child too. At any rate, I didn't pursue getting my own garden plot. Joe wouldn't help, and it might've been too much work for me with Heather to take care of.

Still, I had fresh vegetables all that summer. Two or three times a week, I'd open the downstairs outside door and find a paper bag tagged with a card that said: "From My Garden to Your Table. Enjoy! Mrs. Josephine Powell." In the right upper corner of the card was the cutest little drawing of a hoe and rake. I guess I wasn't the only person getting vegetables from Miss Josie's garden since she'd gone to the expense of ordering printed cards to put on her giveaway produce bags.

I never thought of vegetables as a gift before that summer, but I'm here to say it was the best kind of present. All season I had big, luscious, juicy tomatoes, totally unlike those hard things sold in the grocery store. For a month or so, there was evidently a bumper crop of squash, so much I had to call my mother long-distance. "Mama," I said, "I'm up to my eyeballs in squash. How do you make that squash casserole you always take to family reunions?"

"Where in the world did you get all that squash, Dee Ann?" Mama asked. "I didn't know you have a garden."

"I don't have a garden, Mama. Joe didn't want one. Miss Josie sends me vegetables out of hers, and she's overdone it with the squash."

"Miss Josie, the lady you rent from? I thought you were on the outs with her after she came over and tried to boss you around."

"Well, I guess we're not on the outs when it comes to her giving away surplus vegetables."

"Dee Ann, you shouldn't have spoken to her the way you did. You always were quick to sass people. Haven't you learned it's better to turn the other cheek? Miss Josie was probably just trying to be helpful that day. Don't you feel bad now since she's bringing you vegetables out of her own garden?"

Good grief. As I thought of the clock ticking on my long-distance call, I was sorry I'd ever told Mama about my tiff with Miss Josie. I'd called for a recipe, not a lecture. I ignored her questions, which I don't think she expected me to answer anyway.

"I don't have long to talk, Mama. Do you know that recipe by heart, or are you going to have to look it up?"

"I'll mail it to you today, sugar. And you know it's real easy to freeze squash. Just wash it, slice it up, and put it in those Ziploc freezer bags. You be sure to thank Miss Josie for the vegetables. And it wouldn't hurt to tell her you're sorry for acting so ugly that day she visited."

Thank goodness I hadn't mentioned the Gary Whitt case to Mama or I'd have been on the phone even longer. Mama loves a good murder mystery as well as any kind of gossip and would've wanted every detail.

Later in the summer I got bags of sweet Silver Queen corn but decided I couldn't afford to call my mother to get her corn pudding recipe. When it's fresh, there's nothing better than plain corn on the cob anyway. For a couple of weeks, either Willie or Miss Josie—I never found out exactly which one did the delivering—left me green bell peppers that I used as shells for miniature meatloaf. Joe's favorite, though, was the small cucumbers that I sliced without peeling and marinated in salt, pepper, and vinegar.

No doubt about it, Miss Josie's garden saved our family a bunch of grocery money. Her generosity was, as I said, a real gift to us all summer. I did as Mama told me and wrote Miss Josie a couple of thank-you notes and left them in her mailbox. I knew I should take Heather and go see her in person. After all, she might have some information about the murder of her former contractor.

In addition to furthering my investigation, though, there was another reason I needed to see Miss Josie in person. I hadn't wanted to hear it, but Mama was right: I owed my landlady an apology. But I was too proud to humble myself and ask her pardon. I've always hated to admit it when I've acted unkindly.

*****

The Ladies' Society didn't meet in the summer since everyone was "far too busy with the children out of school and summer travel." Some of the women had homes at the beach, where they promptly relocated "to avoid the awful heat and humidity of Narrow Creek."

I had a child's plastic pool that I filled with water from a garden hose and sat in with Heather in my lap in the yard behind our apartment.

My baby girl was growing in all sorts of ways. She was sleeping in a secondhand crib Joe had bought for ten dollars from one of the tellers at the bank, and the bassinet was sitting in a corner of her room, waiting to be returned to my mother before anything else happened to it. Heather was also beginning to slurp up infant cereal and eat from tiny jars of baby food. It was a sweet sight at lunch to see Joe gently poking a tiny spoonful of pureed bananas or sweet potatoes into her open mouth, wearing an apron around his neck to protect his dress shirt and tie. Someone other than me could finally feed that child.

I'd given up a lot of freedom when I committed to being her main source of food. For sure, I couldn't go far when I was nursing a baby. In fact, I'd left Heather with Joe for longer than an hour only twice since she was born—once to attend my first meeting of the Ladies' Society and then the Saturday I went to work at the bazaar. How was I ever going to find out who killed Gary Whitt when I was stuck at home with a baby?

I needed to get out and mingle, but the only neighbor I'd met was Miss Josie. I kept hoping someone from the Ladies' Society would call to chat, and I could discreetly find out more about the Lisa who was married to an associate minister. But the phone never rang.

Gloria, the membership chairwoman, did send me a postcard from Nags Head, where she was spending several weeks at her parents' cottage. Her note on the back said, "Hope you're having a good summer. Talk to you after Labor Day about club work. Gloria." That was it. I threw the postcard in the trash even though it did have a nice picture of the Wright Brothers Memorial at Kill Devil Hills.

Chapter 10

I knew the minute I laid eyes on it that this letter was something different and special. It was the middle of June, the time of the month when we got mostly circulars from furniture stores and car dealerships. Sandwiched between two such pieces of junk mail, though, was an oversized red envelope, addressed in precise calligraphy to Mr. and Mrs. Joseph Bulluck.

I would've ripped into it right there in the driveway at the mailbox, but I was balancing Heather on one hip and holding the rest of the mail as well. Once I got inside and plunked her in the baby swing, I slit the envelope and pulled out an ornate invitation printed in blue ink on stiff white paper decorated with pictures of American flags and fireworks around the border. It read: "*Mr. and Mrs. Edward Gaylord III cordially invite you to an Independence Day Gala at their riverfront home, Blue Water Haven, on Wednesday afternoon, the fourth of July, from three o'clock in the afternoon until after fireworks.*" There was an RSVP card to be returned by June twenty-fifth.

Ed Gaylord, the president of Joe's bank. Surely Joe would want to go. I was excited about having something to do on the Fourth of July. To me, nothing is more depressing than a holiday with no plans, even a minor holiday like Valentine's Day or St. Patrick's Day. I've always loved a party, especially ones that celebrate special occasions.

I wondered whether to wear my new red sun dress. I didn't think shorts would be appropriate, not when the invitation was so fancy. I'd have to think about my outfit carefully. Believe me, I'd learned the Narrow Creek dress code was tricky business.

At lunch, I couldn't wait to tell Joe about our upcoming social engagement and pounced on him the minute he walked through the door. "Guess what came in the mail today? An invitation to the Gaylords' Independence Day Gala," I answered before giving him a chance to speak. I read Joe the entire card.

"Oh yeah, Ed's Fourth of July party. I've heard it's a big to-do. Nice of him to invite us."

"Exactly what do you mean by a 'big to-do'?"

"I think there's a band, a pig pickin' with all the fixings, and some fancy fireworks to top it all off." Joe took off his suit coat and slipped out of his shoes. "One of the guys at the bank said Ed invites about three hundred people every year. It's definitely the Fourth of July party people go to if they're not at the beach."

"Isn't Ed's wife out of town for the summer?" I remembered all the wives in the Ladies' Society who talked about leaving their husbands home to work while they spent the summer at the coast.

"Ed has a place at Hilton Head, but I believe his wife comes home to throw this party at their river house. Tough life, huh?" Joe shook his head, faintly smiling.

"Wow." The luxury of having two vacation homes, plus a main residence in Narrow Creek. On one of our Sunday afternoon drives, Joe had taken me past the Gaylords' modern split-level brick home that seemed to take up half a block. The story was that the Gaylords had family money in addition to Ed's salary at the bank. I remembered riding in Cynthia's Mercedes to my first Ladies' Society meeting and decided that she and Bill must have family money too. I sure wished Joe and I had some of that supplementary income.

"I assume you want to go then," I said. "Are children invited, or do I need to find a babysitter? The invitation was addressed to only you and me and didn't say anything about family. Do you think we'll be able to find a babysitter on a holiday? What should we wear?"

"Which question do you want me to answer first? Boy, somebody's excited."

I sniffed. "Well, excuse my enthusiasm. You'd be excited too if you sat home every day."

"Okay, okay, don't get all huffy. I've heard it's an adults-only party, so yes, we need to find a babysitter. As far as what to wear, you know I'm no good at fashion advice, but I'll ask at the bank."

"For heaven's sake, don't ask Ed himself. I wouldn't want him to think we don't know how to dress for his party. Just casually mention the party to somebody who's going and ask what that person and his wife are wearing. See if you can get any names of babysitters too."

"Yes, ma'am. Joe Bulluck, super-duper detective at your service. I specialize in getting the skinny on what the dress code is for special occasions without people even suspecting they're being asked. I can also track down the name of every available babysitter in a ten-mile radius, even on a holiday weekend. Now what's for lunch?"

"Oh, Joe, be serious." I rolled my eyes but couldn't help smiling as I reached for the loaf of bread and began making sandwiches with my homemade pimento cheese. Joe didn't know it, but he wasn't the only one who would be doing some detective work relating to this party. With three hundred people invited, I felt I could possibly find out something to help in my Gary Whitt investigation.

*****

Another week passed, and I couldn't seem to shake a summer cold. I struggled to do even basic housework and take care of Heather's needs. I was worn out with sneezing and coughing.

"Why don't you go see a doctor?" Joe suggested. "I hate to see you feeling so bad." I think he was also tired of having his sleep disturbed by my coughing in the middle of the night.

"It just has to wear itself out," I replied. I don't think there's much a doctor can do for a bad cold."

"You don't know for sure what you have is just a bad cold. And even if it is, you don't want your cold to turn into pneumonia. Try to get an appointment with somebody around lunch, and I'll stay with Heather."

I really was congested. And I definitely wanted to get well in time for the Gaylords' party. After Joe left for work, I looked up "Physicians" in the Yellow Pages. What I'd give for old Dr. Cooper. Back home, he'd done everything from treating me for the flu to delivering Heather.

Two groups of family doctors were listed. I called the first, and a chirpy voice informed me that Drs. Walker, Mitchell, and Brown were not taking any new patients at the time. I had better luck with the second group and called Joe at work to tell him I'd made a one o'clock appointment with a Dr. Whitaker at Narrow Creek Family Physicians. Joe would need to take a late lunch to stay with Heather.

At one o'clock sharp, I checked in with the receptionist. No sooner had I picked up a three month old copy of *Newsweek* and settled down in the waiting room than a plump nurse opened a door and called my name.

"Let's get some blood work on you first," she said as she led me to a small area adjacent to a lab. "Have a seat and someone will see you in a few minutes." She disappeared down the hall.

I took the only unoccupied chair in the room where a dozen people were waiting.

"Buck, you heard anything lately about who they think killed Gary Whitt?" asked a woman with a teased blonde updo. She was addressing a crew-cut young man in a Narrow Creek Volunteer Fire Department t-shirt who sat beside her, but the entire room turned to look at her. I held my breath, waiting for a response, wondering exactly who "they" were.

"Nothing more than it won't no robbery. Least there won't no sign of forced entry and nothing was taken," Buck drawled. "Gary musta known who killed him and opened the door for 'em. Whoever shot him done it while lookin' him in the eye. Five bullets to the head. Entry points in the face."

Looking around the room and noticing he was now the center of attention, Buck added, "I can't divulge my source, but let's just say it's official."

An officer of the law? Judging by his t-shirt, I guessed Buck was the kind of guy who might hang around with the law enforcement crowd. Before I could speculate further, however, the lady with the blonde hair abruptly changed the subject.

"I hope taking my blood goes easier this time than the last time I was here." I tried not to stare at a heart tattoo that decorated the arm the woman was slowly massaging as she spoke. "That nurse had a terrible time finding my vein. She said my veins roll."

"My veins roll too," chimed in an elderly black lady. "It sure does make it hard to give blood."

Rolling veins! I studied the insides of my arms.

"Course the worst pain I ever had was my breast biopsy," continued Miss Tattoo. "That doctor just wanted to dig and dig. I didn't have no pain killer either."

"Lord have mercy!" said a woman sitting next to me. "How'd you stand it?"

"It was hard," said Miss Tattoo. "I was pure crying for my mama, and she done been dead ten years."

Out of pure reflex, I put my hand lightly over my heart. Jumping up, I grabbed a *Better Homes and Gardens* off a nearby table. Read and don't listen, I told myself.

It didn't work.

"I hope that nurse with the red hair ain't working today," whispered Miss Tattoo. "She's rough with that needle."

"I know what you mean, girl," the elderly black lady commiserated. "She stuck me four times before she found a vein that worked."

Just then a young nurse with flaming red hair came to the door of the lab. "Geraldine Pittman," she called. Miss Tattoo got up from her seat with an air of resignation.

"Y'all pray for me," she said to the room at large.

I looked at my watch. Why, it was already one-thirty. This trip to the doctor was taking longer than I'd expected. Joe needed to get back to work. What was I even doing here in the first place? All I had was a common cold. Who gets a blood test for a common cold?

If I leave right now, I'll have just enough time to stop by the Rite Aid. I can get something over the counter that'll work just fine. I'll ask the pharmacist. A pharmacist is almost as good as a doctor anyway.

"I've changed my mind about seeing the doctor today," I said as I raced past the check-out counter on my way out. A startled receptionist opened her mouth, but I didn't stick around long enough to hear what she had to say. I was heading for the parking lot, where I slammed the Toyota into first and then second gear, slinging gravel in my haste to get away.

*****

The summer days dragged on as did my cold. The pharmacist at the Rite Aid had told me not to take any medicine since I was still nursing Heather. He said a cold just had to wear itself out most of the time anyway, exactly what I'd told Joe in the first place. I hoped we wouldn't get any kind of bill or insurance information concerning that trip that would tip Joe off that I'd cut the doctor's visit short. When I'd returned home that day, he'd asked whether I'd picked up any medicine, and I'd reported what the pharmacist said.

"Okay, I'm going back to work," Joe mumbled in a distracted sort of way. It's not always a bad thing that Joe, like most men, isn't very inquisitive. Since he didn't ask me what the *doctor* had said, I hadn't had to confess a thing.

Any cheerfulness I'd felt about the upcoming Gaylord party melted in the summer heat. Being home all day with Heather wasn't only lonely, I finally admitted to myself, but also just plain boring a lot of the time. Why hadn't anyone told me that my life would be over once I had a baby? I felt done for at age twenty-five. I had hardly a minute to myself before Heather needed me. I was so tired of doing nothing but tending to that child.

Weeks of breastfeeding Heather, changing her diaper, giving her a bath, soothing her through countless cranky spells, and rocking her to sleep had worn me out. I hadn't slept through the night since she'd been born. No wonder I was sick.

If Joe and I hadn't moved to Narrow Creek, I could've called either my mother or Joe's. Both would've been only too happy to come over and rock Heather for a while.

"Why don't you take a nap?" I imagined Mama saying. "You look worn out. You know you need your rest. You won't be any good to Heather if you don't take care of yourself."

"Go walk around Belk-Tyler's for a while," Joe's mother would no doubt suggest. "Take my car and find something pretty to buy. Here's a coupon I saved for you. Fifty percent off any item that's five dollars or more."

In my dreams.

Some days it was hard for me not to be envious, even resentful, of Joe when he went off to work. I was the one who'd studied hard and made good grades in college. I'm not naturally brilliant; in fact, I even had several professors tell me I was an overachiever, a statement I saw as a compliment. Joe isn't naturally super smart either, but he didn't choose to work very hard and was an average student. Yet he was now the one with a promising career while I was home with a baby. I couldn't help thinking I should be out in the world, too, putting my hard-earned education to use. The only time I used my brain was to think about the Gary Whitt murder, and I wasn't making much progress in verifying a suspect I could report.

But then I'd pause by Heather's door when she was napping, and she always looked like a little angel. I couldn't put that poor darling in daycare. No one would dote on her the way I did.

"It's the most important job in the world," Joe would say to me. "You'll always be glad you took this time to be with her."

Well, why wasn't he taking time to be with Heather? Of course he had to work all week, but he didn't mind going fishing on Saturday mornings with men he met at the bank. He called it networking, but I called it getting out of baby duty. Let him stay with Heather all day some time, by himself. Let him clean up all the messes and get her to quit wailing over who knew what.

The way I felt was kind of crazy, as if I had a split personality. On one hand, I wanted to be content to stay home with Heather, be a devoted wife and mother, and fit in with the women I had met at the Ladies' Society. On the other hand, I wanted more out of life. I'd gone to school for a real degree, not an M.R.S. I wasn't sorry I'd married Joe and I certainly wasn't sorry I now had Heather, but I did have spells when I felt somehow cheated out of my own life. Puzzling over a cold murder case along with dreaming of what I'd do with the ten thousand dollar reward was my only escape from a dreary routine.

Chapter 11

The day of the Gaylord party arrived and not a minute too soon for me. I'd finally kicked my summer cold and was ready to chow down on some barbecue, listen to whatever band the Gaylords had hired, and above all, get out and maybe pick up some clues to further my investigation. Despite moments of doubt about solving the case, I still wanted to find out what I could.

Joe had discovered the dress code was something called "country club casual." Since neither Joe nor I had ever been a member of a country club, I guessed this was what we'd called dressy casual back home, which meant no shorts or any type of denim. Personally, I love denim and feel that you can really smarten it up, but I know that some conservative older people tend to think of it in terms of bib overalls for farmers or ragged jeans worn by hippies.

Not that I'd planned to wear anything denim anyway. My new homemade, red floral sun dress would do for the occasion. I splurged and bought a pair of white sandals at Belk-Tyler's, using a twenty-five percent off coupon. The same day, I found a navy-blue summer handbag in a clearance bin at the Shoe Show. Red, white, and blue. Not only would I be stylish, but patriotic as well. And I'd managed not to charge any of my purchases on the credit card, paying for everything out of the checking account.

Joe hadn't really worried about his outfit. Men have it so much easier than women when it comes to knowing how to dress. He wore what he jokingly called the Narrow Creek gentleman's summer attire: khaki slacks and a light blue polo shirt with a pair of fairly new Topsiders.

I was full of pre-party excitement when Joe left to go pick up the babysitter. Hiring someone to mind Heather had been Joe's job since I didn't know where to begin looking for a babysitter. Joe saw people every day, so I'd delegated him to ask around and find us a suitable sitter.

Sometimes Joe can procrastinate, but two days after we'd replied to the Gaylords' invitation that we were attending, Joe had hired one of his customers, a Bertha Joyner, to come to our apartment on the Fourth of July to babysit Heather.

"She's no rocket scientist," Joe told me, "but I feel pretty sure she knows how to take care of children. She has two of her own, teenagers now."

An older woman. Good. I didn't want some silly teenager who wouldn't change a diaper and instead of watching Heather would spend her time on my telephone talking to her boyfriend. Or worse, sneaking him in and smooching with him on the sofa while my poor baby was left unattended.

But when Joe came in the door that afternoon with Bertha Joyner, I almost told him to go to the party by himself and take that woman back home on his way.

"Dee Ann, this is Bertha Joyner," Joe said, giving us both his best smile.

Bertha Joyner wore a huge yellow tent dress with an uneven hem and ragged white tennis shoes with no laces. The sides of the shoes had holes in them where her bunions stuck out. Her frizzy red hair sprang out in every direction.

"How do you do, Mrs. Joyner?" I managed, while giving Joe the evil eye. I held Heather, who'd been fed and bathed.

Bertha Joyner giggled. "Call me Bertha," she said. She didn't seem to notice that I was glaring at Joe. "That's a right cute baby you got there." She was looking at Heather with cowlike eyes.

"Thank you," I felt obliged to say. "We certainly think so."

"It seems it won't but yesterday that my young'uns was babies." Bertha giggled again. "Now they think they's grown. You know, when they's little, they step on your feet, but when they's big, they step on your heart." Bertha had quit giggling and delivered this little bit of wisdom in a solemn voice.

I let a moment pass. "Yes, well, Heather isn't walking yet."

Joe had wandered off to the bedroom after introducing Bertha and sensing trouble. He now came back in the living room, jingling the car keys and humming under his breath as if he didn't have a care in the world. It was all I could do not to shake that man.

Starved as I was for entertainment, I'd really been looking forward to this party. Bertha was willing to babysit on a holiday. She didn't seem to have good sense, as my grandma used to say, but I figured she did know how to take care of children.

"Around six, you can feed Heather a jar of mixed fruit that's on the top shelf of the refrigerator," I instructed. "Her bottle's in there too, and she'll need that an hour or so after she eats. I prop her up in that little infant seat there on the table when I feed her, and you can hold her to give her the bottle."

"I've written all this down," I said, wondering whether Bertha Joyner could read. "The invitation for the party we're attending is on the refrigerator door. There's a phone number on the invitation in case you need to reach us."

Bertha giggled. This time I noticed she was missing a bottom tooth. "Oh, we'll be fine, Miz Bulluck. You and Mr. Bulluck go on now and have yourselves a real good time. I intend to lock up after y'all leave what with Gary Whitt's murderer still on the loose. I sure wish they'd catch who done it, don't you?"

Before I had time to respond, Bertha beamed at Heather and continued, "Don't worry 'bout me with this little miss. Taking care of babies is my specialty. I ain't never met a baby yet that didn't take to Bertha.

"Gitchee, gitchee, goo," Bertha said as I handed over my child. Heather looked straight into Bertha's face, cow eyes and all, and smiled.

*****

I couldn't wait to get in the car and blast Joe Bulluck from Saturday to Sunday. "What in the world were you thinking when you hired that woman to babysit Heather?"

"What do you mean?"

I hate it when Joe plays all innocent. "What do I mean? Did you get a good look at her? She's like somebody out of a hillbilly movie."

"Now don't go judging people by the way they look." Joe paused to glance both ways at the stop sign at the end of the road. "Bertha and her husband Buddy don't have a lot of money, which is probably why she's available to babysit on the Fourth of July."

"It wasn't only her appearance," I said defensively. "She didn't seem to have all her marbles. All she did was giggle at everything I said."

"She was just nervous. She and Heather will be fine." Joe smiled. "You could've asked Miss Josie to watch Heather if you were going to be so worried about the babysitter," he teased.

That was a low blow. I realized then I shouldn't have told either Mama or Joe about Miss Josie's visit weeks earlier. First, Mama had made me feel bad about my behavior, and now Joe was using that spat for ammunition.

"No, thank you," I snapped. "She'd probably have the entire apartment rearranged and Heather eating a three-course meal by the time we got home."

"Then no more complaining about the babysitter I hired. Let's relax and enjoy our night out together."

I sighed heavily to let Joe know I still wasn't thrilled about his choice of a babysitter but gave up. Joe reached over, and I let him hold my hand as we drove through the countryside outside town. A half hour or so later, after several turns onto a series of secondary roads leading to the river, we finally saw a large hand-lettered sign announcing "Park Here for Gaylord Party."

Joe pulled off the highway and followed a line of cars directed by two police officers into a large grassy lot. Several golf carts were already loaded with guests leaving for the rest of the ride to the river house. Joe and I joined a group waiting for a lift.

"There's some parking at the house, but the overflow is always out here," said a man in royal blue seersucker slacks and red suspenders. "No problem, though; Ed has a fleet of golf carts." A vaguely familiar-looking, middle-aged woman in a white knit, knee-length dress stood by his side. Where had I seen her before? The woman was sizing me up as well.

"I feel like I know you from somewhere," she said. "Did you recently join First Baptist?"

It hit me. I was looking at the receptionist of Narrow Creek Family Physicians. The person I went flying by without so much as a kiss-my-foot the day I rushed out of the bloodwork room.

"We haven't found a church home yet," I replied as another convoy of golf carts arrived and everyone dispersed to find seats. Thank you, Lord.

"Wonder who she was," Joe mused. I didn't answer as Joe, being a gentleman, helped me into the front of a cart. Before he could get on the back, however, the seats were taken. He shrugged and then jumped on another cart that immediately took off. "I'll meet you at the house," he shouted back to me as his cart sped away.

I made a note to steer clear of this woman at the party and keep Joe away from her too for that matter. I didn't want to have to confess what a coward I'd been about having my blood drawn.

"How're you doing, ma'am?" said my driver, a black man dressed in a starched white shirt and creased navy slacks. A white Panama hat with a red, white, and blue band sat at a jaunty angle on his head.

"All aboard," he sang out as he whipped the golf cart down the highway for a quarter mile or so and then around a curve where, for the first time, I saw the Gaylords' white, two-story clapboard river house.

A huge open-air tent was pitched next to the house, and what looked like at least a couple of hundred people were swarming underneath as they made their way down various buffet lines. Bluegrass music blared from the band on a makeshift stage at one end of the tent.

"Here you are, folks," said the driver, as he braked to a stop and the two backseat passengers and I got out. "Y'all enjoy yourselves."

Searching for Joe, I spied him being led to a portable bar by a distinguished-looking older man who'd been standing where the carts were dropping off guests. Ed Gaylord, no doubt. So much for Joe waiting for me.

I'd started to follow them when I heard a shrill voice behind me calling my name and turned to find Cynthia, dressed in a white strapless sun dress that accentuated her golden tan. Beside her was an older woman in a pale-yellow silk caftan. She stood ramrod straight and had the calm, aristocratic air of a person in complete control of every situation.

"Mrs. Gaylord, this is Dee Ann Bulluck. She and her husband just moved here. He's the new collector at the bank. Maybe you've heard Mr. Gaylord mention him. He works under Bill," Cynthia said in a rushed voice. She practically vibrated with energy, her eyes darting all around.

Leave it to Cynthia to put me in my place. But what odd behavior. Evidently I wasn't the only one excited about this party. I smiled and shook the diamond-laden hand of Mrs. Edward Gaylord III.

"I'm pleased to meet you, Mrs. Gaylord," I said. "Thank you for inviting Joe and me."

"My pleasure," replied Mrs. Gaylord, who looked to me as though she thought it no pleasure at all to have to stand out in the heat and meet anyone. "I didn't know Edward had a new employee," she added with a critical look on her face. "Where did you move from?"

Once I said Greenville, Mrs. Gaylord began asking me if I knew this person and that person. In fact, she and Mr. Gaylord had good friends who lived in Greenville, someone with the last name of Aycock, and surely I must know their children, who would be about my age.

"Oh, I know Ginger Aycock," Cynthia interrupted in an almost manic voice. "She and I were suitemates at Randolph-Macon." She was poised to blurt out more but was overcome by sniffles. I briefly wondered if Cynthia was coming down with that bad cold I'd finally shaken. Something was definitely wrong with her.

I hadn't recognized any names and to stop the inquisition, I finally confessed I'd grown up outside the city limits and attended the county high school.

"I see," said Mrs. Gaylord, who seemed to hold that fact against me. "Then you wouldn't know any of my acquaintances." She sighed, obviously having lost interest in me. "I really must move on and mingle. Help yourself to the buffet." With a lazy wave of her hand, she moved away with Cynthia trotting and sniffling behind her.

Over at the portable bar, Joe seemed to be having a great time drinking beer with both Cynthia's husband and Mr. Gaylord. Men are so much nicer to one another. Nobody was making Joe feel like he grew up on the wrong side of the tracks.

Looking down, I noticed a trampled burst balloon. How many more hours would I have to pretend to enjoy myself until the fireworks were over and I could go home? I didn't even have the heart to look for clues in the Gary Whitt murder.

*****

"Ladies and gentlemen, may I have your attention, please?" The lead singer of the Roundabout Boys, a skinny fellow in scuffed cowboy boots and a ten gallon hat, had stepped up to the microphone. All afternoon and into the early evening, the band had played a variety of country and bluegrass tunes, and I'd lingered at the edge of the crowd, singing along or tapping my foot to "Stand by Your Man" and "Foggy Mountain Breakdown."

Joe and I'd finished a dinner of pulled pork, barbecued chicken, baked beans, slaw, and watermelon. The sun had set, and stars were beginning to twinkle. A half moon anchored one corner of the sky. I may have been disappointed in the party, but this Fourth of July night was beautiful. Next to the stage, a bank of spotlights illuminated a large American flag.

"I'm Bubba Evans, and it's been a pleasure to entertain you folks on this proud American holiday. I hope you've enjoyed our playing. Course I know you all really came out to eat that fine spread of food and see the best fireworks show east of Raleigh." Bubba paused as the crowd applauded.

"But before Mr. Gaylord's boys start up the pyrotechnics, it's our tradition to get y'all to help us sing 'America the Beautiful.'

And those of you who are regulars at this shindig know that we always ask a young lady to come up here on stage to help lead the singin'." Again there was a round of applause, and this time, a few whistles.

"So I need a volunteer. If you're female, come on up. It won't hurt none either if you're easy on the eyes. We like to sing with the good lookin' girls, don't we, fellas?" Bubba turned to the other Roundabout Boys, who all agreed by strumming guitars, plucking banjos, or banging the drum.

The crowd murmured, but no one stepped forward. Evidently the volunteer hadn't been arranged ahead of time.

"Why don't you go up there, Dee Ann?" Joe said. "You know the words to 'America the Beautiful.'"

"I haven't sung in front of an audience since college," I protested. "Be quiet before someone hears you." It was too late.

"Here's a singer," Bill yelled, emboldened no doubt by his time at the bar. "And she's good-looking too." Cynthia glared at her husband. I hadn't realized the Fords were standing behind us.

"Hit her with the spotlight, Billy Ray," Bubba said to his light man.

I felt the full blinding force of mega wattage picking me out of the crowd. I had barely enough time to think of how I was going to kill Joe Bulluck—and his boss too— before people began to clap and shout their approval.

"Go for it," someone shouted as my legs began to take me to the front of the crowd. Bubba met me at the edge of the stage and held out a hand.

"Okay, pretty lady, what's your name?" he asked as he led me to center stage.

"Dee Ann Bulluck," I replied in a shaky voice. I searched the crowd and saw Joe giving me a thumbs-up. He's so proud of me right now, I thought. His approval gave me courage.

"All right, Ms. Dee Ann, here we go. Everybody join in."

"O beautiful for spacious skies, For amber waves of grain."

Now I have a nice singing voice, if I do say so myself. I'd performed solos in college when I sang with the Down East Girls. I'd sung solos in high school when I was in Glee Club. I'd also had a couple of beers during the long lonely afternoon while Joe was busy chatting with his cronies from the bank.

I leaned into the mike and gave it my best: "For purple mountain majesties, Above the fruited plain. America! America! God shed his grace on thee, And crown thy good with brotherhood, From sea to shining sea."

Bubba had walked away from the microphone, eyeing me appraisingly. A slow smile spread across his lined face. "Did y'all hear that?" he asked the crowd after two-stepping back to his mike. His question was answered with wild applause and whistles.

"Ms. Dee Ann can belt one out. That was so good, I hate for this gig to end. Is there anything else you want to sing for us, darlin'?"

I checked out the audience. Joe had a huge grin on his face. But it was Cynthia Ford's expression that caught my eye. A look of pure disbelief mixed with jealousy. And something else that looked strangely like despair. She reminded me of that deflated balloon.

"How about 'The Star Spangled Banner'?" I heard myself say.

"You sing; we'll follow." Bubba Evans turned and nodded at his band.

"Oh, say can you see by the dawn's early light," I began. Behind me a guitarist picked out the melody. It sounded like a Jimi Hendrix rendition with a country twist. Not bad, I thought. I could work with this.

"What so proudly we hailed at the twilight's last gleaming." The crowd went completely silent and I saw hands over hearts. The twang of the guitar urged me on.

"O'er the land of the free…" I hit all the high notes.

Just as I finished "the home of the brave" with a flourish, the first firecracker exploded out over the Broad River. I wasn't sure if the exuberant applause was for me or the beginning of the fireworks, but quite a few people surged forward to compliment my singing as Bubba Evans helped me off the stage. Cynthia wasn't among them.

*****

Heather was fast asleep in her crib and Bertha watching television with the volume so low I was sure she couldn't hear a thing. In that regard, she did have better sense than Joe, who'd turn his shows up full blast whether Heather was asleep or not. Bertha was also neater than Joe. Heather's toys had been picked up, and the kitchen was as clean as I'd left it. Of course I had too much pride to tell Joe he'd been right to hire the woman. I do hate to admit it when I've been wrong.

*****

Three days after the Gaylords' Fourth of July party, a letter addressed only to me came in the mail. A folded card embellished with a monogrammed "G" flipped open to a short note written in black ink. It took me a moment to decipher the calligraphy.

July 5, 1979

Dear Dee Ann,

Thank you for volunteering to lead us in the singing of "America the Beautiful" this year at our Fourth of July festivities. Furthermore, your lovely rendition of "The Star Spangled Banner" was quite inspiring.

Edward and I appreciated your willingness to share your talent with all in attendance as we celebrated the two hundred and third anniversary of the signing of the Declaration of Independence. I look forward to seeing you and your husband at next year's event.

Regards,
Tippy Gaylord

I hadn't learned any information at the Gaylords' Independence Day Gala to help me solve the Gary Whitt murder, but I did have evidence to show Joe what a career asset I was.

Chapter 12

A couple of weeks after the Gaylords' party, I sat on the floor in the small hallway connecting the two bedrooms of our apartment. The glow of my performance at the Fourth of July shindig had dimmed considerably. It sounds conceited, but I fancied myself a local celebrity now and expected some accolades. But other than the thank-you note from Mrs. Gaylord, I hadn't heard from a living soul. No one from the Narrow Creek Ladies' Society. No one from Joe's bank. Heck, no one had even called to invite me to join a church choir somewhere.

It was as if I'd never sung. I had only Tippy Gaylord's card to remind me that for a few brief shining moments I'd felt important again. People had paid attention to me and not because I was Joe's wife or Heather's mother.

In fact, I was so down in the dumps I tried to cheer myself up by hanging all my framed certificates from college. Right there in the hallway where I could see them whenever I came out of my bedroom or Heather's bedroom or when I was on the way to the bathroom. Or when I was plopped on the floor in the hallway, which was where I'd ended up.

I leaned back against the wall and studied each one from the top row to the bottom. I was a member of the English Honor Society and the Journalism Club. I was a staff reporter for the school newspaper, an editor of the yearbook, and a soloist in the Down East Girls. I'd graduated summa cum laude from undergraduate school and with honors from my graduate school program.

"What's happened to me?" I whispered. "I used to be somebody. Where's the girl who had the world by its tail?"

I'll tell you where: sitting on the floor having a major pity party as I remembered life before marriage, a baby, and genteel poverty in a small town. And I was the only guest at this pity party. Joe was at work, of course, and Heather didn't count. Instead of commiserating with me, she was on her back beside me on the floor, babbling and merrily waving her plump little arms and legs. Who ever said a baby can pick up on her mother's emotions?

I stretched out to lie down beside her. "I want to be home with you all the time, baby girl, but Mama needs something more. I have to find somebody somewhere in this town like me. I need to talk about more than who's building an expensive house on Sycamore Avenue across the street from his widowed mother. Someone who can talk about poems and plays and novels."

Heather was now giving me some serious attention. "In fact, sweetie pie, I just want to talk to anybody."

At that moment the telephone rang. I picked up Heather and raced to answer it. "Could I speak to Dee Ann Bulluck?" a man asked briskly.

"This is she," I said using my best telephone manners.

"Mrs. Bulluck, how are you today?"

"Fine, thank you," I answered politely although I didn't recognize the voice on the other end of the line.

"I need just a few minutes of your time today, ma'am, to tell you about a wonderful new product our company is marketing. It's called Masonite siding, and I'd like to share with you the advantages of a house built using this material versus one built out of wood or brick."

"I don't think I'll be building a house anytime soon."

"You never know, Mrs. Bulluck. According to my records, you and your husband are currently renting, but statistics show that young couples such as yourselves often buy or build a home within the first five years of marriage."

I wasn't that desperate to talk to an adult. "Just where are you getting this information about my husband and me?"

"It's a matter of public record, Dee. May I call you Dee?"

"My name is Dee Ann, but don't call me anything and don't call me again. I do not make purchases over the telephone." And with that, I hung up.

"A salesman," I told Heather. "And no, I didn't politely decline the offer and thank him for calling, the way your daddy would do. I'm mean."

Heather smiled sweetly. I put her down on the floor again, where she began practicing her latest trick, rolling herself over. There's a technical college just outside of town, I thought. Maybe I need to get on the telephone myself and try to sell something, like my teaching skills. Suddenly I was full of resolve.

If Joe wants to argue with me about going to work, I'll tell him he's not the boss of me. "The boss of me," I repeated aloud. I sounded like a second grader. Lord, I needed a job where I could use my brain before it completely shriveled.

I'll call today to see if there is any part-time work available, I decided. There must be something an English major with a Master's in Education can do. And this family could definitely use more money since I certainly wasn't getting close to earning that ten thousand dollar reward.

The best lead I had to give the police involved the wife of Joe's boss. Before I ever called the Narrow Creek Police Department hotline to report Cynthia Ford as a suspect, I had to be positive she was guilty. A false accusation traced back to me could cost Joe his job.

Unable to flip herself, Heather was getting frustrated and fussy. I reached down and gave her rear a little push. She turned over to her stomach and rewarded me with her special smile. Then the struggle to flip herself began again. This child is never content for long, I thought, sighing wearily.

*****

I couldn't believe how easy it'd been to get an interview at Narrow Creek Technical College. As simple as picking up the telephone and calling the school. Send us your resume, a secretary told me, and then we'll contact you if we have something that matches your credentials. Two days after mailing my resume, I was called by a Dr. Adams to arrange a meeting.

I dressed carefully for my Monday noon interview, opting for the conservative black skirt and white blouse I'd worn when I tried to find a teaching job before Heather came along. My eyes were a bright blue-green as I looked in the mirror to tame my now curly hair by brushing it up on the sides and securing these strands with a clip. I wore a pair of closed toe, black, one-inch pumps I'd bought for seventy percent off at Belk-Tyler's. Joe said I certainly looked like a schoolteacher. I wasn't sure that was a compliment.

Joe left the bank a little early for lunch so he could stay with Heather. "Don't be longer than an hour," he said. "I need to get back to work."

"So what am I supposed to say to a long-winded interviewer?" I asked. "Excuse me, Mr. Person-Who-Will-Decide-Whether-To-Hire-Me, but I see that it's one o'clock, and I really must be going. I don't have any more time for this interview, so as you can probably figure out, I really don't have time for this job."

"Don't be silly, Dee Ann. You know what I mean. Just don't lollygag. Now hurry up and leave so you can hurry up and get back."

With that pep talk, I ran out of the apartment. I tried not to think about being rushed as I asked at the receptionist's desk for the location of Dr. Adams' office. A short young woman with waist-length hair gave me a friendly smile. "Oh, you're the lady who called about teaching a couple of English classes for us," she said. "Dr. Adams was impressed by your resume. Just follow me. His office is right down this hall."

"Come in," Dr. Adams squawked, glimpsing me through his open door. William H. Adams, Dean of Instruction, was a middle-aged man with thinning dark hair parted low on one side and combed over the top of his head in a vain attempt to hide a bald spot. A canary-blue leisure suit hugged his scrawny body, and magnified eyes stared at me from behind a pair of pink-tinted glasses. I needed to get past my first impression of this disco king, or I wouldn't be able to take him seriously.

"I'm Dee Ann Bulluck," I said, extending my hand and using my best professional voice. "I spoke with you on the phone the other day about a part-time job here at the college teaching English." Begin directly with the business at hand. I pictured Joe at home watching both Heather and the clock.

"Yes, I remember," Dr. Adams flipped through several stacks of papers on his desk. "Let me find your resume. Aha, here it is," he said just when, to speed things along, I pulled another copy from my small leather notebook.

"Let's see. Mrs. Bulluck, it appears you have an undergraduate degree in English with a teacher's certificate in this area," Dr. Adams said in an official voice with his head bent over my resume.

"That's correct." A large framed poster of Bobbie Riggs in tennis shorts was the sole picture on the back wall. I wondered what Dr. Adams thought of Billie Jean King.

"You've completed a Master's in Education with a concentration in English," he continued. "And you do have the eighteen graduate hours in literature courses required to teach the college-transfer curriculum at the technical college level." Dr. Adams looked up and trained his magnified eyes on me.

"Yes, and I taught freshman composition classes at the university where I was working on my Master's degree," I added.

"Good, good," Dr. Adams said. "We don't have any English courses available for you in our college-transfer program right now, but remedial English is wide open. There's really more of a need for that type of instruction, I'm sorry to say, than any other."

He frowned and shook his head. "Take my nephew, for example. He graduated high school with decent grades but couldn't get accepted by any four-year college in the state. His SAT scores were too low. When he finally came here to enroll and took our placement tests, he was found to be at the remedial level in all three areas: reading, math, and English. He was insulted when told he couldn't begin the college transfer curriculum until after he took our remedial classes. In fact, he never enrolled. My mother, his grandmother, was quite disappointed. She'd been his legal guardian since both his parents died in a car accident when he was seven."

Dr. Adams paused and cleared his throat. I sneaked a peek at my watch. "Of course, Gary was always a spoiled brat who thought he'd be getting Mother's money one day. He felt he didn't need to work. Mother was completely blind to his many faults. She made excuses for him his entire life."

Something in Dr. Adams' voice made me uneasy. He'd recited this last part in a monotone and his bug eyes had a glazed look. I forgot about watching the time. "Is your nephew Gary Whitt?" I blurted out.

Dr. Adams shook himself and focused his attention on me. "Yes, I suppose you heard he was murdered. I apologize for rambling on about him. His death has been difficult for my mother. She has no other children or grandchildren and my father's been dead for years, so I've chosen to live with her. Mother has only me, you see."

I could've sworn I saw a small, satisfied smile on the man's face. Then as suddenly as the interview had taken one personal turn, it took another.

"Dee, I believe you said on the phone the other day that you're fairly new to the area, didn't you? What does your husband do for a living?"

Are you kidding? I wanted to ask. How did Joe's occupation have anything to do with my getting a job? Evidently, since I now knew Dr. Adams was a middle-aged man living with his mother, he felt entitled to know all about my personal life.

Part of me wanted to ask this sexist pig with the bad comb-over and the tacky leisure suit exactly how in the blue blazes what my husband did for a living mattered. The part of me that wanted a job, however, told me to play the game Dr. Adams had started. It was obvious the man had no regard for federal laws, which forbade asking a female job candidate such questions.

"He works for Narrow Creek Community Bank. And I go by Dee Ann."

"And do you have any children, Dee Ann?"

"A baby daughter," I replied, trying to keep the anger out of my voice.

"I know I'm not supposed to ask this question," Dr. Adams said with a little chuckle, "but what sort of childcare would you arrange if you came to work here?" Something in my face must have revealed my resentment, for he added, "We just want to be sure that you'd be dependable. Over the years I've noticed a higher rate of absenteeism for women with young children."

It's too bad I didn't come wearing a wire to record this, I thought. I could bust this chauvinistic, disco star wannabe for these questions, sue the school, and not have to worry about earning any money for a while. I took a moment to fantasize about the new clothes I could purchase straight off the rack, retail price, at Three Sisters. I could buy myself a Mercedes like Cynthia's, only newer, and I'd get Joe any four-wheel-drive vehicle he wanted, fully loaded. Joe and I would buy our first house, maybe one with that Masonite siding stuff.

A hidden recorder could also have captured his eerie tone of voice as Dr. Adams talked about his murdered nephew, the only other heir to Mother's money.

Since I didn't have a hidden microphone, though, and needed to wrap up the interview as quickly as possible, I told the strange and sinister Dr. Adams I felt sure I could easily find some sort of daycare for my child...should I get the job.

Chapter 13

D r. Adams called the next morning. Would I be interested in teaching three remedial English classes three mornings a week? I couldn't accept fast enough. A job! Monday, Wednesday, and Friday mornings from eight until eleven.

And possibly a chance to find out more about Dr. Adams' former relationship with his murdered nephew. A death that conveniently left him as the sole heir to Mother's money—and her affection.

Joe just shrugged at what he saw as my sudden decision to go to work. "I thought you wanted to be home with Heather. But whatever you decide. I want you to be happy. A few mornings a week with a babysitter might even be a good thing for Heather."

I wasn't quite sure what that babysitter comment meant, but I let it go since I was getting my way about going to work. The only problem was that fall semester would begin August fifteenth, three weeks away. I had to arrange that childcare I'd told Dr. Adams I'd have no trouble finding.

I got out the telephone book and looked under "Childcare," which told me to look under "Daycare." Two options were listed: Kiddie Care and Narrow Creek Children's Center. Both had part-time rates that were half of what I'd be making at the college. Also the five-to-one "caregiver" to baby ratio shocked me. How could one woman watch five babies? I could barely keep up with one.

Joe came home with the names of a couple of ladies who kept children in their homes, but when I spoke with them, no one had a vacancy for a part-time baby. "Why don't you see if Bertha can help you?" Joe asked. "I know you think she's a little rough around the edges, but you have to admit she did a good job keeping Heather for us that Saturday when we went to the Gaylords' party. I think she said something the last time she was in the bank about setting up a daycare business."

Somehow I couldn't picture Bertha as a businesswoman, but I figured by setting up a daycare business she probably meant keeping a baby or two at her house. I was getting desperate, so I called to see if she was indeed in the childcare business.

"I am," she said, "even though I don't have no babies yet. Little Miss Heather can be my first. I won't charge you much neither, since you ain't gonna be workin' full time out there at the Tech. Maybe twenty dollars a week if you think that's a fair shake." The woman had answered my second question, her rate, without my even having to ask. We arranged a time that I could visit her daycare establishment, which I had correctly guessed to be her house.

On a steamy summer morning, I loaded Heather in her carrier and using the directions Joe had given me, set out to pay a professional call. Joe'd bought himself a repossessed Jeep from the bank for five hundred dollars three days after I'd decided to go to work. We were now officially a two-car family like almost everybody else in America, even though Joe had borrowed that five hundred dollars from his dad to pay for the Jeep. I wondered how long I'd have to work at my part-time job to repay that debt.

Bertha lived only a mile or so away in a neighborhood of small brick houses, all identical with their boxy appearances and attached carports. Joe had told me many of the people in the neighborhood had been able to buy a home only because they qualified for assistance from the Farmers Home Administration. "Solid, hardworking folks live there, Dee Ann," he'd said. "They're just people who don't make a lot of money at what they do for a living and never will."

Bertha's house was the fourth on the left on Penny Street. She had one of those plywood lawn ornaments where an old lady is bending over and her skirt has blown up to reveal a rather large rear end encased in polka-dot bloomers. Oh boy, I thought. Wonder what the inside of the house looks like.

I knew that Bertha was married to someone named Buddy, and they had two teenagers, Jimmy and Tiffany. Buddy was a highway worker for the state.

Bertha must have seen me drive up because she had the door open by the time I got Heather out of the car. She lumbered out to meet us, wearing a bright red cotton house dress and an even brighter smile. She was sporting a pair of tube socks with the same pair of worn-out Keds I'd seen before. At least with those socks I didn't have to look at her bunions. Her frizzy red hair was secured by a rubber band into a ponytail that stood up on the top of her head. No doubt it was going to hurt to get that rubber band out later.

"Come on in the house, Miz Bulluck, and let me show you around. Hey there to you too, little Miss Heather, Bertha's sweet potato pie. I could just eat you with a spoon, yes, I could, yes, I could."

Heather practically beamed at Bertha, who'd delivered that affectionate greeting while hovering right in front of the baby's face. I caught a whiff of stale coffee, but Heather didn't seem to mind as she flailed her chubby arms in Bertha's direction.

"Can I hold her, Miz Bulluck?"

"Sure," I said, handing over a squirming Heather. "And call me Dee Ann." Goodness, this woman is probably only ten years older than I am, I thought. It was time to end the Miz Bulluck business.

Bertha gave me a full tour of the house: eat-in kitchen, living room, three small bedrooms, and one and a half baths. The paneled walls throughout the house were decorated with scores of photographs. The woman must have hung every baby and school picture Jimmy and Tiffany had ever had taken. The only break in the photo gallery was a large print of *The Last Supper* in a black plastic frame, positioned behind a couch upholstered in brown Naugahyde.

What Bertha lacked in decorating skills, however, she made up for in housekeeping; everything was as neat as a pin. The bedroom furniture might have been old and nicked, and the sofa arms patched with duct tape, but there wasn't a speck of dust or a dirty dish in the whole house.

"I know my home ain't nothing fancy," Bertha said. "Me and Buddy don't have much. We spend what Buddy makes on the young'uns. You know, when you have young'uns, you ain't gonna have much else. Course I wouldn't trade 'em for nothing." Bertha paused a moment after this declaration of motherly love.

"I been keepin' house for ol' Miz Adams, but every since her grandson Gary got shot, it's just too sad around there for me. I feel bad 'bout leavin' her with no house help and that growed-up son to take care of—he's one strange bird in my book—but my nerves couldn't take much more."

I snapped to attention: Bertha had worked for Gary Whitt's grandmother?

"That woman won't doing nothin' but cryin' all day," she continued. "She don't need house help as much as she needs a psychiatric."

Psychiatrist, I mentally corrected. I regarded Bertha with new interest, wondering what else I could find out from her about Gary's former relationship with his "strange bird" of an uncle. Before I could frame a question, though, Bertha rattled on.

"So's I told Buddy I wanted a happy job for a change. I decided to set myself up keepin' babies here at the house for these young mamas what's got a job," she continued. "Babies is my specialty anyway. I plan to call my business Bertha's Babies. Don't that have a nice ring to it?"

Bertha searched my face, obviously wanting approval. "Yes, that's a very catchy name," I said. The two B's did give it alliteration.

I noticed something else. Bertha wasn't giggling. She had smiled plenty and her cowlike eyes had a naïve look, but I hadn't heard a single silly titter out of her. But Sensible Bertha suddenly vanished.

"You know, every year I enter that Reader's Digest Sweepstakes, but I don't never seem to win nothing. Do you think that contest is real?" She leaned toward me as if I had the inside scoop.

"I guess there are winners," I answered, flustered at the turn the conversation had taken, "but the odds are something like oh, one out of twenty million that a person's number would be drawn."

"Well, no wonder I don't never hear nothing back from them folks. One out of twenty million! Who knew? Boy howdy, it's a good thing I done decided to keep babies instead of waitin' for that ship to come in." For the first time that day, Bertha giggled.

"Does anyone in your household smoke, Bertha?" I asked, trying to steer things back to childcare.

"No, ma'am! Me and Buddy don't smoke and we don't drink neither. We're good Christian people who fear the Lord and praise His holy name. And those young'uns of mine better not be smokin' or drinkin' neither, or me and Buddy will git their hides good." Bertha folded her arms and nodded her head.

"Yes, uh, Bertha," I said, again trying to get the interview back on track, "Heather will be awake for a couple of hours when she first arrives, and then she'll need a morning nap from ten until eleven. Please don't let her sleep longer than an hour, or she won't go down for her afternoon nap. When she's awake, she likes to be held some and talked to and played with." I didn't want my baby parked in a playpen and ignored.

"You don't have to worry about ol' Bertha doin' her job. I'll treat that baby just like she's my own flesh and blood. I never could understand these women who just want to put a young'un in a playpen all day and go on 'bout their business like there ain't no baby around."

I blushed a little. Had Bertha been reading my mind?

"No indeedy, right now Heather is my only baby to mind, and me and her are gonna have our own selves a big time. Us two are gonna read picture books and play with toys and go strollin'. I already got Buddy to haul my young'un's old baby buggy out of the attic, and I wiped it down good with Clorox, so's on nice days, I can take Heather outside."

"Well," I said, faced with such enthusiasm and no other options, "Heather will be here on August fifteenth."

*****

I hadn't realized how hard it would be to get myself up and dressed as well as have Heather ready to go to Bertha's by seven-thirty on those three mornings I'd agreed to teach an eight o'clock class. Good grief, how do women do this five days a week with more than one child?

True, Joe helped some. He was in charge of the coffee and even scrambled the eggs and made toast. And since he didn't have to be at the bank until eight-thirty, it was his job to deliver Heather to Bertha's house on his way to work.

"You have the happy Heather job," he said. "You get to pick her up. I get the hard part of having to leave her. She doesn't fuss, but I still feel like I'm abandoning her."

I couldn't believe Mr. Sunshine himself was complaining.

"Now Joe," I lectured, "don't you remember telling me that you thought it would be good for Heather to get out of the house a little? It's not like we're leaving her forty-plus hours a week at an overcrowded daycare. She's with Bertha only three mornings a week, and I feel sure she has the woman's full attention, such as it is. I thought you were the big Bertha fan here, although I must admit she's winning me over. Even though she doesn't always seem to have all her marbles, she does have a way with babies. So don't go and make me feel bad about leaving Heather to go to work."

Truth be told, though, I did feel guilty about leaving a seven-month-old. Neither my mother nor Joe's mom had ever held a job once they'd had children. Of course, both had married right out of high school, forgoing college. I'd worked hard to get my college degrees, and I intended to use them.

And we needed the money, too, little bit that it was. Especially since we now owed Joe's dad five hundred dollars, and I wasn't exactly closing in on that ten thousand dollar reward money. When I'd quizzed her, Bertha claimed she didn't know about any conflict between Dr. Adams and his nephew. Being the housekeeper for Mrs. Adams meant she went on Tuesdays to do the laundry and on Thursdays to clean.

"Except during lunch time," she'd told me, "Dr. Adams was always at the Tech, and Gary won't there much at all since he had his own place. I can't ever remember seein' both of 'em together in the same room."

At least Bertha was turning out to be a better babysitter than informant. In fact, I found myself a little jealous of the time she spent with my child. "She's a right happy baby, Dee

Ann," Bertha reported. "I just love to hear that young'un laugh. And she's such a smart thing. Today I saw her hold on to the side of my couch and almost pull her little self straight up."

Standing? I hadn't noticed Heather trying to pull herself up at our house. What if she took her first steps for Bertha?

In addition to jealousy, I was trying hard not to get that working mommy guilt that I'd read about in women's magazines and seen discussed on *The Phil Donahue Show*. So it didn't help me any to run into Miss Josie the second Wednesday morning I was leaving for school. I came out of the apartment side door precisely at 7:30, just as I'd been doing each morning I went to work, and suddenly I heard the sliding glass door of the Powells' house open. Miss Josie strolled out with a watering can.

"Where are you going all dressed up so early in the day?" she called out to me without so much as a good morning. She eased down her porch steps and crossed the yard to my car.

"I have a part-time job teaching at the technical college." Since she hadn't said good morning to me, I wasn't going to initiate a polite greeting.

"Really?" Her eyebrows shot up and her mouth hardened. "What are you doing with Baby Heather?" She might as well have said Poor Baby Heather. "I've seen Joe leaving with her in the mornings. Surely he's not taking her to work with him?"

"She goes to a lady's house while I'm at school. Bertha Joyner. It's just three mornings a week," I said defensively. Why was I explaining all my business to this busybody? And what was that crack about Heather going to work with Joe supposed to mean?

"I see," said Miss Josie, her voice full of disapproval. "Bertha Joyner? Don't know the woman. Have a nice day at school." And with that she turned to go back inside, without watering a single plant. Pretty sloppy detective work in my book.

I could imagine the conversation she'd have with Mr. Powell as soon as he got home from his morning trip to Ernie's Grill. "Floyd," she'd say, "I can't believe she's leaving that poor little baby to go to work. I wonder who in the world this Bertha Joyner is. I know plenty of women with young children work these days, but still, I hate to see a baby go to a stranger's house."

"Miss Josie made me feel guilty about leaving Heather to go to work," I reported to Joe at lunch. I told him about the encounter, even what I suspected she would say to Mr. Powell.

Joe laughed. "I'm sure she was just curious about where you're going so early in the morning. That's how it is in small towns. Everybody has to know everybody else's business. And we do live in their backyard."

Everybody knowing everybody else's business didn't seem to be helping me in solving the Gary Whitt murder.

"Maybe Miss Josie does have some old-fashioned ideas about working women," Joe continued. "But you can be sure Floyd Powell doesn't care who's working over here as long as he gets his rent check on time. Heck, he'd put Heather to work to line his pockets. Believe me, I've seen that man argue for the highest rates he can get on his accounts at the bank. He loves a dollar."

Joe was grinning. He wasn't considering how bad Miss Josie had made me feel. He was getting a kick out of thinking about what a wheeler-dealer Floyd Powell was.

Chapter 14

Although I was only a part-time teacher, several people at the technical college stopped me in the hall or caught me in the faculty lounge or at the mimeograph machine to introduce themselves and say welcome. I guess in a school with just eighteen full-time faculty, anybody new on campus—even part-time—was bound to be noticed.

And commented on. During my second week I was in a bathroom stall when I overheard a couple of ladies talking about me as they entered the restroom.

"She's young but seems enthusiastic. And heaven knows, we can certainly use some enthusiasm around this place." That sounded like Vivian Harris, the head English instructor, who was serving as my mentor.

"It's easy to be bursting with energy when you first get here," a less kind voice responded. "Let's see how well she holds up over the long haul." Was that Edna Perry, Vivian's best friend and the school's other full-time English instructor, who I'd already sensed was a little jealous of me?

I had a tense couple of minutes before each participant in this conversation chose a stall and I could flush, quickly wash my hands, and escape. I didn't want anyone to be embarrassed even though a certain person in that conversation would've deserved it.

The most interesting introduction at the college, though, was a re-introduction. One day that second week when I was walking down a hall, I passed Scarlett Hood, the very pretty woman I'd met at the Kut and Kurl.

We looked at each other and laughed.

"Dee Ann, is it? We meet again. So you're the new instructor. Your hair looks good. Welcome to Narrow Creek Technical College, Exhibit A in the graying of America. It's nice to see another employee here under the age of fifty."

I laughed again. "Thanks. Yes, I'm the new part-time person in the English Department, and yes, I've noticed a lot of the employees here are, shall we say, somewhat mature. Where are all the younger teachers?"

At that moment a tall, slender black lady came out of a nearby classroom. "Where are all the minority teachers would be a better question," she said.

I flinched a little. She had a point. I'd already noted that although over half of the student body was African-American, I had yet to meet a single black instructor.

"I didn't mean to startle you, girlfriend. I'm Hazel Hood, the token minority faculty member here. I teach history, so at least I get to educate these students about Harriet Tubman and Frederick Douglass."

"Oh Hazel, quit singing the blues," Scarlett said. "The school would hire more black instructors if minorities would apply. Young black teachers are just like young white teachers— they've moved to bigger and better-paying technical colleges in cities.

"Me," Scarlett continued, "I'm stuck here. I married a local farm owner whose family has lived in this area since the days of the King's land grants or some such drivel, and he's not about to leave."

"Yeah, that family history is why Scarlett and I have the same last name," Hazel added. "Her husband and my husband aren't exactly cousins. No, ma'am, my husband's ancestors were slaves who took the Hood name when, Thank God Almighty, they were freed at last."

"Honestly, Hazel, you're making Dee Ann uncomfortable. What's got you in such a Black Panther mood this morning?"

Hazel cackled. "Scarlett, girl, you crack me up. I love that you come right out and say what most white people think." She paused for a moment, and her smile faded. "But since you asked, I'll tell you what's got me riled up. Just about every black male over the age of twelve has been a suspect in the Gary Whitt murder. You white folks wouldn't believe how many brothers have been hauled down to the police station for what the police chief calls questioning." Hazel rolled her eyes. I blushed as I recalled the day I heard Miss Josie report that one of her friends suspected the "coloreds" in a robbery gone bad.

"People in our community keep up with each other," Hazel continued, "and if one of us had shot that man, somebody would know it and, poor as most of us are, call that hotline and collect the reward. A white person killed Gary Whitt, and the sooner the police accept that, the faster they'll solve the case."

Although I'd become more than a little ill-at-ease with such a frank conversation, Scarlett was unfazed. "Why don't you call up Chief McSwain and tell him that?" she asked.

Hazel gave a cynical snort. "You think he'd listen to a black woman? I'd just be inviting him to haul in any man I'm related to for more questioning," she said, putting air quotes around the word *questioning*. "My mama didn't raise a fool."

Hazel suddenly seemed to remember I was standing there. "Excuse my ranting, Dee Ann. I meant to welcome you to Narrow Creek Tech. I didn't intend to get all side-tracked on race relations in Narrow Creek, but Scarlett is about the only white woman I've met who can hear the truth without squirming about how white folks mistreat black people around here." With a sad shake of her head, Hazel Hood turned and walked on down the hall.

"So Dee Ann, what's brought you to this god-forsaken country? I don't think I got all the details that day I met you at Vee's shop."

I was still a little shaken from the conversation, but evidently Scarlett had indeed taken the encounter in stride.

"We moved here for my husband's job at Narrow Creek Community Bank," I managed to say. I'd learned "Where does your husband work" was a standard question in a small town.

But Scarlett didn't seem to care where Joe worked other than the fact that maybe in time he'd be transferred. "Lucky you. You might get out of here one day. You do know there is absolutely nothing interesting to do in this town, unless you want to go to someone's dinner party and talk about everyone who's not there."

I hesitated before answering. I knew there was some truth to what Scarlett was saying, especially the part about people gossiping, but I also knew it probably wasn't a good idea for me to come right out and criticize the small town where my husband was a bank employee. At least not to anyone but Joe, who got a constant earful, bless his heart, and always sighed, "I know, Dee Ann, I know."

But I liked this bold, sassy woman with raven hair, emerald-green eyes, and a short skirt. Maybe I could be myself around her instead of a bland banker's wife who was always polite and socially correct.

Still, better to play it safe. "I don't think we're moving anytime soon. And we have a baby girl—you remember Heather—so even if there were places to go, it's hard for us to leave the house right now." I didn't mention that we also didn't have extra money for entertainment.

"You have to drive at least an hour out of Narrow Creek to get to a city with any kind of nice restaurant or night club," Scarlett said as though she hadn't heard me. "Tell you what, though. You and your husband should come over for dinner. What are y'all doing Saturday night? My husband J.T.—that's short for John Thomas—can grill steaks. Bring Heather to play with my little boy. He's four. I promise I won't talk about *anyone* in Narrow Creek." Here she paused, and I saw that mischievous smile I remembered from the Kut and Kurl. "I'll talk about *everyone* in Narrow Creek.

"Got to go to class. I teach remedial reading, by the way. Big business here. I'll check with you again tomorrow about Saturday night." Scarlett gave me a little wave as she entered a classroom on the left. I glanced at the clock in the hallway and saw that I had two minutes before my basic English grammar class to mull over Scarlett's invitation—as well as what I'd learned from Hazel Hood about the police investigation in the black community.

*****

"We've been invited to dinner." One good thing about having my last class end at eleven was that I had plenty of time to pick up Heather and get home to see Joe when he came rolling in at noon.

"Where?" Joe asked before taking a big bite of his bologna sandwich. Heather sat in her infant seat, her tiny mouth open for the next spoonful of pureed bananas.

"Remember that woman, Scarlett Hood, I told you about meeting when I went to the Kut and Kurl? Guess what? She works at the technical college. We started talking and she invited us to dinner this Saturday night. Her husband's name is J.T., short for John Thomas, and he's a farmer."

"J.T. Hood," Joe said slowly. "I recognize the name. He's a big-time landowner. I see him in the bank now and then, talking to Fred in the Farm Department. I didn't know his wife worked, though. I wouldn't think they needed the money, that's for sure."

"Honestly, Joe. Maybe there are other reasons to work—personal fulfillment, for example." Sometimes Joe can't see past dollars and cents.

Joe gave me that funny look he gets when I've said something he considers off the wall. But he nodded. "If you want to go, then sure. Even though I've been introduced to J.T. only once at the bank, and I wouldn't know his wife if I passed her on the street."

Chapter 15

Saturday night arrived and Joe, Heather, and I were headed to the Hoods. I'd gotten directions from Scarlett, and it turned out that her house was quite a ways from town, fifteen point two miles, to be exact. Joe clocked it on the odometer. For some reason he's always liked to see how far somewhere is from somewhere else.

No wonder Scarlett, being stuck out in the boondocks, felt the way she did about living in Narrow Creek. Still, the drive through the country was pretty in the gathering dusk, and when the huge brick manor house surrounded by acres of lush farmland finally appeared, Joe and I were quite impressed.

"She said the house was sort of antebellum," I told Joe. "But she didn't say she lived on a plantation."

"These folks have some serious money," Joe replied. "Do they know we don't?"

"For Pete's sake, Joe, don't reduce everything to a dollar," I scolded, though I was already worrying about a reciprocal invitation to our four-room apartment with the commercial-grade carpet and worn-out furniture.

Scarlett met us at the mahogany double front doors. She was dressed in a chiffon blouse with a fall leaf pattern and gold palazzo pants that hugged her curvy figure. Her peaches-

and-cream complexion glowed, her green eyes sparkled, and her dark hair was casually feathered back from her face.

"Y'all come in," drawled a man as good-looking as Scarlett was beautiful. This solid-built young gentleman farmer standing behind her was the epitome of tall, dark, and handsome. "I'm glad you found us out here. I'm J.T. Hood. Joe, I believe I met you at the bank."

"That's right," Joe said, shaking hands with J.T. "Good to see you again, J.T. This is my wife Dee Ann."

"Aren't you a pretty little miss," J.T. said, shaking my hand also. Behind him Scarlett rolled her eyes. I guess it was the "pretty little miss" part she didn't like. It was patronizing, especially coming from someone not much older than I was who should've known something about women's lib, but I was there to enjoy myself. At least the man hadn't tried to hug me.

"And here's my bride Scarlett," he said to Joe, using the local expression to describe a wife of however many years. As J.T. turned to her, Scarlett barely had time to replace her eye rolling with a smile. It was all I could do not to laugh.

"I love your house, Scarlett." I gazed at the two-story foyer with its huge brass chandelier. An impressive spiral staircase was lined with oil portraits. Hardwood floors gleamed beneath a tastefully worn Oriental rug. "Feels like I'm at Tara."

"I could be Scarlett O'Hara, the name fits, but J.T.'s sure no Rhett Butler," Scarlett said. Thankfully, the men had already walked into a wood-paneled den I glimpsed from the foyer, so J.T. missed this bit of venom.

"Come on, and I'll show you the place. Bring Heather, and Ida can watch her. She's upstairs with John Thomas."

"What'll you have to drink, Joe?" J.T. boomed as I followed Scarlett up the curved grand staircase.

"Sorry about that 'pretty little miss' crack. J.T. can be a sexist pig. Sounds just like his father used to." We'd reached the second floor, where another impressive reception area was furnished with a camelback sofa and two wing chairs. Scarlett's second floor foyer was bigger than my living room.

"No offense taken. On the scale of chauvinist behavior, that hardly registers." Heather had grown still in my arms, as overwhelmed by the house as I was.

Several spacious bedrooms opened from the hall, and Scarlett led me into one where a little boy with dark, curly hair sat on the floor playing with plastic action figures dressed like pirates. Near him, sitting somewhat uncomfortably in a child-sized chair, was an old black woman in a faded cotton dress and worn-out bedroom shoes.

"John Thomas," Scarlett said, "I've brought you a little friend to play with. Say hello to Heather and her mother, Miss Dee Ann."

"Hullo," John Thomas said. "I don't want to play with a baby," he added in a sullen voice, frowning at his mother.

"You just help Ida watch her then. Be nice now, John Thomas. Ida, this is Mrs. Bulluck. She and her husband are having dinner with us. Let me know if there are any problems," Scarlett added, inclining her head toward John Thomas.

"Yes, ma'am, Miss Scarlett," Ida said. "I'll be watchin' these children good. Y'all go on down now and have a good time." Without getting out of the chair, she held out her arms for Heather.

I handed Heather to her and studied the room. Everything was decorated in a pirate theme. Fabric featuring swashbuckling pirates on ships flying the Jolly Roger had been made into a bedspread with matching curtains. A life-size statue of a pirate waving a papier-mache sword stood in one corner.

Scarlett saw me eyeing the room and laughed. "John Thomas loves his pirates. The decorator had the window treatments and bedspread custom-made. We found Mr. Pirate in a Neiman-Marcus catalog." Coming from anyone else, this information might've seemed boastful, but Scarlett was so nonchalant she could've been talking about the weather rather than expensive interior decorating.

I glanced at Heather, who seemed content with Ida holding her. "I'm right downstairs if you need me, Ida. Her bottle is in the diaper bag if she gets fussy."

"She'll be fine. Don't you worry yourself none," Ida said with a nearly toothless smile.

Downstairs, Joe and J.T. were standing next to a well-stocked bar in a corner of the den, discussing bow hunting. An open bottle of Jack Daniel's stood beside a couple of cans of Coca-Cola. Judging by Joe's heightened color, I suspected he and J.T. were already on their second round. "Would you girls like a drink?" J.T. asked.

"I'll have the usual, a vodka tonic," Scarlett said. "What about you, Dee Ann?"

"A glass of wine if you have a bottle open." I'm not one for hard liquor, even if it's watered down with soda or fruity mixes.

J.T. poured our drinks as he and Joe cranked up a conversation about black-powder season. Scarlett gave me another eye roll. "Come on," she said, "let's go to the library."

Of all the rooms I'd seen, this was my favorite. Built-in mahogany bookshelves held leather-bound classics interspersed with Chinese porcelain vases and bowls. The Hood family coat of arms hung on one wall, flanked by oil portraits of portly gentlemen in riding habits and ladies in sweeping gowns with low-cut décolletage.

"J.T.'s ancestors," Scarlett said. "The men grew cotton and the women looked pretty. Actually, the men didn't do much of anything either. They had overseers and slaves. Yep, slaves, just like Hazel Hood told you." Scarlett laughed cynically. "J.T. keeps up the tradition as best he can. He has a farm supervisor, poor white tenant farmers, and black day laborers paid less than minimum wage whenever possible.

About all he ever does is ride around in his big air-conditioned truck and in his words, 'check on things.'"

I was saved from having to respond to these disturbing comments as J.T. and Joe strolled into the library. "Sorry to interrupt the hen party, but Joe wants to see my guns and hunting trophies." J.T. nodded toward a collection of enormous deer heads mounted on the wall behind a massive gun case filled with all sorts of firearms.

"Where'd you kill these, J.T.?" Joe asked. He was admiring the deer heads as much as I'd admired the books.

As J.T. began a recitation of his hunting exploits, Scarlett moved across the room and I followed. "I don't need to hear those hunting stories for the two hundredth time," she said. "For that matter I didn't want to hear them the first time. Hunting, hunting, always hunting! Do you think he's ever read any of these books? He wouldn't know Shakespeare from Edgar Allan Poe unless one of them wrote a good deer story. In large print using easy words."

"Scarlett! Shhh." I glanced at J.T. Fueled by whiskey and an attentive audience, he was giving Joe a blow-by-blow account of how he'd killed each deer on the wall, pointing in the gun case to the rifles he'd used.

"Honestly, I don't know why we have these books in here," Scarlett continued as though she hadn't heard me try to shush her. "I've never read them either and don't intend to. I really don't like to read.

"I know that sounds awful coming from a reading teacher, but in college I knew I sure didn't want to teach English, math, or science. I just sort of drifted into majoring in reading education."

I couldn't think of a word to say to this confession. I would've loved to own her collection. These were the books I'd read and discussed in so many college literature classes. It had never occurred to me that some people owned books only for display. It had certainly never occurred to me that a reading teacher wouldn't like to read.

"Just like I drifted into marrying J.T. and living out here in the backwoods," Scarlett continued. "When I first laid eyes on him six years ago, he was the most handsome Kappa Sig at NC State and wealthy to boot. Mother and Daddy had scraped together enough money to send me to Meredith College, an all-girls' school, you know. I was a senior, looking around for a suitable husband, and thought J.T. was a catch. He wasn't hard to reel in. We got married six months after we met, two weeks after I graduated. I didn't think it through."

Scarlett's eyes hardened as she looked across the room at J.T. "I didn't really know him." I thought it best to say nothing to this confession.

Scarlett gave a little shake. "Let's go see how dinner's coming along. Ruby is making stuffed potatoes and a tossed salad. She might need me to help her set the table. She doesn't always get the forks in the right place."

"J.T., have you put those steaks on yet?" she barked as we walked past the men.

J.T., interrupted, looked confused for a moment but then responded, "On my way, darlin'. Ruby's had them marinating in my secret sauce."

*****

"I had a good time tonight," Joe said. Heather was fast asleep in the back seat. I was tired too, but Joe, having consumed several rounds of Jack Daniel's and Coca Cola, was wound up.

"That J.T. is a talker. Man, he's got some nice deer heads, not to mention his gun collection."

"Everything is certainly first class around there," I replied. "That house is absolutely to die for. Did you like Scarlett? Isn't she pretty?"

"Not as pretty as my lovely wife, one Dee Ann Bulluck, my chauffeur for the evening. I love a woman who can drive a man home. 'I only have eyes for you,'" he began singing off-key. Joe is a terrible singer and tries only when he's had too much to drink.

"Be quiet. You'll have every dog in the county howling besides waking up Heather."

Joe laughed. He quit singing, but I could hear him humming.

"I can't imagine living in a house that big," I said. "And two maids there to help her entertain! One to babysit and one to cook."

"They've got the good life, no doubt about it. You can't beat being born into money."

"Unless you make it yourself," I said. "But that's called nouveau riche, a label that's not usually a compliment. Why is it that people consider those who inherited money to be a notch above those who worked hard to make it themselves? Seems to me there would be more prestige in earning a fortune than in having one given to you."

"I'd take it any way I could get it," Joe said. "And in this neck of the woods, be careful about bashing old money. There are quite a few people around, your new friend and her husband included, who are what's left of the old gentry. People with lots of land. The few lucky haves—and a lot of unlucky have-nots."

I thought about Ida with her faded dress and Ruby working in someone else's kitchen on a Saturday night. And Willy, who limped around the Powells' yard, calling me Missus every time he saw me. The only black person I'd met in Narrow Creek who wasn't impoverished was Hazel Hood.

There also seemed to be something a little sinful about having so much wealth. Didn't the Bible say love of money is the root of all evil and that it would be harder for a rich man to enter heaven than for a camel to go through the eye of a needle?

It would be nice, though, to have a few more material comforts in this life. A bigger house, for example. Heck, any kind of house, for that matter. Even if I happened to solve the Gary Whitt murder, ten thousand dollars wouldn't begin to buy the lifestyle I'd just seen.

Joe and I would have to make a whole lot of money to ever have what the Hoods seemed to take for granted. But I also knew that despite the big house and the help, my new friend wasn't happy.

Chapter 16

"**D**ee Ann, telephone!" I rushed out of the bedroom, where I'd been folding laundry while thinking about a lesson plan for dangling participles.

"I'm just around the corner. You don't have to shout," I hissed in an undertone. I didn't want whoever was on the phone to hear me reprimanding Joe although he deserved it, yelling at me as if I were three states away.

"Hello," I said sweetly.

"Dee Ann, this is Gloria Smith. I hope you've had a good summer."

Gloria Smith, the Narrow Creek Ladies' Society membership chair. Darn! It was time to talk about club work. But maybe I could also steer the conversation to find out something about the mysterious Lisa, the woman I'd overheard arguing with Cynthia in the First Baptist kitchen.

"I'm calling to give you some options for fulfilling your civic requirement for the upcoming year," Gloria continued. "Let's see. We have playing Bingo with the residents at the nursing home, ringing the Salvation Army bell during the Christmas season, volunteering to tutor at the middle school, and working at our thrift store. You'll probably need to do at least three of these to get all your hours in.

"You don't have to sign up for everything right now. I just wanted to touch base to let you be thinking about how you want to complete your volunteer requirement." Gloria finally paused.

"Oh, okay," I said, trying to sound enthusiastic. Over the summer, I'd put thoughts of the Ladies' Society out of my mind. I'd especially tried to forget that, come early fall, civic work would start. But I'd agreed to serve a year of probationary membership. And I'd been raised better than to renege on my word, so I accepted that it was now my duty to play Bingo with the old folks and sell gently used clothing at the club's secondhand store.

"I know we'll have some openings in the volunteer schedule since Cynthia is no longer with us," Gloria stated. "Now that I think of it, you could really help the club if you'd fill in the slots she signed up for last spring."

I forgot all about civic work as well as pumping my caller for information about the identity of Lisa. "What's happened to Cynthia?"

"You haven't heard?" Gloria exclaimed. "It seems Cynthia Ford has resigned after helping herself to the club's money."

"Helping herself to—what?"

"She stole from the club, to put it bluntly."

"Are you kidding me?" My mind was reeling. Cynthia cheats on her husband, smokes dope, and now she's a thief.

"I wish I were. It's a sad, sad tale," said Gloria in a hushed, tut-tut voice. "The club is missing over three thousand dollars. We discovered our money was gone when our checks started bouncing. Cynthia wrote one for two hundred dollars to our annual scholarship recipient, and when the poor girl went to deposit it in her college account, the bank told her the check was worthless." Gloria's voice was rising as she relished each detail. "The girl's mother called Barbara Highland, who, of course, went down to the bank and found out we had several checks that had come back due to insufficient funds.

"Barbara didn't get to be club president by being meek and mild. She marched straight into Cynthia's husband's office and said, 'Bill Ford, your bank says the Narrow Creek Ladies' Society has a zero checking account balance. I'd like to find out what's going on here. Either your bank has made a huge mistake or our treasurer has, and I want you to get to the bottom of this.'" Gloria paused dramatically before continuing. At my end of the line, I nervously twisted and untwisted the phone cord around my index finger as I processed every detail.

"Barbara said Bill didn't even know Cynthia was the club treasurer, but once she informed him that yes, his wife had been in charge of our money for the past year, he turned white and started stammering that he'd correct the situation immediately.

"According to Barbara, he called an hour later and said Cynthia had forgotten to make several deposits, but our money was now in the checking account and we wouldn't be charged any fees for bounced checks. Barbara said he apologized over and over and declared Cynthia was so embarrassed she thought it best to resign from the club. He said he hoped her resignation would allow the club to forgive her." Gloria gave a derisive snort.

Why would Cynthia need to steal money from, of all people, the Ladies' Society? That was like robbing a church. I decided to play devil's advocate. "Maybe Cynthia really did forget to put the money in the bank."

"Forgot to make deposits? Give me a break!" Gloria exploded. "That woman is an accountant. That's why we elected her to be treasurer. She was excited to get the job, and now we know why."

"But why would she take the money," I countered, "knowing that the club would eventually find out?"

Had Cynthia needed drug money? Or maybe she'd been blackmailed by Gary Whitt. Maybe he threatened to reveal her infidelity or her drug habit. It wasn't hard to think of reasons she'd be so desperate.

"I'm betting she made herself a temporary loan with the money," Gloria replied, "intending to pay it back before the money was missed. Then whatever she was counting on to replace our money didn't happen. I've heard embezzlers often rob Peter to pay Paul. I saw a very similar case on *The Rockford Files* just the other night. I absolutely love James Garner on that show, don't you?"

"I'm a *Columbo* fan myself, but my husband likes *The Rockford Files*," I answered automatically. Why was I allowing myself to get sidetracked discussing cop shows?

"Didn't Bill tell Barbara he'd found the money and deposited it in the bank?" I asked, getting the conversation back on track. "Sounds to me as if it was just a mistake on Cynthia's part," I added, still pretending disbelief in any wrongdoing.

"Oh, Bill found some money all right and put it in the bank to smooth things over, but I'm pretty sure that money wasn't ours," Gloria said. "Poor Bill had to fork up the money himself to cover what Cynthia had already spent. It's quite coincidental that she's no longer driving her fancy Mercedes around town anymore. She's in an old Buick sedan that looks like something somebody's spinster great-aunt would drive. It's obvious Bill has taken that Mercedes away from her as punishment. I bet he's trying to sell it to help cover what she's cost him." Gloria sounded proud of herself for offering this evidence.

"She's guilty, plain and simple, Dee Ann," she continued in a self-righteous voice. "I know she brought you to the club and maybe is your friend, so it's been my Christian duty to make you aware of her true colors. We're judged by the company we keep, you know, and I don't want to see your reputation tarnished by associating with a known embezzler."

Cynthia was certainly no friend of mine; she was my prime suspect, in fact, but I wasn't about to tell this woman that.

"I do trust you won't discuss this situation with anyone outside of our club," Gloria said haughtily. "We don't want word to get out that we had a thief in our midst. It wouldn't be good publicity. The Ladies' Society has a certain image to maintain, so we try to avoid being associated with anything unpleasant. We agreed to hush up this scandal in return for the money being replaced along with Cynthia's resignation."

You don't even know the half of it, I so wanted to say. Instead, I assured her I wouldn't breathe a word of scandal to anyone. Hanging up the phone, I made a beeline for my husband.

*****

"You won't believe what I just learned." Joe and Heather were on the floor together in her room, where he'd retreated after calling me to the telephone. Normally I would've paused a moment to enjoy the sight of Joe playing with his daughter, but I was so bursting with this exciting development in my investigation the sweet scene barely registered with me.

"Whatever it is, it's got you in a stew," said Joe. "Bridge club met at Miss Josie's house last week? Somebody's cousin from California home for a visit? You know they put stuff like that in the Narrow Creek newspaper."

I hadn't realized Joe read the "Social Notes" column. "This is serious," I said, filling him in on the call.

Joe sat up. "I hate to think the worst of people, but that explains a few things," he mused once I'd finished.

"What things?" I demanded.

"Bill's been acting a little funny at work. He's been downright gloomy, in fact. The tellers love to gossip, and they've all been saying he has marital problems. They say Cynthia loves to spend money they don't have and has gotten them in big-time credit card debt."

My husband, bless his sweet heart, seemed genuinely sorry for Bill. "Joe Bulluck, why haven't you told me this?"

"It's gossip. You know I don't like to talk about people."

"Okay, let's just stick to the facts here, then." I sounded like one of those detectives on the cop shows Gloria and I'd discussed. "Is Cynthia still driving her Mercedes?"

"She's not. Bill turned it in to the leasing company and borrowed the bank's old company car for her to drive. He said it was costing him an arm and a leg to lease that car each month and that Cynthia didn't deserve to drive it anymore."

Joe looked a little sheepish revealing this damning bit of evidence, so I didn't chide him for not telling me earlier. He really doesn't like to discuss other people's business. I must admit, Joe is often a better person than I am. Then again, he wasn't secretly conducting a murder investigation.

Had Cynthia been embezzling and going into credit card debt to pay for nice clothes and the lease on her Mercedes? Maybe I was jumping to conclusions about drug and blackmail money. Those weren't exactly expenses she could put on MasterCard.

Unless she'd run up her credit cards with cash advances. If only I were a teller at the bank and could get a look at her statements—or I could just ask Joe.

"Do you know whether any of that credit card debt involved cash advances?"

"How in the world would I know that, Dee Ann?" Joe exclaimed. "I don't even know for sure she and Bill are in debt; I was repeating what the tellers have said. This is exactly why I don't like gossip."

He paused and gave me a suspicious look. "What difference would it make whether Cynthia's charging expensive pocketbooks or making herself a credit card loan? And why do you want to know?"

"Just curious," I said, faking nonchalance. "Does Heather need a diaper change?"

Chapter 17

"**E**quality under the law shall not be denied or abridged by the United States or by any State on account of sex." The bold letters jumped off the flyer tacked to the bulletin board in the faculty lounge. I leaned closer to read the smaller print:

> *Learn how you can help in the battle to ratify the Equal Rights Amendment in North Carolina. Members of the state chapter of the National Organization for Women (NOW) will hold a meeting on Monday, September 17, 1979, at 7 p.m. in the Harold Booker Assembly Room at the Narrow Creek Public Library. All are invited to attend.*

"What are you reading?" I'd been so intent on the flyer I hadn't heard Scarlett come in the lounge on this ho-hum Wednesday morning.

"This announcement," I said. "I can't believe people from NOW are actually coming to Narrow Creek. I don't exactly picture this town as a hotbed of feminism."

"Maybe that's why they're coming," Scarlett replied. "Maybe they're trying to broaden a few minds, stir things up."

"Why don't we go? I support the ERA. At least, I think I do. I'd like to hear what someone from NOW has to say about it. Lord knows, we don't get many opportunities to hear out-of-town speakers." I usually saved my criticism of Narrow Creek for Joe, but that flyer had me riled up.

"Politics isn't my thing," Scarlett said. "And I'm sure I'd have to lie to J.T. about where I was going. He likes that Phyllis Schlafly woman, the one who's always going around the country telling other women they should be home waiting on their husbands and tending to their children.

"He'd go with me himself to hear her speak, but I'd have a fight on my hands if I told him I wanted to attend a NOW meeting." Scarlett shook her head. "I have to pick my battles."

I hadn't even considered whether Joe would object. Oh, he sometimes made comments to me about my "women's lib soapbox" when I fussed at him for not doing more around the house. But he didn't disagree with me when I'd point out that it wasn't fair all the manager positions at the bank were held by men and all the teller jobs by women. He said that was the way things were, and there was nothing we could do about it.

But maybe there was. Going to this meeting could be enlightening, even empowering. There was no way Joe could object to a meeting that talked about how to help women be treated fairly in the workplace. He wouldn't mind my going to a NOW meeting, and on the slim chance that he did, too bad.

*****

Monday night, I left Joe home in charge of Heather and drove the short distance to the one-story, 1960s-style, red-brick building that housed the Narrow Creek Public Library. Joe had laughed when I told him I wanted to attend a NOW meeting to discuss the Equal Rights Amendment.

"What are you ladies going to do? Burn your bras there in the library? Don't send the stacks up in smoke."

I told Joe he wasn't being the least bit funny.

"Don't let them turn you into a man-hater," he then said. "Or convince you that you don't need a husband and a baby. We don't want Mommy to leave us, do we, Heather?" This time he didn't seem to be joking as he knelt to kiss Heather, who was sitting in her baby swing.

"The women's movement isn't about leaving your husband and children. It's about women having the same opportunities as men in the work force. And in other areas of life, too. For example, I've heard you say how hard it is for a woman to get a loan without a man co-signing even if she qualifies on her own salary."

"I've seen that happen at the bank," Joe conceded. "Go to your meeting, Dee Ann. I'll be interested in what you learn."

So there I was in the Harold Booker Assembly Room on the front row in one of the thirty or so folding chairs that had been set up for the event, waiting for all the other women in Narrow Creek—and maybe some broad-minded men— to show up. At 7:05 when the meeting began, there were four of us total. All women, no men. I didn't know anyone there. The other three women looked to be close to my age, but I'd never seen them at a meeting of the Ladies' Society or bumped into them at the Winn-Dixie. Did they live in Narrow Creek, or had they driven in from somewhere else?

The two women from the NOW chapter in Raleigh didn't seem perturbed by our small number, but I was embarrassed for them. At least those of us in attendance had the courtesy to sit together on the front row to show our eagerness in hearing all about the ERA.

The older of the two ladies, a stern, gray-haired woman, introduced first herself as Betty Johnson and then her companion, a young, attractive, blonde woman named

Gloria Parker. "Just call us Betty and Gloria," she said. "We're proud to share first names with two of the most famous feminists of our time." Of course I knew she was referring to Betty Friedan and Gloria Steinem. The two women did resemble the famous Betty and Gloria a tad bit.

Betty started by handing out information. The cover of one pamphlet featured an older lady wearing an apron and standing over a stove. The caption read, "What would happen to this woman if her husband suddenly died?" Another hand-out contained a list of North Carolina representatives with phone numbers and addresses. "Write to these congressmen today urging them to vote YES to the ERA!" screamed a banner headline.

"Despite what Phyllis Schlafly and her Stop-ERA cronies would have people believe, the Equal Rights Amendment is simply about guaranteeing women the same rights, benefits, and privileges as men," Betty began. "To quote Alice Paul, who spearheaded the passage of the Nineteenth Amendment giving women the right to vote, 'There is nothing complicated about equality.'"

Suddenly a voice came from the back. "Who wants to be equal to men? Most women enjoy being put on a pedestal. I know I do." I turned to see who'd interrupted the speaker and locked eyes with none other than Tippy Gaylord.

"I'd appreciate the chance to speak before fielding comments from the audience," Betty replied, unruffled.

"Personally, I'm not going to sit through whatever communist propaganda you intend to spout off. I came only to warn these impressionable young women here tonight not to believe anything they hear from you liberal feminists." Tippy Gaylord made the word *feminists* sound like a profanity while glaring at us "impressionable young women." Her disapproving stare lingered on me. I hoped she didn't recognize me from her Fourth of July party. Maybe all the wives of the men who worked for her husband looked alike to her.

"Common sense dictates that we respect the differences between the sexes," Mrs. Gaylord proceeded in a haughty voice. "Do you women know that if the ERA passes, you could be drafted? Forced to use public unisex bathrooms. And if you found yourself divorced, your ex-husband would no longer be required to pay alimony."

"Madam, I'm asking you to respect our right to speak," Betty interrupted. "We reserved this room tonight and advertised our meeting. We've traveled from Raleigh to meet with those interested in the passage of the Equal Rights Amendment. You're certainly entitled to your opinion, but I think it common courtesy that you schedule your own meeting to express your misinformed views."

I had to admire Betty. She didn't bat an eye the entire time she was reprimanding Mrs. Gaylord. Then again, she didn't know Mrs. Gaylord from Eve. She had no clue this was a woman with plenty of money and influence who in all probability had never had anyone tell her to get her own meeting.

Mrs. Gaylord snorted. "I'm far from misinformed." She gave Betty a withering look before again addressing us four delinquents: "Young ladies, please read what Phyllis Schlafly has to say about the ERA before you commit yourselves to supporting this radical piece of legislation. Good evening. I sincerely hope you'll follow me out."

Clutching her alligator purse, Mrs. Gaylord swept from the room, letting the door slam behind her. Betty immediately regained the momentum of the meeting, informing us that for every dollar a man made, a woman made only fifty-nine cents.

I wondered if that pay discrepancy was because most women were teachers, nurses, and secretaries, jobs that didn't pay all that much. Why were these low-paying jobs for that matter? Who decided that a truck driver or a brick mason should earn more than a first-grade teacher or an ER nurse?

Gloria's part of the meeting was her testimonial about the discrimination she'd suffered in the corporate world. She'd graduated with a degree in business administration from a prestigious university, but when she applied for jobs, found herself being offered secretarial work instead of management trainee positions. Men in her class whom she'd outperformed academically were starting in those management positions at salaries far higher than what she was being offered as an administrative assistant.

"I've learned the title 'administrative assistant' is code for 'secretary,'" Gloria said. "I'm not belittling the secretaries of the world, but I didn't attend college for four years only to go into a position I could've had straight out of high school. I was even told by one interviewer that after a few months, I could help train new managers since I had a degree in business." Gloria paused with tears in her eyes. "Why would I want to train a man for the same job I'd been denied?"

The meeting concluded with a question and answer session, which caused me to forget all about the ERA. The attractive petite woman with sky-blue eyes and a chin-length bob who sat next to me piped up.

"My name is Lisa Strayhorn, and I'm married to the associate minister at First Baptist Church here in town."

I knew that voice. Lisa, married to an associate minister. This was the woman I'd overheard confronting Cynthia that Saturday at the Ladies' Society Arts and Craft Show.

"The information you've presented tonight has made me realize just how oppressed I am in my marriage. For ten years, since the day I said, 'I do,' I've built my entire world around my husband."

Not entirely, I wanted to interject.

"People don't realize how confining it is to be married to someone in the church. You ladies talk about a woman being paid less than a man. When you're the wife of a clergyman, you're expected to work for nothing. Parishioners seem to think there's a buy one, get one free deal."

How about marry one, have a fling with another?

"Most members serve the church in some capacity, but I'm always expected to do more. Any job that nobody wants, my husband volunteers me. Nursery duty, visiting the shut-ins, heading up Vacation Bible School, organizing the Wednesday night suppers.

"It's been a full-time, unpaid job, and I'm sick of it. And I'm sick of my husband for signing me up for all the church grunt work just to impress his boss, the senior minister. Tonight's meeting has given me the courage to leave the church and my husband."

Betty and Gloria were nearly spluttering, insisting that the ERA wasn't about leaving husbands and forsaking churches, but Lisa was too busy planning her future to listen to their disclaimers. "I'm moving back to Raleigh as soon as I can pack my bags, and I'll stay with Mother and Dad until I can get a job. I have an art history degree. Surely I can find something related to my field in a city as big as Raleigh."

Lisa didn't mention that her lover had been murdered, and it might be a good time to get out of town.

Chapter 18

J oe was asleep when I got home shortly after nine. I've never understood how that man can go to bed so early and be unconscious in two minutes' time. If I go to bed before eleven, I lie awake and think of every problem I have and become so worked up I finally decide to get back up.

But this was one night I was glad my husband had observed his early bedtime. I didn't want to tell him about Tippy Gaylord's appearance at the NOW meeting. I was sure Joe wouldn't want Mr. Gaylord knowing about my attendance at an event so heartily disapproved of by his wife. And I certainly wasn't going to inform him of Lisa Strayhorn's outburst.

Maybe Tippy Gaylord hadn't recognized me, I told myself as I lay awake in bed at midnight beside a snoring Joe. Or maybe she doesn't fill her husband in on everything she does and everywhere she goes. And was Lisa Strayhorn really leaving town because she was sick of serving her husband and a demanding church, or was there another motive?

I finally got out of bed and read a couple of chapters of *Sophie's Choice*, which I'd found under the new releases at the library and hurriedly checked out right before the meeting. The book was so absorbing I forgot all about my own distress and was finally able to wind down enough to go to sleep.

Joe was in the bathroom shaving when I approached him the next morning. I'd decided to 'fess up about Tippy Gaylord being at the meeting in case Mr. Gaylord confronted Joe at work. Better Joe be warned than blindsided. I tried a lighthearted approach. "You might want to call the bank to be sure you still have a job before you go in today."

Joe's half-shaven face in the bathroom mirror was quizzical. "What are you talking about?" He scraped the razor across his cheek.

"One Mrs. Tippy Gaylord crashed the NOW meeting last night. And I mean crashed. She didn't show up to support the ladies from NOW, but to interrupt them. The meeting had barely started when she stood up and started spouting off anti-feminist rhetoric."

The part of Joe's face that wasn't still lathered looked almost as white as the part that was. "Let me get this straight," he said. "Tippy Gaylord was at the meeting last night. What specifically did she say?"

"She advised all of us young women—all four of us there—not to believe anything we heard from the NOW speakers, the 'communist feminist liberals.' Evidently she considers feminists and liberals to be as bad as communists." To avoid meeting Joe's eyes, I busied myself with picking up his bath towel off the floor and hanging it on the rack.

"Did Tippy Gaylord say anything to you specifically?" Joe asked.

"No. I'm not sure she even recognized me." I adjusted the towel so the edges were folded inward and the towel hung evenly. "She saw me only that one time at the Fourth of July party."

"You were pretty high profile that night, though," said Joe with a touch of irritation. "Your performance with the band probably marked you as someone she'd remember."

"Well, what if she did recognize me last night? It's a free country. I have a right to attend any meeting I want to as long as we're not plotting the overthrow of the government."

To my surprise, Joe concurred. "You know, you're right. Now that I think about it, I agree with you. I work for a conservative bank in a conservative town, but Ed Gaylord doesn't own me. I give the bank forty plus hours of honest work each week, but I'm not going to let what I do for a living rule our lives."

Joe turned around to finish shaving. The color had returned to the already shaved part of his face.

"To tell you the truth, I'm not sure I even support the ERA," I confessed. "Mrs. Gaylord made a couple of points about what might happen if it passes that, if true, are disturbing to me. Like women being drafted into the army. I need to study the bill more. Maybe read some impartial information, if there is any. I'm not ready to put on my marching boots and go to a rally in Raleigh. For either side, pro or con."

If Lisa Strayhorn's decision to leave her marriage had really been sealed by just one meeting about the Equal Rights Amendment, then this bill was pretty powerful stuff.

Joe dried his face with the towel I'd just carefully hung up, absentmindedly dropped it on the floor again, and followed me out of the bathroom. "I like a woman who thinks for herself," he said, smiling. "Even if having my own little Gloria Steinem might make my life hard at times." I looked back at the towel on the floor. Gloria Steinem certainly wouldn't be hanging up any man's towel for the second time in five minutes. She wouldn't have hung it up the first time.

*****

Two days after the NOW meeting, Joe came home at lunch whistling. He's a naturally cheerful person, but this Wednesday he was practically beaming.

"What in the world happened at work this morning to put all that pep in your step?" I asked as I poured our iced tea.

"A conversation with Ed Gaylord."

Uh-oh. Although Joe had given me his little speech about not caring whether Mr. Gaylord heard I'd been at the NOW meeting, I felt sure he was at least a little concerned about any repercussions. I'd certainly been worried about causing any problems for Joe at work. Our family needed his job; in fact, we needed him to get a promotion.

"This conversation didn't happen to be about me, did it?" I asked in a small voice.

"Actually it didn't, although it did concern a certain meeting you attended." He paused, having fun in dragging out his explanation.

"Spill it, Joe, if you want any lunch today."

Joe chuckled at my idle threat. "It seems Ed Gaylord thinks it's funny his wife went to a NOW meeting to protest. He said there's not much in life that gets her stirred up, but mention the Equal Rights Amendment and she goes ballistic." Joe fiddled with a loose button on his shirt, and I made a mental note to sew it on tighter before putting the shirt in the laundry.

"Ed said she's jealous of professional women, and she equates working women with the ERA. He said Tippy has never had to lift a finger her whole life, other than to arrange a vase of flowers or make out a grocery list for the maid."

Joe paused to pick up Heather, who'd been crawling around his feet. "Anyhow, Ed was pretty amused that his wife had taken the trouble to go down to the library and put in her two cents' worth. He said she came home fussing about those young women being brainwashed by feminists."

That might have happened, I thought, picturing Lisa Strayhorn.

"Did you admit one of those young women was your wife?"

"I did. Ed just laughed and said Tippy told him she didn't recognize anybody. It seems she couldn't see all that well since she won't wear her glasses in public."

I wouldn't have guessed Tippy Gaylord was so vain she'd rather walk around in a blurred world than let anyone see her in glasses. I also wouldn't have guessed Ed Gaylord would be amused by something that distressed her. "But doesn't Ed care about his wife? He doesn't seem concerned about what's obviously important to her."

Joe was quiet for so long I almost thought he hadn't heard my question. When he spoke, he picked his words carefully. "I don't know how Ed feels about the ERA. He didn't say. But I get the feeling he doesn't respect his wife. Today wasn't the first time he's made fun of her. I don't think he values the home she's kept for him or the children she's raised while he was working."

What a disappointment to give your life to a man who belittles you. Maybe Tippy Gaylord needed the Equal Rights Amendment as much as any professional woman. Maybe she should've been the one at that meeting who declared she was leaving an unappreciative husband rather than Lisa Strayhorn.

If indeed, I reminded myself, Lisa Strayhorn had been telling the truth about her reason for fleeing Narrow Creek.

Chapter 19

Three weeks after our visit to the Hoods' house, Joe and I were watching Walter Cronkite on the *CBS Evening News* when Joe suddenly suggested we reciprocate their hospitality by taking Scarlett and J.T. out to dinner. I'm the one who usually plans what little social life we have, so I was surprised. Other than activities that involve sports, Joe doesn't care about going anywhere much.

I jumped on his suggestion. "That's a good idea." It was a good idea. By taking the Hoods out to dinner, I wouldn't have to show Scarlett my less than luxurious apartment.

"How do we pay for it, though?" A big night out for the two of us was Pizza Hut. We'd want to take the Hoods somewhere more upscale, but we didn't have an upscale budget.

"Here's the beauty of the plan," Joe said, rubbing his hands together in an exaggerated fashion and smiling. "The bank will pay for it."

"The bank?"

"The bank," Joe repeated. "Bill and I were drinking coffee the other morning, and I mentioned I'd been to dinner at J.T. Hood's house. He got excited and told me the bank would love more of J.T.'s business, and that if I wanted to, you and I could take J.T. and his wife out on the bank's tab."

"Are you kidding? That's great. Where can we go?" Being a banker's wife was finally beginning to pay off.

"We'll do something special," Joe said. "We can drive over to Rocky Mount and eat at that new Chinese restaurant that has booths set up like seats in a train car. I've also heard there's a great seafood restaurant over in New Bern. We could belly up to the bar for some steamed oysters. September is an R month, so we should be able to get some fresh ones."

"I don't know if the Hoods have ever tried Chinese," I said, thinking of myself. "Maybe we'd be safer to take them to eat oysters. Do you want to go this Friday night if they're available?"

I assumed a Friday night restaurant trip to another town meant no children, and Joe and I needed an adults-only night out anyway. "After I make sure Bertha can stay with Heather, I'll ask Scarlett since she was the one who invited us to their house."

"Bertha, is it? I guess you've overlooked her, what was it, 'hillbilly appearance' and 'lack of good sense'?"

I just hate it when my own words are used against me.

*****

The ever-faithful Bertha said she could come Friday night. Scarlett and J.T. were free for the evening too, so the party was on. On Friday, Joe came home driving the bank's Lincoln Town Car, and I felt downright affluent as we rode off to pick up the Hoods.

"What pretenders we are," I said without a bit of guilt.

"I'm going to let on that we're in the bank's car, but I don't intend to tell them how dinner is being paid for," Joe said. "No need for J.T. Hood to think I'm asking him out just to get his business."

"And we're not. I, for one, am in this strictly for a good time. A night with my charming husband, new friends, and steamed oysters. What more could a girl ask for?"

Joe reached over to squeeze my hand. I squeezed his in return. Once in a while I did let Joe know I appreciated being married to him.

Like us, the Hoods were in jeans. "Since we're going out of town, let's be scandalous and not dress up," Scarlett had suggested.

"Fine with me," I'd agreed, so now we were all comfortable in denim.

What was not comfortable, I soon noticed, was the vibe between Scarlett and J.T. "Girls in the back," said Scarlett, opening the rear door. "I want to talk to Dee Ann. J.T., you ride up front with Joe."

"How are you tonight, Miss Dee Ann?" J.T. asked.

"She's fine and drop the Miss. The Old South is dead and gone," snapped Scarlett before I could open my mouth.

For a moment, there was silence in the car. Then J.T. spoke. "I'm sorry, y'all. Scarlett's upset with me tonight for some reason. Lord knows what I've done now."

"J.T., just talk to Joe, and let Dee Ann and me have some girl time."

I couldn't believe Scarlett would speak that way to J.T. with Joe and me sitting right there. Everybody gets mad at a spouse now and then, but you should keep those squabbles at home. Goodness knows Joe could upset me sometimes, but I'd never say hurtful things to him in public. Joe would never intentionally embarrass me in front of other people either.

But Scarlett didn't seem to realize how awkward she'd made everyone feel as she started gossiping about the faculty meeting we'd endured that afternoon. "Can you believe how worked up some teachers get over nothing? Honestly, I just wanted to stuff an eraser in Edna Perry's mouth when she kept going on and on about how everyone should know it's a 'professional courtesy' to leave a clean blackboard for the next instructor. Big deal! How hard is it to erase someone else's notes before you get started? If you don't feel up to the job, ask a student to do it.'"

I didn't want to admit to Scarlett that having to erase someone else's scribbled-filled blackboard was one of my pet peeves too and I totally agreed with Edna. Instead, I gave a detailed account of my job interview with Dr. Adams.

"He asked me not only what Joe did for a living but also what I intended to do for child care," I concluded. "Hasn't this man been to any Equal Employment Opportunity workshops?"

Scarlett laughed. "He probably has, but I doubt any information can penetrate that bad comb-over. He's too busy preening in front of a mirror to worry about how to conduct a professional, legal job interview. But he's harmless. In fact, he's really quite easy to wind around your little finger if you play along." Scarlett smiled and wiggled her eyebrows.

"I go in to see him occasionally and compliment him on whatever tacky leisure suit he has on that day," she confided. "I ask some stupid question about teaching and pretend he's given me a brilliant answer. It's all I can do to keep from laughing as he puffs up, thinking he's smart and handsome. Then I mention something I want, like travel money or classroom equipment. I've been to some nice conferences over the last couple of years, and I've got a humdinger overhead projector."

I was shocked, but Scarlett added, "You should try it, Dee Ann. Flirt with him a little, and see what you can get. He'd love the attention of someone as cute as you are."

Up front, Joe and J.T. were in a deep discussion of money market rates, thank goodness. Joe would tease me to no end if he heard Scarlett suggesting something so counter to my women's lib beliefs. And I wasn't sure how J.T. would take it if he heard his wife blatantly admitting to flirting with another man, even one who looked as ridiculous as Dr. William H. Adams, Dean of Instruction.

Since we were on the subject of Dr. Adams, I decided to see what Scarlett could tell me about the man. "Did you know Dr. Adams lives with his mother? And that his nephew was Gary Whitt, that guy who was murdered back in the spring?" Joe glanced over his shoulder at me as J.T. roared on about some land deal.

"Oh sure," Scarlett said in a flippant voice. "Dr. Adams talks about 'Mother' all the time. I don't think he misses his nephew, but it's going to be a sad day for him when he buries old Mrs. Adams." Scarlett shook her tousled hair and reached for her purse. "Or maybe not—since he now stands to get all her money. Gary was the only other heir."

"I wonder if the police consider him a suspect." I spoke in a low voice. "You know he mentioned Gary to me the day I interviewed, and he didn't sound too fond of him. Combine dislike, competition for his mother's affection, and the desire to be the sole heir, and you may have a motive for murder." I studied Scarlett to gauge her reaction.

"Are you kidding?" She laughed. "Dr. Adams is afraid of his own shadow. He'd never have the nerve to do anything remotely violent. We're talking about a man who grows orchids and plays the violin."

She dug through her purse, finally producing a lipstick case engraved with the initials "TB" and "S" with hearts on either side. Scarlett saw me eying the inscription. "A gift from an old college boyfriend." She seemed so totally convinced of Dr. Adams' innocence, I felt foolish asking any more questions.

At the restaurant, Scarlett maneuvered the seating arrangement at the bar so she and J.T. were at either ends of our row of four with Joe and me in the middle. "Keep me as far away from that man tonight as possible," she told me. "He's gotten on my last nerve."

Parked on the other side of Joe at the noisy bar, J.T. was fortunately out of earshot, and I hoped Joe would keep him talking so he couldn't hear anything his wife was saying. Frankly, I didn't want to hear it myself. I like to be around happy, positive people, and Scarlett was lacking both of those qualities. Also, the last thing I wanted to do was get in the middle of someone's marital squabbles.

"I'm so sick of hearing about how wonderful his mother is," Scarlett said as if I'd asked why she was upset with J.T. "It's Mama Hood this and Mama Hood that. That woman can do no wrong as far as J.T. is concerned.

"'Mama Hood was always happy staying home with her family. She never left a child to go to work. She knew God made women to serve their husbands. Why can't you be more like Mama Hood?'" Scarlett did a pretty good imitation of J.T.'s boisterous, drawling voice as she mocked what J.T. considered his mother's merits.

What man is crazy enough to tell a wife to be more like his mother? I wondered. Evidently Dr. Adams wasn't the only grown man still tied to his mother's apron strings. I was beginning to understand how Scarlett had a legitimate beef with J.T.

"The worst part is the way J.T. lets her keep our son any time and for however long she wants. That's why I'm steaming right now. This afternoon, when I got home from school, John Thomas wasn't there. I asked Ida where he was, and she said that Mama Hood had taken him to her house again. She'd come over not long after I'd left for school and told Ida to pack John Thomas' suitcase for the weekend.

"I marched myself outside where J.T. was smoking a cigar by the pool and asked him whether he knew his son wasn't home. 'Of course,' he said. 'Mama Hood's got him.

She was feeling lonely and wanted some company for the weekend.'

"'What about me?' I said. 'Did it ever occur to you I might want to spend the weekend with my son?' I tell you, Dee Ann, I was ready to take a shovel and whack that man's thick head.

"And do you know what he had the nerve to say to me?" Scarlett drew in her breath dramatically. "He looked me dead in the eye and said just as sweet as you please, 'Well, darlin', if you want to spend time with John Thomas, then why don't you quit that job you don't need and stay home with him like a good mama ought to?'

"I threatened to go to his precious Mama Hood's house right then and there and get my son, and then J.T. reminded me that my car is in his name—oh, he owns everything we have—and that if I wanted to get to work next week, I'd better calm down and go back in the house."

Scarlett's hand was shaking so badly she put down her glass of chardonnay. "Either I let his mama have John Thomas all weekend, or I don't have a car to drive to work. Can you believe he's blackmailing me this way? And then he has the gall to tell you and Joe he doesn't know why I'm upset with him tonight."

I was seeing J.T. in a different light. Joe and I didn't have much, but what we did have, we both agreed we owned jointly. I couldn't imagine Joe ever telling me I couldn't drive the Toyota, even if he was the one making most of the money. When I started teaching and needed a way to get to work, Joe'd given me the car and gone out and found that old five hundred dollar, beat-up Jeep for himself. And Joe would never let his parents take Heather for a weekend without talking to me about it first.

I swiveled around on my bar stool and sneaked a look at J.T. He was digging into his first batch of shucked oysters, an oversized napkin tucked into the neck of his shirt, completely oblivious to the airing of his dirty laundry that was going on three seats away. Thank goodness.

Chapter 20

After "Where does your husband work?" the second question Narrow Creek natives asked when meeting me for the first time was "Where do y'all go to church?"

Joe's family had skipped around some between the Methodists and the Presbyterians. I'd been baptized, total immersion as the Baptists do, when I was nine, which at my home church of Fair Grove Baptist was deemed the appropriate age to make a public profession of faith and join the church.

Joe had never officially been baptized but said he considered himself a Christian. It bothered me that he'd never made a public profession of his faith, but I didn't press the issue with him. I'd fallen away from the church myself during college and didn't have any high ground to stand on.

Becoming a mother, though, or perhaps people asking me the church question so many times made me want to find a church home in Narrow Creek. I missed being part of a congregation. A good congregation cares about one another, and I needed some people in Narrow Creek who cared what happened to my family. Of course, I'd have to be concerned about them in return. You don't go to church just to get support but to help others too. Every good Christian knows it is more blessed to give than to receive.

When I mentioned my idea of finding a congregation to Joe, however, I found out he didn't feel my urge to look for a church family. "Joe," I said, testing the waters, "why don't we visit First Baptist tomorrow morning?"

"Visit, as in go there?"

"Yes, visit, as in attend the eleven o'clock service. We need to be part of a church. The Bible says to 'train up a child in the way he should go: and when he is old, he will not depart from it.' Just the fact that I remember that verse from my own church-going days and want to find a congregation proves my point. If we never take Heather to church, she won't know how to be a good Christian. She might even grow up to be a heathen."

"We certainly wouldn't want that," Joe said, smiling as he watched his baby girl smear her face with mashed bananas. Heather grinned, exposing the nubs of her new teeth. "Although Heather the Heathen does have a certain ring to it, don't you think?"

"Honestly, Joe, teaching a child about the Lord is no joking matter. Tomorrow morning, we need to be ready to leave at ten-thirty for First Baptist."

"No need for the drill sergeant voice. If visiting a church is that important to you, then we'll do it. Heather's too young to know whether we go or not right now, and as for me, I find the Lord out in the woods on a pretty fall morning when I'm hunting. But I guess it won't hurt to visit First Baptist. I do have a lot of customers who go there," he added.

I almost told Joe that we weren't going to drum up business for the bank, but I'd picked First Baptist to visit for a reason other than finding a church home myself. The illuminated sign in front of the sanctuary building listed a Reverend Gregory Strayhorn as the associate minister. I wanted to see whether Lisa was still at First Baptist or whether she'd made good on her vow to leave town.

The next morning, I put on my most conservative dress, a black A-line sheath I'd had forever. Since it wasn't meant to fit at the waist, I could still wear it after having Heather. I had a pair of suntan pantyhose and my low-heeled black pumps to complete the outfit.

I dressed Heather in a pink frilly dress that Joe's mother had given her and clipped a tiny white bow in her few sprigs of hair. Little white cloth shoes made her look like somebody's doll baby.

"You're Mama's precious girl, yes, you are," I cooed. "Are you excited about going to see the other babies at church?"

"Let's hustle if we're going," Joe said, coming out of the bedroom in one of his dark blue banker suits. "We've got to find the nursery and then the sanctuary." Joe hates to be late for anything, especially anything official.

"For someone who doesn't want to go, you sure are in a hurry," I couldn't help but comment.

After rushing me out the door, we pulled up on the street beside the impressive brick structure of First Baptist with time to spare. We spied a young couple with two toddlers opening the door of the fellowship hall, the same entrance I used when attending meetings of the Ladies' Society.

"I'll bet they're on their way to the nursery. Let's follow them," Joe said. We went down a long hall, meeting the parents we'd seen going into the building, who evidently had already dropped off their children.

"The nursery's to the right at the end of the hall," the mother said with a pleasant smile, eyeing Heather. "You can't miss it. You'll hear the children."

Sure enough, as soon as we turned the corner, the squeals of preschoolers and babies escaped from behind a closed door with a brass plate inscribed Nursery.

Joe rapped on the Dutch door. The top half swung open, revealing an elderly woman with tight gray curls and squinty eyes. Unlike the smiling mother in the hall, this woman looked like she'd been weaned on lemons, as my grandma used to say. She glared at Joe and me with her screwed-up eyes and spit out questions.

"Has this baby been fed recently? Diaper changed? We're full to busting open this morning, and I'm not going to have time to do either one."

So much for good morning and welcome to First Baptist. The old bat hadn't even asked me for my child's name. Joe was as stunned as I was, but he nodded yes to both questions.

"Good then. Give her to me. I'll put her in that crib over there so she won't get stepped on." Behind her, half a dozen children were chasing each other around the room. "The girl who's supposed to be in charge of the babies didn't show up this morning. And I can forget getting any of these prissy First Baptist mothers to volunteer in her place."

Heather clung to me as she studied the nursery lady's grim face and the chaos behind her. "I used to call Lisa Strayhorn when I got in a bind. She was the wife of our associate minister. Up and left both him and the church a few weeks ago and moved to Raleigh." The old woman's thin lips were set in disapproval. "At least they never had children."

Leaving Heather with this woman wasn't going to be easy. I was beginning to have doubts about whether Joe and I really needed to find a church home. Still, I'd persuaded Joe to make the effort. We were there, dressed up, on time, and all set to sit in the sanctuary. Besides, although I'd just learned Lisa Strayhorn had indeed left town, I wanted to get a look at her husband and listen for any possible gossip from church members.

"Heather, Mommy and Daddy will be back in an hour. This lady will take care of you. Be a good girl." I always talked to Heather as though she could understand every word I said.

That morning, I think she did understand. Only too well. She started screaming as soon as I peeled her off and handed her over.

"Go on and leave now, and she'll quit making such a fuss," the woman scolded Joe and me. "As long as she sees you two here, she'll keep crying. Give me her things." Joe was holding Heather's bag and blanket. He still had that stunned look on his face and made no move to give up Heather's possessions.

"Hush now, stop this foolishness," the woman said to Heather. "You're not being thrown to the wolves."

Finding out more about Lisa Strayhorn would have to wait. "We've changed our mind about attending church today. I'd like my child back, please. Now." A woman I recognized from the Ladies' Society was coming up to the door with her toddler, and my face flamed with embarrassment.

"Here she is," the nursery lady said. "She would've been fine if you'd just left. Parents today let their children rule the roost."

I was at the point of saying something very unchristian to this old battle ax, but being in the house of the Lord, I held my tongue. Joe, Heather, and I were back home by the time the eleven a.m. service started at Narrow Creek First Baptist Church.

Chapter 21

Monday morning in the faculty lounge, I was telling my church disaster tale to Scarlett and Hazel when Elizabeth Tucker, the remedial math teacher, strolled in and overheard.

"Oh, honey, you got tangled up with Hilda Moore," she said. "That old dingbat thinks she owns First Baptist. She's probably grumpier than ever since she doesn't have the associate minister's wife to help her in the nursery anymore. I heard Lisa Strayhorn left town, telling both First Baptist and her husband she'd had enough of serving."

I perked up at this information, but before I could steer the conversation to learn more about Lisa Strayhorn, Elizabeth rolled on. "I don't know why First Baptist allows Hilda to work in the nursery. She's not good with children and doesn't know how to be nice to their parents either. She certainly doesn't do anything to help recruit young families."

"No kidding," I said. "I was so upset yesterday I went home and cried."

"Why don't you visit my church, St. James Methodist?" Elizabeth said. "We're smaller than First Baptist, but we know how to put out the welcome mat."

"I've never been anything but Baptist," I hedged. "Is the worship service very different?"

"Almost the same. Don't worry, Baptists make good Methodists. I used to be Baptist myself. You won't miss a beat during the service. The congregational responses and the Apostles' Creed are all printed in the bulletin. Come this Sunday and I'll meet you at the door. We'll take Heather to the nursery together. We have two sweet ladies watching maybe five children at the most."

"I'll see if I can talk Joe into another church excursion," I said. "He's not excited about going anywhere, to tell the truth, and yesterday's experience at First Baptist didn't help sell him on the idea."

"He sounds like me," said Scarlett, who'd been listening to Elizabeth's invitation with a frown. "I used to be Episcopalian. I loved that communion wine purging the sin as it slid down my throat. When I married J.T., though, he was a card-carrying member of First Baptist, so to make him happy, I moved my membership. Had to be re-baptized, too. The whole dunking thing. Baptists are funny about that. My Episcopalian sprinkling wasn't good enough for them."

"That's where we go now. Or I should say, J.T. goes. I didn't last long with those Baptists either, Dee Ann."

"I'd invite you to my church, St. Mark AME, but you and your husband would be the only white people there," Hazel chimed in. "I've read that eleven to twelve on Sunday morning is the most segregated hour in America. It's a shame. You'd have a good time at my church, singing and praising the Lord, and you wouldn't have to worry about a nursery. Babies are welcome at the service. We believe what the Lord said, 'Suffer the little children to come unto me.'"

"If a child gets fussy, the mama takes the baby out," Hazel continued. "We all kind of come and go anyway. It's hard to stay seated for two or three hours or however long the service is going to last. We don't watch the clock; we keep going as long as the Spirit moves us."

"That sounds very inspirational," I said weakly. Being the only white people at Hazel's church wouldn't be Joe's greatest concern. Staying at a service past noon would be his biggest problem.

"I think you and your husband would like St. James," Elizabeth said, ignoring both interruptions. "Our minister is a good man, not pushy or stuffy. Everyone in the congregation loves him."

"Thanks for the invitation," I said. "I'll see if I can persuade Joe to give church another try." Elizabeth smiled. I liked her sunny disposition. She was a little older than Scarlett and me, married, but with no children. She had short brown hair and carried a few extra pounds, which I'd heard her joke about losing one day.

Unlike Scarlett and me, Elizabeth had grown up in Narrow Creek, but she didn't seem cliquish about being one of the natives. Instead, she laughed about some of the pretentious women in the Ladies' Society and would give me the lowdown on how someone's father had swindled a friend in a land deal or someone's mother had left her husband for another man. She wasn't being mean; she was just showing me that these women's families weren't as perfect as they pretended.

"Duty calls," Scarlett said. "Time for Reading Fundamentals."

"I'm right behind you, girlfriend," Hazel said, following Scarlett out the door. I had a class coming up too, but I returned to the topic of Lisa Strayhorn as I began gathering my books.

"Do the folks at First Baptist believe Lisa's reason for leaving her husband?" I casually asked Elizabeth. "Does anyone think there might've been another man in the picture?"

Elizabeth looked startled. "I haven't heard anything other than she was tired of all the obligations involved in being a minister's wife." Elizabeth paused. "Did you know her?"

"Oh no," I hastened to say. "Just curious."

"How well do you know Scarlett?" Elizabeth asked. It was my turn to be startled.

"I don't know anyone in Narrow Creek all that well since I've been here only a few months. But Joe and I've had dinner with J. T. and her a couple of times. She's been my first friend here."

"Scarlett can be a lot of fun," Elizabeth said. "And she's not a snob, which is saying a lot in this town. But she's a free spirit, sometimes too free, if you know what I mean." I felt Elizabeth watching for my reaction.

"I'm not sure I do," I said truthfully. "I know she's not thrilled to be living in Narrow Creek. I think she's bored here."

"The town is not the only thing she's bored with. I know it's unchristian to gossip, and here I've just invited you to church, but you should know it's common knowledge that she'll step out on J.T. when given half a chance. Poor man, I don't think he suspects a thing."

I was stunned. I'd seen how she treated J.T. and heard how ugly she talked about him, but cheating on him was another matter entirely. "I can't believe that," I sputtered, remembering what Veronica had said at the Kut and Kurl. "People are probably making up stuff because they're jealous of her being so pretty and having such a nice house."

"Maybe there's an element of that," Elizabeth conceded. "But it's true that Scarlett has been unfaithful to J.T. I've worked with her now for three years, and I've seen her in action. I'm telling you this only to warn you. I don't want you to get caught in the middle of something that's bound to get ugly one day when J.T. finally opens his eyes."

Elizabeth picked up her book satchel and headed for the door of the lounge. She paused with her hand on the handle and regarded me for a moment. "And for what it's worth, I can be your friend too."

*****

That Sunday, I put on my good black dress again and gussied up Heather in her frilly pink outfit. As predicted, Joe wasn't excited about trying another church, but as usual, he wanted me to be happy, so he humored me by going.

Elizabeth met us on the front steps of St. James United Methodist, a tidy white clapboard with stained glass windows, and walked us around to the side door that led to the nursery, a bright, cheerful room staffed by two smiling women. The door to this nursery was wide open; parents were welcome to step inside. One of the ladies, a plump grandmotherly type, immediately reached for Heather and sat down with her in a rocking chair. Snuggled on this lady's lap, Heather didn't even look at us when we left.

"I want to introduce you to my husband," Elizabeth said once we were almost back at the sanctuary. "He's waiting for us in the vestibule." She opened the simple wooden front door of the church, and there stood a short man with warm brown eyes and a slightly receding hairline.

"Dee Ann, Joe, this is my husband, Benjamin Tucker."

"Pleased to meet you," Benjamin said, shaking hands with both of us. "Welcome to St. James. I hope everyone was nice to you in the nursery." He gave me a mischievous smile. Evidently Elizabeth had told him about my experience at First Baptist. Benjamin turned to Joe. "I hear you're the new man at the bank. How're they treating you down there?"

As Joe and Benjamin began to talk in that jovial sort of way men do when they first become acquainted, Elizabeth took my arm and steered me into the sanctuary. "You've picked a good day to visit," she said. "There's someone here I want you to meet—Miss Annabelle Jenkins. She's our oldest living member and doesn't get to church but once or twice a year when she feels up to it. She was my Sunday school teacher when I was a child, and I have some of the best memories of her lessons. She's one of the finest Christians I know."

We approached a frail, white-haired woman slumped in a wheelchair. "Miss Annabelle," Elizabeth said, "this is my friend, Dee Ann Bulluck. She's visiting our church today."

Miss Annabelle slowly raised her head and peered at us through rheumy eyes. "Who are you?" she asked Elizabeth.

Elizabeth's eyes widened. "Why, you know me, Miss Annabelle. I'm Lizzy Benton," she said using, I assumed, her childhood and maiden names. "You taught me in Sunday School and Vacation Bible School back in the late '50s."

"Lizzy Benton, Lizzy Benton. When did you get so grown up? Have you graduated from high school?"

Elizabeth laughed. "Miss Annabelle, I'm almost thirty. I've graduated from college and been married for seven years."

"Married! I was never married. Never in my whole life. Are you married?" Miss Annabelle asked, staring at me.

"Yes, ma'am, I am," I admitted. I felt Miss Annabelle would've liked me better if I had matched her single status.

"I wish I could have been a bride," Miss Annabelle announced. "I never found anyone suitable." She raised a gnarly hand and pointed it at me. "Do you know the most important verses in the Bible for a married woman?"

"No ma'am, I can't say as I do," I thought it safe to reply.

"Proverbs 31: 10-12," Miss Annabelle declared. In a quavering voice, she recited:

> *"Who can find a virtuous woman? For her*
> *price is far above rubies. The heart of her*
> *husband doth safely trust in her, so that he*

*shall have no need of spoil. She will do him
good and not evil all the days of her life."*

She leaned forward and grabbed my arm with clawlike
fingers. "Is your husband's heart safe with you? Will you do
him good and not evil all the days of your life?"

Although I was somewhat rattled, I put my hand on
top of hers and gave her a little pat. "That's what I promised
the day I married him," I managed to say. "I like to think I'm
keeping my word."

She released me and fell back in her wheelchair. "Too
many women straying these days. Too many divorces. No
one used to leave a husband. I never had a husband to leave.
Did you know I never got married?"

"Yes ma'am, we know," said Elizabeth. "Dee Ann and I
need to find our seats now. Good to see you, Miss Annabelle."

As we crossed the church to join our husbands,
Elizabeth whispered, "Sorry if she made you uncomfortable.
She's gotten a lot more senile since I last saw her. This is the
first time she hasn't recognized me."

Joe and Benjamin were already settled in a pew in the
middle of the sanctuary. "Is this location okay?" Elizabeth
asked. "Benjamin and I always sit here, but we can move
somewhere else."

"This is fine," I assured her, glad that we weren't too
close to the pulpit. I've never been comfortable perched right
under the minister, and I felt sure Joe didn't want to be too
near the front either.

As parishioners filled the surrounding pews, Elizabeth
introduced us. One old man recognized me from my
performance at the Gaylords' Fourth of July party and
suggested I join the church choir. I was flattered but explained
I had a baby and a part-time job and didn't know how I could
possibly fit choir practice in my schedule.

"She can sing, Mr. Bailey?" Elizabeth asked the elderly gentleman, cutting her eyes at me in surprise. "We'll definitely work on getting her in the choir. That baby won't be a baby forever."

Joe recognized quite a few people from working at the bank. Maybe people were using their church manners, but everyone was just as nice as they could be. It's funny how sweet and kind some folks can be in church on Sunday, and then on Monday morning when they get back out in the world, forget every bit of religion they have and turn mean and selfish. Of course, some people, like the nursery lady at First Baptist, don't even bother to be nice on Sunday.

The organ prelude began, and the congregation became still. When the last notes died away, the church bell tolled three times. Then the choir, clad in black robes and wearing large crosses around their necks, processed from the rear of the church and down the aisle to the front choir loft. I was filled with a sense of peace as I stood and sang with the choir. Gary Whitt's murder seemed very far away.

Chapter 22

"Ten Arrested in Local Drug Bust" shouted a banner headline in the Wednesday morning *Narrow Creek News and Views*. The two-inch letters caught my eye the minute Joe tossed the newspaper on the kitchen table. I snatched up the paper while Joe poured his coffee.

"Listen to this," I said. 'A four-month drug investigation conducted by the Narrow Creek Police Department and the State Bureau of Investigation has uncovered a drug ring operating in the Narrow Creek area, resulting in the arrest of ten federal offenders.'"

"Wow," Joe exclaimed, sloshing coffee on the counter. "Drug dealers in Narrow Creek? I thought that was big-city stuff."

I had too before the Gary Whitt murder. There were quite a few things about the seamy side of life in Narrow Creek that I knew and Joe didn't.

"Any names given?" Joe asked. "I wonder if these dealers are locals or people who pop in off the interstate."

"No names, but this tidbit is interesting: 'The arrests were made through a sting operation where informants posed as drug buyers to catch dealers in the act of peddling marijuana and cocaine.'"

Joe raised his eyebrows. "Informants posing as drug buyers? It would take a mighty brave person to rat out and then frame a drug dealer. That informant was probably someone caught with drugs who gave up the big guy to save his own skin."

I dropped the newspaper and stared at Joe. "How in the world did you come up with that?"

"Hey, I watch *Hawaii Five-O*." Joe shrugged. "That scenario has happened on more than one episode."

The rest of the story featured quotes from Police Chief Roger McSwain bragging about how the drug bust was a result of the excellent detective skills and expertise of his department. What about the detective skills and expertise of the State Bureau of Investigation? An agency brought into town to help solve the Gary Whitt murder, or so I thought.

Were the two related? Did the cops discover the drug ring in the course of their murder investigation? Maybe one of the dealers was also Gary Whitt's killer. Suddenly I realized Joe was asking about breakfast.

"Earth to Dee Ann. Do you want eggs or cereal?"

*****

All morning, I taught avoiding comma splices and run-on sentences with only half my mind. The other half was busy thinking about a possible connection between the big Narrow Creek drug bust and the Gary Whitt murder investigation.

I didn't have long to speculate. At lunch, I'd just strapped Heather into her high chair and fed her a few spoons of pureed sweet potatoes when Joe burst through the apartment door. He paused for a moment as if considering whether to speak. "What I'm about to tell you can't go any further than this room," he finally began, giving me a stern look.

I nodded, wondering what the usually tight-lipped Joe was about to divulge.

"Bill and I went to collect payments from a car dealer this morning, and you won't believe what he told me on the way back to the office about the drug bust. Specifically, his wife's involvement."

"Cynthia?"

I remembered hearing her tell Lisa Strayhorn that she called Gary Whitt to buy marijuana, but caught up in a drug raid?

"Yeah, Cynthia. Seems she has a problem with cocaine. Not marijuana, but the hard stuff. I knew plenty of potheads in college but nobody who used cocaine."

"From what I've heard on the news, it's the new illegal drug that's become popular," I said. Heather fussed, wanting more sweet potatoes, and I quickly gave her another spoonful. I was eager for Joe to get on with the story. "So did Cynthia get caught buying cocaine from a dealer?"

"That's exactly what happened. Well, not exactly," Joe hedged. "She thought she was buying from a dealer, but the guy was an undercover cop. Cynthia was hauled down to the police station, where she called Bill who then called his attorney, Ray Williams. Bill said he and Ray got there about the same time, finding Cynthia in an interview room."

I had a hard time picturing prissy Cynthia Ford seated across a cheap table from a stern cop in a sterile interview room. I hoped she'd had to wear an orange jumpsuit and handcuffs.

"Ray advised her to cooperate fully with the police. He worked out a deal so that instead of being prosecuted, Cynthia could go to rehab. She had to turn state's evidence and help the SBI set up a sting operation."

"My word!" I stared at Joe, wide-eyed. "Bill told you all this?"

"In the strictest of confidence. The poor guy has to spill his guts to someone. Imagine how torn up he is finding out his wife has a drug problem. This explains at least part of Bill's money problem. I imagine a cocaine habit can be expensive. Bill thought Cynthia was just overspending on clothes and jewelry."

I forgot all about opening a jar of Gerber peaches. "So Cynthia's not going to jail but to rehab?"

"That's what Bill said. She had enough information about the drug ring in Narrow Creek that she could bargain her way out of prosecution. I imagine being a pretty, white, professional woman didn't hurt any either. And Ray Williams is a sharp attorney."

I pleated a paper napkin on the table as I absorbed this news while Heather, giving up on more food for the moment, played with her baby spoon. "Bill expects all this to remain a secret, right? How does he propose to explain Cynthia's absence when she goes to rehab? I would think she'd be away for at least several weeks."

"He's going to tell everyone that Cynthia's mother is on her deathbed in Atlanta, and that Cynthia is taking a leave of absence from her job to help care for her." Joe shook his head. "Personally, I wouldn't go to the trouble to lie to protect her, but I guess despite the hell she's putting him through, he still loves her."

I wondered if Bill knew his wife had been unfaithful as well, with a man who most likely supplied her with cocaine. I wasn't going to divulge that piece of information I'd overheard while hiding in a kitchen, though.

I was also willing to bet the investigation of Gary Whitt's murder had uncovered the drug ring in Narrow Creek. Gary was a drug dealer, so the police had investigated this angle, catching Cynthia, one of Gary's former buyers.

"I'd like to know how long she's had a cocaine addiction," I mused. "How did Bill not notice? Surely he'd have seen some change in her behavior. I wonder what people on cocaine act like." Suddenly, I remembered Cynthia's darting eyes, manic speech, and excessive energy the day of the Gaylords' Fourth of July party. Had she been high?

"He didn't say. I guess she hid it well. As far as I know, she still went to work every day." Joe reached for the loaf of Sunbeam and started unwinding the twist tie. "We need to eat lunch before I use up my whole hour on the Cynthia saga." After putting two slices of bread on a paper plate, he paused with his hand on the refrigerator door. "You know, Dee Ann, this story beats anything I've ever seen on *Hawaii Five-O*. Truth really is stranger than fiction."

*****

After Joe left for work and Heather went down for her nap, I picked up the telephone. While I'd been eating my bologna sandwich and Fritos, I'd come to a decision: it was time to call the police department hotline and report what I knew about the Gary Whitt murder.

After months of what I thought had been no action on the part of the police, I now suspected, due to the drug bust, the investigation had been ongoing. Chief McSwain—or more likely, somebody from the SBI—was probably closing in on the killer. If it wasn't one of Gary's drug dealing cohorts, then maybe it was a former paramour.

I had two names: Lisa Strayhorn and Cynthia Ford. My palms were sweaty as I dialed the hotline number, which I'd copied the first time it was given in the newspaper and then kept on a slip of paper in my jewelry box. If I had any chance of collecting that ten thousand dollar reward, the time might be now.

"Narrow Creek Police Department, Chief McSwain speaking," a voice barked after the second ring. Oh my word. I had the chief himself on the line.

"Yes, Chief McSwain," I began in a high-pitched, nervous voice. "My name is Dee Ann Bulluck, and I have some information about the Gary Whitt murder."

"Do you spell your last name with an *o* or a *u*, Miz. Bulluck?" the Chief blared.

"Uh, a *u*. B-u-l-l-u-c-k." I gulped.

"Did you know the victim Gary Whitt?"

"No, no sir. Well, I met him once briefly, three days before he was killed," I clarified. Why was the Chief asking me all these questions? I was getting even more nervous than when I dialed.

"Under what circumstances did you meet Gary Whitt? Were you buying drugs from him?"

"I most certainly was not. I was introduced to him in my landlady's backyard. He was working on a bathroom in her house. Miss Josie—Mrs. Josephine Powell, that is—told me he was a contractor."

"Oh wait, I know who you are. You live behind Floyd and Josie Powell. Your husband is the new man down at the bank. Been there just a few months now. How do you like living in Narrow Creek? Dee Ann, is it?"

"Fine, ah, just fine," I stuttered. Here I'd screwed up my courage to make this phone call and instead of being allowed to spill my guts about two very viable leads in a murder, I was first treated like a suspect myself and then subjected to a dose of the Welcome Wagon.

"Yes, Narrow Creek is normally a nice, quiet place to live," the Chief continued in his town booster voice. "Both a murder and a drug bust in the same year is highly unusual for us. Never has happened before, in fact." He paused as if reconsidering. "Not the drug bust anyway.

"Did you say you have some information? You won't believe how many hair-brained calls we've had. Talk about wild goose chases. That ten thousand dollar reward has done more harm than good. Everybody and his brother has called. Whatcha got for me today, little lady?"

Hardly encouraged, I stammered my suspicions about both Lisa Strayhorn and Cynthia Ford, relaying the conversation I'd overheard in the kitchen of First Baptist. Respecting the trust Joe had placed in me, I didn't let on that I knew Cynthia had been caught in the drug raid, although I did repeat her words to Lisa about calling Gary to buy marijuana.

"Hmm. You've got the scoop on that conversation you overheard, but the rest of what you're telling me is old news," the Chief commented when I finished. "Like I told you, we've had tons of tips due to that reward money. Both of these ladies have already been reported as women who were stepping out on their husbands with Gary Whitt.

"Seems he was quite the ladies' man and didn't care whether a woman was married or not. Didn't mind dumping one for another either, which can make a woman madder than a wet hen.

"Just between you and me, that's the direction this investigation is taking now. We've cleared both Lisa Strayhorn and Cynthia Ford, along with their husbands. Airtight alibis, all of 'em. But we've got a list we're working through. If you hear of any other girlfriends, let me know. That man got around."

I was so shocked I hardly heard the Chief thank me for my call. Bill Ford hadn't told Joe everything. Not only was his wife interrogated by the police in the Gary Whitt murder investigation, but he'd been too. So Bill did know about his wife's affair with Gary Whitt.

I was disappointed. My two leads, which I'd sat on for weeks dreaming of a ten thousand dollar pay-off, were duds. Enough with amateur sleuthing. I hadn't liked keeping secrets from Joe and being sneaky about getting information from others, anyway.

I was in such low spirits that I raided Joe's supply of Little Debbie's, eating first an oatmeal cream pie followed by a Swiss roll. Then with Heather still napping, I went to bed myself, burying my head under the pillow.

Chapter 23

My amateur investigation had been a bust, but on the positive side, I was finding my niche in Narrow Creek. For one thing, Elizabeth was becoming a good friend. We gabbed at school between classes. She loved blue, especially Williamsburg blue when decorating, and wrote poetry. During breaks in the lounge, she taught me how to cross-stitch, and I made a sweet sampler that said, "If Mom says no, ask Grandma," which I planned to give to Mama from Heather for Christmas.

Each Sunday, Joe and I sat with Benjamin and Elizabeth in the same pew at St. James United Methodist. Although I'd sworn off any more sleuthing, I couldn't help occasionally studying the dozen or so attractive young women in the pews. Had any of these women had an affair with Gary Whitt? Could one possibly be a jilted lover who'd sought the ultimate revenge? If someone as straight-laced as Lisa Strayhorn and as status-conscious as Cynthia Ford had fallen for a drug-dealing playboy, other unlikely candidates could be out there.

Often I thought about Miss Annabelle Jenkin's prophetic words from Proverbs: "Who can find a virtuous woman? For her price is far above rubies." According to Chief McSwain, there were quite a few not so virtuous women in Narrow Creek, a whole list. I'd always believed fidelity went with being married, but I was learning a lot of women didn't share my opinion.

I'd decided we needed to visit St. James for a while before joining. I wanted to make sure Joe and I were ready to be faithful, active members instead of people who picked a church because they wanted to say they belonged to such-and-such congregation.

But after a month of attending, I felt sure St. James was where the Lord wanted me to be, and Joe agreed to join. He and Heather were baptized together—thanks be to God, as the Methodists say.

I simply transferred my membership from my childhood Baptist church. Since I'd been dunked when I was nine, I didn't have to be sprinkled.

I was so proud of Joe for making his profession of faith, and Heather was such a good baby that day too. When the drops of water from the baptismal font hit her sweet head, she looked a little startled but didn't start screaming the way I'd already seen a couple of Methodist babies do.

The only rain on my Methodist parade was my mother, who made it her business to tell me that my Baptist relatives back home had all said that Heather was obviously too young to make a profession of faith and therefore wasn't really being baptized. Mama was a little ugly about the whole situation, in fact.

"Dee Ann, I can't believe you're turning your back on your Baptist faith and letting your baby be sprinkled," she'd said. "If you want to dedicate her to the church, that's fine, but don't go calling it baptism when it's clear that baby can't accept the Lord as her Savior. Show me the verse in the Bible that says a baby can be sprinkled and have it count as baptism."

Mama didn't think sprinkling counted as baptism for Joe either. "Jesus was put under the water, dunked in the

River Jordan, by none other than John the Baptist. Who's sprinkled in the Bible? Name just one person."

Now I'd asked these questions myself, and Reverend Shaw had explained it all to me. But Mama just got mad when I told her the word "immersion" isn't found in the Bible, and there are plenty of references to "sprinkle" when it comes to being baptized. And it didn't seem to make her any nicer when I said that Heather would go through a confirmation class when she was in the sixth grade and then go in front of the church to renew and reaffirm her faith.

No, ma'am, she declined coming to Narrow Creek to witness Heather and Joe being baptized. My feelings were hurt by her decision. It's a shame that religion can make people hard-hearted.

After that ordeal, Joe didn't tell his parents he and Heather were being baptized. They weren't Baptists, but Joe didn't pursue asking them, and I was so disappointed in Mama I didn't have the heart to call them myself. So it was just the Tuckers who went up front to stand with us the day we joined the church. The minister had asked them to be our fellowship friends.

Once church was over, we went to celebrate at the K&W. I had meat loaf and mashed potatoes, and Joe got the baked spaghetti. Elizabeth said she was on a diet and picked up the eight-layer salad. I'm not sure how many calories she saved since her choice was covered in huge dollops of sugared-up mayonnaise.

Benjamin wasn't on any diet, though, that was for sure. He got half a fried chicken, macaroni and cheese, fried okra, and a slab of chocolate cake. Along with Elizabeth, Joe and I passed on dessert, and I was glad we did since the Tuckers insisted on paying for our meals.

I always like to return hospitality, so I approached my newest friend at school one morning. "Are you and Benjamin free for lunch after church this coming Sunday? I'm planning to bake a ham on Saturday and make deviled eggs and potato salad."

Elizabeth's brown eyes lit up. "Why, that sounds wonderful. How nice of you to ask us. What can I bring?"

I smiled at her gracious reply, complete with the polite Southern question of what she could add to the menu. "Just bring yourselves. I have it all under control." Baked ham, potato salad, and deviled eggs were three items from my short list of specialties. I figured I could simmer some green beans with country ham seasoning early Sunday morning before church and then warm them back up when we got home. I even planned to make a loaf of beer bread, an easy recipe that usually turned out well for me.

I wondered what Elizabeth, who'd told me she was a teetotaler, would think if she knew she was eating bread made with a can of beer. All the alcohol evaporates, though, I told myself. It's like rum cake. If I had time on Saturday, I planned to make a pineapple cake too. Miss Josie wasn't the only one with a family recipe for this dessert.

"Do you know where we live?" I asked.

"In the apartment behind the Powells' house," Elizabeth said without a moment's hesitation. She laughed at the surprised look on my face. "Don't you know everybody knows where everybody lives in Narrow Creek?"

"Let me warn you," I confessed. "I've done the best I can with the place, but my apartment will never be featured in *Better Homes and Gardens*. Unless it's the 'before' model in a redecorating article." I thought of Cynthia Ford's condescending looks and remarks the time she picked me up for my first Ladies' Society meeting.

"You and Joe are just starting out. You're not supposed to have anything," Elizabeth said. "Heck, Benjamin and I've been married for seven years, and we just bought our first home six months ago. We still don't have any furniture at all in the dining room and one of the bedrooms, and I have a wish list a mile long of what I want to buy for the house."

"Really? I haven't invited anyone over because I felt our house was sort of shabby, but you've made me feel better."

"I'm sure your home is just as cute as it can be. The important thing is that you have Joe and that precious Heather."

Elizabeth was right. I wouldn't have traded Joe and Heather for the nicest house in Narrow Creek. Especially now since Joe had joined the church.

*****

That Sunday Elizabeth and Benjamin followed us home from St. James. Miss Josie peeped out her kitchen window as the Tuckers got out of their car. I was surprised she'd already beaten us home from the service at First Presbyterian, where, I'd heard, she served as president of the Ladies' Circle. Mr. Powell stayed home and told Miss Josie he watched the television evangelists. He told everyone else who asked about his church attendance that he wasn't much on going.

"Look at her, Joe," I hissed as we got out of the car.

"Look at who?" Joe was loosening his tie as he walked to our downstairs door.

"Miss Josie, there in the window. Oh my word, now she's putting on her glasses so she can see who's with us. You'd think we had robbers in the driveway the way she's craning her neck. What a busybody!"

The Tuckers joined us before Joe could answer. He glanced at me, shook his head, and grinned. He knew Miss Josie got my goat.

But my irritation faded as the ham, deviled eggs, potato salad, green beans, and beer bread were all eaten and praised.

My pineapple cake was a huge hit, if I do say so myself. Elizabeth rocked Heather to sleep in the Boston rocker that had been my one furniture purchase since Joe and I'd been married.

Elizabeth yearned for a baby in the worst way. She'd told me she and Benjamin had been trying for years, and she worried they would never be parents. All the tests had been run, she'd confided, and nothing had been found wrong with either Benjamin or her.

"The doctor says the best thing to do is just relax and let nature take its course," she'd said one day in the lounge at school. "Easy for him to say. He's not a woman staring thirty in the eye with no baby in sight."

I watched her rocking Heather. Her face glowed when she laid my sleeping child in the crib. We tiptoed from the room and gently closed the door.

Elizabeth, her eyes shining, whispered, "Don't tell anyone, but Benjamin and I are going to start adoption procedures this week."

"That's wonderful news."

"It may be a while." Elizabeth fiddled with her Ten Commandments charm bracelet. "The process is a blizzard of paperwork, and there's a waiting list a mile long. But at least I'm on my way to becoming a mother."

"And you'll be a good one, too," I said as I thought of the joy I saw in her face when she held Heather, another woman's child.

Chapter 24

A sense of dread came over me as I read the note left in my school mailbox. Dr. Adams was asking to see me. Even though Scarlett had insisted the man was harmless, I couldn't help but remember his creepy behavior concerning his nephew during my interview. Maybe I should give his name to the tip line, I thought, before reminding myself that I was no longer trying to solve the Gary Whitt murder.

And there was also the unpleasantness of having to deal with his chauvinism. I avoided him whenever possible, but he'd sneaked up behind me in the hall a couple of times and told me how much he liked my dress or my hair. Maybe Scarlett could flirt with him to get a few perks at work, but no way could I bring myself to bat my eyelashes and compliment him in return. I'd rather live without chalk than stoop to that. I hoped today's encounter wouldn't be too demeaning.

"Come on in, Dee Ann, and have a seat," Dr. Adams squawked. Thankfully he didn't ask me to close the door. "I like that skirt you have on today." He winked at me with one of his magnified eyes, and I gulped down a gag. If he was waiting for me to compliment him on that canary yellow suit he was wearing, we'd be there until hell froze over.

A moment of awkward silence ensued before Dr. Adams cleared his throat and sat up straighter in his chair. "I asked you in today to see if you'd be interested in attending the annual conference of the Remedial Educators' Association. You're doing an excellent job here. I'd like to hire you full-time whenever a position becomes available. For now, if you can plan to be away from your family for three days, the college wants you to get some professional development at our expense. We can even pay you for the extra hours you'll be attending the conference."

Dr. Adams beamed as if he'd just handed me that bonus check for those extra hours, and I did feel excited at the prospect of an educational road trip. Not exactly a real vacation, but a vacation from routine. Just myself to take care of for a change. And what was that Dr. Adams said about becoming a full-time employee one day? Was there a catch somewhere? I seemed to be getting some of those perks Scarlett talked about without having to flirt with this buffoon.

"Where's the conference being held?" I asked. "And what are the dates?"

"Boone. Mountain country. November 14 through 16, Monday through Wednesday. Elizabeth Tucker and Scarlett Hood are going, and they'd be happy to have you join them. Scarlett specifically asked about the possibility of your attending. She's a big fan of yours." Dr. Adams winked at me again, and I realized that Scarlett had probably done some flirting on my behalf.

"Thank you for the opportunity," I said, using my best professional voice. "I'll let you know tomorrow, but I'm almost certain I can make arrangements to attend."

Why not? Bertha could keep Heather all day while I was away. And Joe could certainly figure out what to do with her when he picked her up after work. It would be a good bonding experience for the two of them.

A little to my surprise, Joe thought so too. "Heather will be fine," he said when I explained the trip. "She and I will be best buddies. I can handle taking care of her."

"I'm sure you can," I agreed. "But I hate to be away for three days. What if she thinks I've abandoned her?"

"You can call at night, and I'll let her hear your voice. Then we'll both know you're alive and kicking."

I realized that if Joe had wanted to leave for three days, I'd probably pout and make him feel guilty. But not my sweet-natured husband.

"You're a good man, Joe Bulluck. Heather won't be the only one I miss."

*****

"Welcome, Remedial Educators" read the marquee in the parking lot of the sprawling Mountain View Inn. Elizabeth and I picked up our registration packets in the lobby while Scarlett wandered into the adjoining cocktail lounge.

"We're going to have fun here tonight, ladies," she said as Elizabeth and I joined her, lugging our suitcases.

"For Pete's sake," Elizabeth said, "it's only noon. The bartender isn't even on the job yet."

Scarlett rolled her eyes. "I said tonight, Elizabeth. Loosen up a little, and you'll find out how much fun life can be."

"What makes you think I don't have fun?" Elizabeth huffed. "I enjoy every day the good Lord gives me. Don't roll your eyes at me."

"Okay, okay." Scarlett sighed. "If you're going to bring God into it, let's move out of the bar and take our suitcases upstairs. Why didn't you girls get a luggage cart?"

Our one room on the third floor came with two double beds and a sleeper sofa. Scarlett appraised the tidy but small room. "First-class accommodations, as always. Staying within the allotted reimbursement, one of the many benefits of working for the state. Oh well, it'll be like a pajama party. Let me have the fold-out sofa. I haven't slept on one of these in years." She threw both her suitcase and herself down on the brown suede couch.

"Come on, ladies," Elizabeth said. "Let's freshen up and then go down for lunch and the afternoon opening session." Scarlett rolled her eyes again when Elizabeth turned to go into the bathroom. "What a stick in the mud," she whispered.

At four o'clock the last workshop, "Teaching in the 1980s: What to Expect in the Next Decade," ended, and we visited the vendors' displays. Elizabeth struck up a conversation with a textbook company representative who was discussing the merits of a new series of math tutorials. Scarlett and I walked on, looking for the reading and English booths.

"How are you two ladies this afternoon?" asked a handsome, dark-haired man behind a table displaying reading textbooks. "Anything I can help you with?"

"Well, let me see," Scarlett replied in a sassy little voice I'd never heard. She gazed boldly into the stranger's lively brown eyes. "What exactly do you have?"

The salesman returned her brazen look along with a charming smile. "Here's the Chester series, beginning at grade level eight and going through college-level reading. If you've got the time, I'd love to tell you all about it. It's not every day I get to talk to such a pretty teacher. Where are you from? I love that accent."

Scarlett tittered and moved closer to the booth. "A little town you've never heard of in the eastern part of the state. Nothing ever happens there, and I'm bored out of my mind all the time." The sassy voice now had an extra dose of Southern drawl.

Not wanting to be a part of where this conversation was going, I moved down the aisle in search of an English textbook booth, preferably one manned by an overweight bald guy or a woman wearing sensible shoes and thick glasses. Someone who was interested in selling books instead of romancing the customers.

A few minutes later when I looked for Scarlett, she was gone. And so was the handsome, dark-haired salesman with the lively brown eyes.

My arms were loaded with complimentary textbooks and pen and pencil sets when I found Elizabeth close to where Scarlett and I'd left her, discussing the Mad about Math series with another salesman.

"Excuse me," I interrupted. "Elizabeth, I'm going to the room to drop off these books and call home."

"I'll come too," she said. "Thank you for the materials," she told the vendor. "I'll be in touch."

"Where's Scarlett?" she asked as we walked toward the elevator. Before I could answer, we turned a corner and there she sat in the bar, twirling a glass of white wine.

"Dee Ann, Elizabeth, come meet my new friend," she called. I really didn't want to go into a smoky cocktail lounge at five o'clock in the afternoon with my arms full of textbooks, and behind me, I heard Elizabeth let out an exasperated breath. But Scarlett had seen us, and there was no escape.

"Ladies, this is Trey Phillips," she said giddily. Most of her glass of wine was gone, and I wondered if it was her first. "He works for Scott Publishers, and he's told me all about their remedial series in English, math, and reading."

I'll just bet he has, I thought.

"How do you do, ladies?" Putting down his bourbon on the rocks, Trey Phillips stumbled to his feet and offered us his hand. Like Scarlett, it seemed he'd forgotten I'd met him already when Scarlett and I first strolled by his booth.

"Trey has invited us all to dinner at the Beef Master Inn," Scarlett said. "He's trying to butter us up to get our business." She giggled.

"We'll talk about textbooks a little, and then I can claim the dinner as a business expense with a clear conscience," Mr. Smooth said. "Although having dinner with such lovely company could hardly be called work by any stretch of the imagination," he added, smiling at Scarlett.

"Thank you for the invitation, but I think I'll pass," Elizabeth said primly. "I'm on a vegetarian diet, so I don't want to tempt myself by going somewhere that sounds like a steak house."

Going out to eat at a nice restaurant on a book company's tab sounded like a great idea to me. The state allotment for dinner didn't cover anything fancier than somewhere like the Western Sizzlin. What was Elizabeth's problem? A vegetarian diet? She wasn't worried about eating meat when she'd had that double cheeseburger at lunch.

Still, there was something a little dangerous in the way Scarlett sat next to Trey Phillips, sipping her wine and fawning over him. I suddenly felt like a high school third wheel, tagging along on her best friend's Friday night date.

"I guess I'll have dinner with Elizabeth," I said reluctantly. Neither Scarlett nor Trey Phillips urged me to change my mind.

Chapter 25

ater in the evening after eating chef salads in the hotel restaurant, Elizabeth and I sat on the double bed in the room watching a ho-hum, made-for-television movie. "Where do you suppose Scarlett is?" I asked.

Elizabeth shrugged. "I have no idea." She got up and strolled to the television. "Are you interested in this? I brought my senior yearbook. I thought we could get some laughs looking at the clothes and hairstyles of the Narrow Creek High School class of '66."

I grinned. "By all means, turn off the television. What could be more entertaining than penny loafers and bouffant hairdos?"

But Peter Pan collars and cardigan twin sets were not all that caught my eye. Near the beginning of Elizabeth's yearbook was the Senior Superlative section, and there, staring at me with laughing eyes and a cocky half smile, was an eighteen-year-old Gary Whitt. He was kneeling on top of a children's slide, holding the ankles of a pretty girl who pretended to be gliding down on her stomach. The caption read, Biggest Flirt. Turning the page, I saw that Gary had also won the male half of Best Looking.

"I didn't know you graduated from high school with Gary Whitt," I said, recovering from my surprise.

Sitting beside me, Elizabeth studied Gary's Best Looking photo. "Yes, but he didn't get my vote for either of these superlatives. I was probably the only girl who was never a Gary Whitt groupie.

"A lot of the boys didn't like him either," she continued, "but practically every female in my class was under his spell at the beginning of senior year. He had that bad boy appeal, I guess, and he was a handsome guy. By the time we graduated, though, he'd two-timed so many girls, his star was fading."

"Why didn't the boys like him?"

Elizabeth stared straight ahead at the dark television screen. "Gary was a spoiled kid who liked to brag. He rubbed a lot of the guys the wrong way. And he was a hothead who was always quick to pick a fight.

"To tell you the truth, I wasn't completely surprised when I heard he'd been murdered. He was always brawling. 'Live by the sword, die by the sword,' you know. I'm betting he finally crossed somebody with an even shorter fuse than he had."

"Do you think that person was a woman he two-timed or somebody's jealous husband?" I asked.

Elizabeth leaned back on the bed, propping herself up with her elbows. "Either is possible, or he could've made one of his drug dealing buddies mad." She laughed at the shocked look on my face.

"I know I have a reputation for being a goody two-shoes, but I hear Narrow Creek gossip. Gary Whitt's drug dealing was no secret. About the only two people in town who didn't seem to know what he was up to were his grandma, who thought he hung the moon, and Chief McSwain, who never arrested him.

*****

I dutifully looked at the rest of Elizabeth's yearbook, but my mind was elsewhere for the rest of the evening. Was there a jilted woman or a husband who'd been cheated on who had a hair-trigger temper that matched Gary Whitt's? Or had Gary been killed, execution-style, in a drug dispute?

By eleven, I felt like it'd been an eternity since I'd kissed Joe and Heather goodbye in Narrow Creek at seven that morning. I was ready to go to bed.

"What's keeping Scarlett?" I looked at Elizabeth as I stifled a yawn. "Dinner can't be taking this long."

"Let me tell you what's going on," Elizabeth said in a disapproving tone. "You may not see Scarlett again tonight. She's on a date, shall we say, with this Trey Phillips."

"Do you mean she's going to spend the night with him?" I found it hard to believe that Scarlett could be so bold.

"If not all night, then most of it. She's pulled this prank before at these conferences. I just go on about my business and ignore what she's doing." Elizabeth shifted uncomfortably.

"So this is how you know she's unfaithful to J.T.?"

"Exactly. I should've warned you, but I thought that maybe with you along this year, she'd behave. You're a good influence on her, but I guess there's something about being out of town with access to a good-looking man that's just too hard for her to resist. I'm sorry you've had to see for yourself what a cheat she can be." Elizabeth walked over to her suitcase, picked out her nightgown and toothbrush, and went into the bathroom.

There was nothing for me to do but find my own pajamas and try not to think about where Scarlett was and what she was doing.

"Who can find a virtuous woman? For her price is far above rubies." First Lisa Strayhorn and Cynthia Ford, having affairs with Gary Whitt. And now Scarlett, doing her running around out of town.

Sometime in the middle of the night I heard Scarlett's key in the lock. I was vaguely aware of the sliver of light shining underneath the bathroom door while she got ready for bed. The next morning she sat on the pullout sofa in a pair of black silk pajamas, drinking hotel room coffee and reading *Cosmopolitan.*

On her way to the shower, Elizabeth walked past Scarlett without so much as a good morning. "What happened to you last night?" I asked. "I was worried."

"I wasn't aware I had a curfew." Scarlett tossed her dark, tousled hair. "But if you must know, service was slow at the restaurant, and then Trey and I talked for a while after dinner. I didn't want to run right off after that wonderful meal he'd paid for."

"I just expected you to be back before Elizabeth and I went to bed. I don't mean to sound like your mother. You're a grown woman and can stay out as late as you like."

"Thank you for your mature view on the matter," Scarlett said in a mock-prim voice with a mischievous smile turning up the corners of her pretty mouth. "It's good to know I can count on you to be broad-minded." Was she was making fun of me for quizzing her? Even first thing in the morning, with no make-up, uncombed hair, and having had only a few hours of sleep, she looked lovely. And innocent. "Why don't we get dressed and go find some breakfast?" she said. "I'm starved."

I wanted to ask whether she was being honest with me about how she'd spent all those hours with Trey Phillips and whether she thought J.T. would approve of her going out to dinner with another man.

Even if the evening was nothing more than a long dinner and conversation, what about appearances? Elizabeth was bristling with disapproval right now, thinking the worst. Didn't Scarlett care about her reputation?

I studied my friend, casually laying out her clothes and searching through her jewelry bag. She pulled out a pair of large gold hoops. "What do you think about these earrings with this outfit?"

Faced with such nonchalance, I couldn't bring myself to question her any further.

*****

"I don't care what she told you," Elizabeth said later as we waited for a workshop to begin. "Do you know what time she came in? Three a.m. I heard her and looked at the clock. I'll bet that restaurant closed by eleven if not sooner. Maybe you don't want to believe the worst, but Scarlett is not telling you the whole truth. She and Mr. Handsome weren't talking until three in the morning. 'If it looks like a snake and crawls like a snake, then it's a snake.'

"Now it's her business," Elizabeth continued, "and contrary to what she may say about me, I'm not Chief of the Morality Police. I'm past caring, other than feeling sorry for J.T. and her son. But I do hate to see her make you any kind of an accomplice to her shenanigans."

"An accomplice!" I was shocked. "How in the world am I an accomplice?"

"You're not—yet. But you may be caught in the middle of something ugly first and last. Just be careful, Dee Ann."

*****

The ride home was subdued, in sharp contrast to the jovial mood on the way to the conference just two days earlier. Although there'd been no sign of Trey Phillips after the first day, and Scarlett had dutifully eaten dinner with us and stayed in the room the second night, Elizabeth hadn't directed a single comment to her since the evening she'd disappeared with the man. It was what the Amish call shunning.

For her part, Scarlett acted as though nothing was wrong and seemed oblivious to the fact that I was the only one still speaking to her. Before leaving, we rode around on the Parkway looking at the mountains, but no one seemed to be having much fun. After a dizzy hour on narrow winding roads gazing up at peaks and down into valleys, we were all ready to go home. The apartment I'd been delighted to leave on Monday morning had never looked so good to me.

Joe met me at the bottom of the stairs, holding a smiling Heather dressed only in a diaper and t-shirt. "How was your trip, Mommy?" he asked, using a baby voice and waving Heather's arms as if she were speaking.

"It's a long story. Let's just leave it at I'm very, very glad to see my husband and my Heather."

Holding Heather between us, Joe pulled me close. "We missed you, too." I breathed in a combination of shaving cream and baby shampoo and knew I was home.

To celebrate my return, Joe had cooked spaghetti, his specialty. His recipe consisted of browning a pound of hamburger, pouring off the grease, and then adding a jar of grocery-store spaghetti sauce. He was proud that he knew how to boil pasta to just the right degree of firmness.

He'd also made pear salad by opening a can of pear halves, dumping them onto iceberg lettuce, and adding grated cheddar cheese and a dollop of mayonnaise. The table was set, and I noticed that rather than tossing the silverware beside our plates as he usually did, Joe had taken the time to line up the knife on the right and placed both a dinner and salad fork to the left.

The apartment was tidy, with Joe's newspaper folded on the kitchen counter and Heather's toys stacked neatly in the corner. "Let me put a pair of pants on Heather and then we can eat," Joe said. "I'd just finished changing her diaper when I heard you drive up."

For more than one reason, my eyes filled with tears.

*****

"So how was the conference?" Joe asked as we sat down to steaming plates of spaghetti.

"Enlightening in more ways than one. I found out one of my new friends cheats on her husband."

Joe put down his fork. Heather stopped gumming her chopped noodles and was looking intently from one parent to the other.

"It's Scarlett. I hadn't told you anything before because I thought it was just idle gossip, but now I've seen it with my own eyes."

"Seen what?"

"Scarlett spent most of a night out with a book salesman. I'm fairly sure she goes outside her marriage, to use the least vulgar term. Elizabeth says she has a history of being unfaithful."

"Wow. Poor J.T. Does he know?"

"Supposedly not, according to Elizabeth. She told me weeks ago that Scarlett had something of a reputation for, as she put it, stepping out on J.T. I should've told you then, but I didn't want to believe it."

Joe and I regarded each other for a minute. "What do I do now?" I asked. "How can I still be friends with this woman?" I thought of Elizabeth's warning. "Maybe I need to distance myself from her. I don't want people to think I condone her behavior."

"You don't have to stop being Scarlett's friend," Joe said thoughtfully. "She needs someone like you. Turning your back on her doesn't accomplish anything, except maybe make you feel self-righteous. It's okay to like Scarlett without liking what she's doing."

"But how do we act around J.T.? I'll feel like I'm condoning her behavior if I pretend everything's hunky dory."

"That's a tough one," Joe conceded. "I sure don't want either you or me to be the one to inform him his wife's a two-timer. Why don't you talk to Scarlett? Tell her she either needs to quit running around or separate from J.T. It's not fair to the man to be made a fool of, especially in a town this small."

"I'll think about it. Maybe it's time someone called her attention to how badly she's behaving."

*****

As I was putting the leftover spaghetti in the refrigerator, I noticed a disposable aluminum pan containing the remains of some type of chicken casserole.

I scurried to the bathroom, where Joe was soaping a slippery Heather in three inches of bath water. "Where did that covered-dish food in the fridge come from?"

"Miss Josie brought it," Joe said, without looking up. "Something with chicken and noodles in it that I've had for supper the last two nights. It was pretty good."

"Boy, she doesn't miss a thing," I fumed. "She sees me in the morning loading my suitcase in a car and before the sun sets, she's brought the poor helpless husband and the deserted, motherless baby a casserole."

"Now, Dee Ann, she was just being nice. She talked about her children when she came over. They all live out of town and don't ever come to visit. She hardly ever sees her own grandchildren. I really think she made that casserole just to have an excuse to spend a few minutes with Heather."

"Maybe Miss Josie is a little lonely," I admitted. "I haven't seen anyone who looks like they could be her children or grandchildren over at the house."

"Tell me again who it is that spies on the neighbors," Joe teased.

Chapter 26

I was glad the next day was Thursday, one of my days off, and I didn't have to go to school and face the Scarlett problem. Besides, I felt I needed a whole day to be with Heather. And I had another situation I needed to rectify.

I scraped the rest of the chicken casserole into Tupperware and carefully washed and dried Miss Josie's aluminum pan. I changed Heather's diaper and brushed her cap of blond curls.

Holding the pan with one hand and balancing Heather on my hip with the other, I crossed the short distance from the apartment to the back door of the Powells' house. Miss Josie looked startled to see me along with her pan.

"Gracious, Dee Ann, you didn't have to wash that and return it. It's disposable. But how thoughtful of you. Most young folks today use something just once and then toss it. Like gift-wrapping paper and bows. Lordy, I never buy bows. I have a whole box full of bows that have come off gifts people have given me. And wrapping paper. I open presents gently so as not to rip the paper. Then I can cut off the edges where the tape has been, iron out the paper if it needs it, and use it again. I never have to buy gift-wrap."

I nodded. I knew all about saving bows and wrapping paper. I'd seen my mama and grandmama do it all my life.

"Floyd thinks I'm foolish to hold on to things the way I do," Miss Josie continued. "'The wolf ain't at the door,' he says. But I lived through the Depression, and learned to waste not, want not. Young folks today don't even know what I'm talking about." I started to tell her I was one young person who did understand, but before I could say anything, she changed the subject.

"Goodness, come on in. I didn't mean to keep you out here on the porch while I rattled on. And here's little Miss Heather. You're getting to be such a big girl."

Heather looked at Miss Josie, burped loudly, and then giggled at her accomplishment. Miss Josie and I both laughed too.

"We'll visit for a minute if we're not interrupting anything."

"Lillian's here, but I think she's leaving soon," Miss Josie said, nervously patting one side of her stiff bouffant. "You're no interruption."

Lillian? Who was Lillian? I hadn't seen a visitor's car in the driveway.

Miss Josie led me into a den cluttered with country decor. Cross-stitched samplers hung on the walls while a pie safe stood in one corner and a quilt rack claimed another. A wallpaper border featuring geese wearing pink bonnets waddled around the room.

Sitting on a red plaid sofa was a shrunken, white-haired woman with piercing blue eyes, which she immediately trained on me.

"Lillian, I'd like you to meet my back-door neighbor, Dee Ann Bulluck," Miss Josie said. "Dee Ann, this is Mrs. Lillian Adams."

"Mrs. Arthur Adams," the woman corrected, looking me up and down. "Are you one of those hussies that used to call my house looking for Gary?"

"I beg your pardon," I gasped.

"Lillian, for heaven's sake, Dee Ann is a married woman who just moved here in April," Miss Josie rushed to say. "I'm not sure she ever met your grandson."

My word! I'd been called a hussy by none other than Gary Whitt's grandmother. I wasn't about to correct Miss Josie by reminding her that I'd encountered Gary in her backyard the day I'd arrived in Narrow Creek. I'd rather Mrs. Adams thought I never made his acquaintance.

"I apologize," the old woman said, not sounding one bit apologetic. "I'm not in my right mind these days. The shock of Gary's death was just the beginning of my torment. The investigation has almost put me in my grave beside my precious grandson." With a ropy, blue-veined hand, Mrs. Adams lifted a dainty handkerchief to dab the corners of her eyes.

"My house was searched from top to bottom by those state investigators. They wouldn't tell me what they were looking for. Oh no, they wouldn't answer my questions, but they had plenty for me.

"Who were Gary's friends? Did he mention any enemies? Did anyone ever call the house looking for him? I don't know why Roger McSwain had to call in those pompous SBI agents from Raleigh."

I eased myself and Heather down into a navy leather wingback chair. Miss Josie took a seat on the sofa beside Mrs. Adams.

"My Teddy Bear had lots of friends, I told them over and over. I never heard him mention an enemy. Why, he was such a sweet boy."

Others had painted Gary as a spoiled braggart, a two-timing skirt chaser, and a drug dealer. I'd certainly never heard anyone call him "Teddy Bear." His grandmother, bless her heart, held a completely different opinion of the boy she'd raised.

"Even though he had his own apartment with a telephone," Mrs. Adams continued, "I did get some calls for him, especially from women. They'd never give their names, but always wanted to know if I'd seen Gary lately. They acted as if he'd vanished.

"Girls were always chasing Gary. He was such a good-looking boy." Mrs. Adams sighed.

"He was a handsome fellow," Miss Josie chimed in, no doubt trying to be a comfort.

"What really tore up my nerves was how those investigators treated my son as if he had something to do with Gary's death," Mrs. Adams said without acknowledging Miss Josie's comment. "Why, William loved his nephew."

So I was not the only one who'd had suspicions about Dr. Adams, my creepy dean of instruction at the technical college. Heather was beginning to squirm, so I sat her on my knees and gently bounced her.

"Those SBI agents had the impertinence to ask me all sorts of questions about my will at the time of Gary's death." Mrs. Adams glared at me as if I were one of the agents. "They wouldn't leave me alone until I told them that my estate was to be split equally between my two boys. Not that either really needed my money.

"William has a nice salary at the college, and Gary was doing well in his construction business," she said with a touch of pride in her voice.

Gary was doing well in his drug business, I couldn't help but think.

A slight rap on the back door followed Mrs. Adams' explanation of her will. "That's probably Cecil," she said to me as Miss Josie left the room. "It's four-thirty on the dot, and I told him not to be late fetching me. I sent him down the road to buy collards out of James Smith's fall garden while I paid Josephine a visit."

Miss Josie returned with a slim black man wearing a white shirt with frayed cuffs and a skinny tie. "You ready to go, Miz Adams?" he asked. Offering his arm, he eased her up from the sofa. As they slowly made their way to the door, Gary Whitt's grandmother gave me a backwards glance.

"I hope you're a virtuous woman," she said. "I feel Gary met his death at the hands of one who was not."

*****

"Whew, I've never been so glad to see a visit end," Miss Josie said, returning to the den. "I was counting the minutes until her help came back to pick her up. I'd almost rather she kept my Tupperware. She'd certainly taken her sweet time returning it anyway. I sent that marinated vegetable salad months ago, just a few days after Gary was killed." Miss Josie took a deep breath and shook her head back and forth as if to dispel the gloom left by her visitor.

"I apologize for her unkind remark to you as well as her monopolizing the conversation," she said, sitting down at the end of the sofa closer to my chair. "Lillian has always been one to never let anyone else get a word in edgewise, and since Gary's death, she's even worse." Miss Josie pressed her lips together in disapproval. I put Heather on the floor, where she began inspecting the braided rug.

"I don't mean to sound harsh, but it's downright rude not to let anyone else speak, even if you do have a dead grandson. We all have our crosses to bear."

Miss Josie obviously didn't know just how interesting I'd found the one-sided conversation. It was also ironic hearing this woman who was fond of monologues herself fault others for that vice.

"Why, I've had heartache in my own life," Miss Josie went on. "It may surprise you to know I once had a career.

I was twenty-eight when I married Floyd. In those days, I was considered an old maid by many folks, but I preferred to think of myself as a professional woman."

Miss Josie sat up a little straighter. "I was a nurse at the hospital here in town. Daddy hadn't wanted me to train for nursing; he said it wasn't a respectable profession. But I begged so much I finally wore him down, and he let me go to Raleigh to nursing school for two years.

"Those were probably the happiest two years of my life. Oh, I had to study hard, and we girls had strict rules at our dorm with curfews and what we couldn't wear when we went downtown, but compared to the life I had here with Mama and Daddy, I was free."

Miss Josie paused to pick up Heather, who was crawling at her feet. "I had such fun with the other girls, and we always had plenty of suitors from State College calling at our dorm. We would sit in the parlor with our young men and play bridge or listen to the radio. Of course, we had our dorm mother chaperoning any time a man was on the premises. On Saturday nights we were allowed to sign out and go to the movies if we went on a double-date and were in by ten o'clock."

I leaned back in the soft leather chair and slipped my arms out of my jacket. Heather was busy examining the buttons on Miss Josie's sweater.

"Oh, I could tell you stories all day long about those two years," Miss Josie continued. She paused and then her voice, which had been loud and gay, became quiet and serious. "During the last year of school, I had a special beau, Adam Whitaker II. He was the most handsome thing I'd ever seen. And smart! He was from Charlotte and was studying at State College to be a chemical engineer. I'd never heard of such a profession.

"I was head over heels, absolutely smitten. I thought he felt the same way, but the day before I was to graduate, he sent me a letter, a Dear Josie letter, you might say. It seems there was some girl back in Charlotte he'd promised to marry when he finished school. He told me not to wait around Raleigh for him."

The den was still. Heather, lulled by Miss Josie's quiet voice and gentle patting, was drifting off to sleep, her sweet head on Miss Josie's shoulder. Somewhere, I heard a clock ticking.

"It was a blow, I'm telling you," Miss Josie said sadly, "but there was nothing to do except pack up and go home after graduation. I was too embarrassed to stay on in Raleigh. I was supposed to start working at Rex Hospital there, but I told them I'd changed my mind. I came back to Narrow Creek and got a job on the maternity floor at the hospital."

Miss Josie swallowed hard. "Mama and Daddy had known about Adam and me. They'd even met him once when they came to Raleigh to visit. And I'd confided in Mama that I expected to get an engagement ring once I graduated.

"I didn't tell her how it ended, though. I was afraid if Daddy found out how Adam had jilted me, he would've come to Raleigh with a shotgun. Times were different then. A woman's honor was protected—sometimes foolishly. And Daddy had a hot temper.

"So I told Mama I was the one who'd called things off. I said I'd decided Adam wasn't the man I wanted to marry, and no matter how much Mama nagged me to change my mind—she thought he was a good catch—I stuck to my story."

Miss Josie sighed. "I didn't move back in with Mama and Daddy, either, which made Mama even more unhappy. I found a room to rent in Miss Annabelle Jenkins' house instead. Miss Annabelle had never been married and was in her early fifties then. Since she'd stayed home to nurse her mama and daddy in their old age, they'd left her the family homeplace—it's that big old white house on Church Street where the Baileys live now—and she'd rent rooms to all the unmarried lady schoolteachers in Narrow Creek.

"I know it was a little selfish on my part to get my own place, but if I'd moved back home with Mama and Daddy, I would've been expected to take care of my younger sisters and brothers whenever I wasn't at the hospital. I was the oldest in a family of eight children."

I imagined Miss Josie, young and disappointed in love, living in a room in a spinster's house, trying to make a life for herself.

"I stayed at Miss Annabelle's house for eight years. I earned my own keep being a nurse. I saw a lot of babies born healthy, and I saw some tragedies, too. I was good at my job. Women asked for me when they came in to deliver. I got along well with the doctors, too, and some of them were pretty ornery, let me tell you." Miss Josie shifted a dozing Heather from one shoulder to another.

"One Saturday I was eating lunch at the counter in Woolworth's with my girlfriend June Hill when I noticed Floyd Powell sitting by himself several stools away. Floyd had been two grades ahead of me at Narrow Creek High School, and everybody knew everybody in Narrow Creek, just like now. But somehow it struck me that day that he was rather handsome. Floyd was thirty years old then and had never been married. Folks said he was a confirmed bachelor.

"I'd not courted any young man seriously in the eight years since I'd fallen in love with Adam Whitaker in Raleigh, and believe me, my mama was plenty worried about that fact. She didn't want me to be an old maid. Not a week went by that she didn't ask whether anyone was courting me and why not." Miss Josie gazed at an old black-and-white framed photograph of a stern woman in a high-necked blouse on the end table between us.

"When I noticed Floyd that day in Woolworth's, I was at the point I wanted to get married. Not because of Mama, but I'd finally let Adam Whitaker go. For years, I'd kept thinking—foolishly, I know—that Adam would come to Narrow Creek one day and tell me he'd made a big mistake. I dreamed he'd show up at the hospital with a dozen roses and on bended knee ask me to forgive him for ever thinking he could live without me and then beg me to marry him.

"That happens only in the movies, though. My Adam was gone. I decided I wanted a family. I wanted to be the woman having the babies instead of helping to deliver them. That day in Woolworth's, I asked Floyd to come sit with June and me, and I made a special effort, I'm not ashamed to say, to flirt with him. He wasn't a confirmed bachelor, I found out; he was just shy around girls. Six months later we were married, and a year after that I had my first child." Miss Josie lightly rubbed Heather's back.

"Floyd has been a good husband, and I think I've been a good wife. I've never told him about Adam Whitaker. I wouldn't want him to think he was my second choice."

"No, ma'am," I agreed. "He doesn't need to know that story."

"The only bad part about being married and a mother was that I gave up nursing. Floyd didn't want me to work, and in my day women who were married stayed home. It was hard, though, to give up my own paycheck and depend on a man for money. You're doing the right thing, working at the college. Keep part of your life for yourself. I'm glad young women today can have both a job and a family, although sometimes, to tell the truth, I'm a little envious that I didn't have that choice."

Heather stirred and I realized it was almost noon. Joe would be home any minute for lunch. "Miss Josie, thank you for the chicken casserole and the visit. The next time Heather and I go to the Dairy Queen, why don't you come with us? Do you like ice cream?"

"I love it," said Miss Josie with a faraway look in her eyes. "It's absolutely my favorite."

*****

That night, my normally sound sleep was interrupted by nightmares. In one, an old woman with piercing blue eyes and ropy-veined hands was trying to wrestle Heather away from me. "Hussy," she kept saying, "you have no right to be a mother. I'll take her to raise. I need another child. My Teddy Bear is gone."

Then a man with a handlebar mustache appeared. He was dressed in a white shirt buttoned all the way to a starched collar. He wore a black coat and a scowl. "How dare you dishonor my daughter, you scoundrel!" He raised a hillbilly shotgun and fired it five times—right into the handsome, pleading face of Gary Whitt.

I woke up in a sweat. Miss Josie's father had the wrong man.

Chapter 27

A week passed after our return from the conference, and I felt awkward every time I was around Scarlett. Her probable tryst with Trey Phillips was the white elephant in the room. I could hardly bear to look at her.

But Scarlett seemed oblivious to any chill in our friendship. She chitchatted to me each day at school as if nothing had ever happened. She showed absolutely no signs of remorse that I could see but was her usual sassy self. Finally, it was more than I could take.

I caught up with Elizabeth in the parking lot one morning and told her I was going to have a come-to-Jesus talk with Scarlett about the salesman incident.

"And say what, Dee Ann?" She pulled her bulky sweater tighter against the blustery wind. "Are you going to tell her it's wrong for her to be cheating on J.T.? Shouldn't that be obvious even to Miss Free Spirit Scarlett? I'm sorry. I don't mean to sound so sarcastic. You're probably doing the right thing in confronting her. I don't think anyone else has the gumption to do so. Or wants to get involved. I know I don't."

"On one hand, it's none of my business," I admitted, "but then again, she's my friend and I feel as though she's in trouble. Or will be one day when J.T. hears the gossip." Dry leaves skidded across the parking lot. My eyes watered in the wind. "Joe said I should tell her she needs to either shape up or separate, that it's not fair to make a fool of J.T."

Elizabeth squinted at me and then spoke thoughtfully. "In the years I've known her, you're probably the best friend Scarlett has had. Most women don't want to get close to her, either because they're jealous of her looks or they don't approve of her lifestyle. You're a good person, not a busybody, to want to help her."

I didn't let on to Elizabeth, but I also wanted to find out whether Scarlett had ever been involved with Gary Whitt. Despite telling myself that I was no longer investigating the murder, I still toyed with the idea of identifying the killer. That ten thousand dollar reward was such a lure. Never mind my disappointment in supplying two false leads to Chief McSwain. According to him, I'd been correct in suspecting a jilted woman; I just didn't know the right one. Yet.

Had Scarlett been one of Gary Whitt's many paramours? Had she been one of the "hussies" who'd called Mrs. Adams' house looking for Gary?

Was she capable of murder? If she really was a playgirl, wouldn't she have let Gary go without looking back?

"Why are you two ladies so serious on such a sunny day? And what's this about Dee Ann being a busybody?" Elizabeth and I had been so intent on our conversation that we hadn't noticed Hazel Hood.

"Let me guess: that crazy Scarlett has been up to no good again." Hazel laughed at the startled expression on Elizabeth's face. "Elizabeth, I can look at you and know in a minute when you're talking trash about our girl Scarlett. What's she done now?

"That's okay," Hazel went on without waiting for a reply. "Y'all don't have to tell me. I have my sources. White folks don't seem to notice that the people who work for them have eyes and ears, too. I know more about what goes on in

Scarlett's house than the two of you put together. And I'm here to tell you that husband of hers needs to wake up and smell the coffee, as Ann Landers says." Hazel pulled up the collar of her coat and then wrapped her arms around herself.

"Blessed Jesus, it might be sunny out here, but it's cold. I'm going in," she said as another blast of bitter wind hit us. "I'll leave you two to figure out what to do about Miss Scarlett."

"Good grief!" I exclaimed after she hurried away. "What in the world has Hazel heard? It's bad enough that everybody white in Narrow Creek talks about Scarlett, but now it looks like there's gossip in the black community as well. I'm going to ask her to go to lunch tomorrow, just the two of us, and speak to her frankly about the whole ugly situation. She has to come to her senses before something awful happens." My teeth began to chatter.

"I'll be praying for you," Elizabeth replied. We scurried to the school's nearest entrance.

*****

Scarlett and I sat in the corner booth at the Pizza Hut. Scarlett had ordered only a trip to the salad bar, but I'd signed up for the whole buffet and helped myself to the salad bar too. Why eat in a restaurant with pizza in its name if I wasn't going to enjoy several slices?

I'd finished my fourth and last piece of pizza, and we were waiting for our check. It was now or never. I'd practiced what I wanted to say and hoped I wouldn't sound judgmental. "Lord," I prayed, "have me speak as you would speak."

"Something's been bothering me since we went to the conference the other week," I began. I looked my friend dead in the eye. "I want to know the whole truth about your evening with the book salesman."

"We've already discussed that, Dee Ann. I went to dinner with Trey Phillips of Scott Publishers, service was slow at the Beef Master Inn, and we talked for a while after we finished eating," Scarlett recited in a breezy voice, looking away. She began to twist the chain of her long gold necklace.

"Scarlett, you got in that night at three a.m.! I didn't just fall off the turnip truck." The chain was getting tighter and tighter around her neck. "You couldn't have been sitting in the Beef Master Inn half the night. I'm sure the place closes by midnight or so. Or at least the restaurant does. I don't know about the inn part."

I wasn't sure I was speaking as the Lord would speak. He wouldn't have mentioned falling off the turnip truck. But in my rehearsal, I'd imagined Scarlett immediately confessing instead of repeating the same story she'd already told me. She'd thrown me off by refusing to come clean.

"I never said we were at the Beef Master Inn the entire time," she replied after a moment's pause. "And quite frankly, I don't like your tone of voice or what you're implying. What's this sudden concern on your part about my private life?"

"It's not a 'sudden concern.' I've wanted to talk to you for quite a while about what you're doing behind J.T.'s back," I countered. "From what I hear, this salesman isn't the first man you've gone out with. Apart from the fact that it's just plain wrong to disregard your marriage vows, it's also only a matter of time before J.T. finds out you're cheating. Then what are you going to do? Do you think it's fair to treat him this way? You're making a fool of him."

I was on a roll. My plan to speak calmly and compassionately had fallen apart. The devil had certainly taken over my tongue.

"Dee Ann, you and everybody else in this godforsaken, gossiping town can go straight to hell." Scarlett stood up with tears in her bright green eyes. Her necklace spun itself straight. "I'll take care of my check at the counter and wait for you in the car."

Stunned and ashamed, I sat in the booth by myself. I'd made the situation worse. Scarlett had admitted to nothing, and I'd just alienated her. So much for asking whether she'd had a fling with Gary Whitt.

Scarlett stood outside my car, drying her eyes with a lipstick-smudged tissue. I unlocked the doors, and we got in without looking at each other.

I drove in an icy silence halfway back to school. Scarlett sat sideways in her seat with her back to me, staring out the window. I felt like crying myself.

"I didn't mean to upset you," I began. "I brought up the subject because I'm your friend and want to help you."

"If you want to help me, then quit being so damn judgmental." Scarlett turned, and I could sense her studying me as I kept my eyes on the road. "What I liked about you was the fact that you were different from all these catty women in town. You seemed open-minded about life. Live and let live. I guess I was wrong." She sniffed and then blew her nose.

"This conversation shouldn't be about me." I stopped at a red light, one of the two in Narrow Creek. "I'm trying to talk to you about your marriage. Maybe you don't want my advice, but I feel it's my responsibility as your friend to warn you that sooner or later J.T. is going to hear some nasty gossip. Not from me, I promise you, but some meddler is going to tell him."

Scarlett didn't miss a beat. "He can believe some fool, or he can believe me. The truth is I like to flirt. I like for handsome men to think I'm attractive. When I was a little girl, my daddy treated me like a princess. I had three older brothers, so I was special. There was nothing I wanted that I couldn't get, including plenty of attention. I was spoiled past rotten.

"Then I grew up and married J.T., who worshipped me for a while. Gradually, though, he didn't pay me the attention he had when we were dating and first married. I wasn't his whole world." Scarlett's wan smile when she'd been remembering her adoring daddy had been erased by the hard look she often got when she talked about J.T. "I'd been replaced by hunting and fishing and football. I know J.T. loves me, but he doesn't treasure me, not the way I was used to being treasured by my daddy, my brothers, and my mama."

Scarlett sniffed. "I like the attention of handsome men. That's all. It makes up for not having my daddy to spoil me anymore and for not being the most special thing in the world to my husband. I know my behavior gives people in a small town a chance to talk about me, but I don't care about appearances," she concluded defiantly.

I was shocked into silence. Could this explanation be true? Could it be that Scarlett was all talk and no action? "But I still don't understand where you were until three o'clock in the morning."

"Flirting, Dee Ann, just flirting." Scarlett smiled. "Oh, Mr. Trey Phillips thought he was going to score, but it's just a game for me. I guess I'm guilty of being a big tease, and maybe it's not nice of me to lead men on that way, but then again it's kind of funny when they think I'm easy and find out otherwise."

I shot my friend a sideways glance. "This is a dangerous game. You could play the wrong person and get hurt." Had she ever flirted with Gary Whitt? I was afraid to ask. I didn't want a repeat of the scene in the Pizza Hut.

"Oh, I'm careful about choosing my prey," she said as I drove into the college's parking lot. "Book salesmen aren't known to be the violent type."

I parked in a faculty spot and removed the key from the ignition. "I'm beginning to think you're crazy."

"Now to that accusation," she said with a shrug, "I plead guilty."

Chapter 28

Giant plastic candy canes hung from the lamp posts on Main Street the Saturday morning I'd arranged to meet Elizabeth for breakfast at Ernie's Grill. It was early December, and once Thanksgiving Day passed, Narrow Creek embraced Christmas in all its commercial glory. Mannequins dressed in black velvet pants and red sweaters crocheted with holly leaf patterns stood guard in the storefront windows of Three Sisters Dress Shop. Bob's Ace Hardware had an assortment of children's sleds stacked right outside the front door.

"As if it snows more than once or twice a season at best around here," said Elizabeth, eyeing the display.

"Kids want to be ready for even a flurry," I replied. "And Santa loves to deliver sleds."

"Maybe we'll have more than an inch this year," she allowed. "I love a snow day myself. School is dismissed at the first flake, and we don't go back until it's all melted." Elizabeth pushed open the old wooden door with the faded Pepsi logo stenciled on it. "Here we are."

Ernie's Grill wasn't much more than a laminated counter where customers ordered their food before sitting down in one of the half dozen booths on the other side of the room. Behind the counter, Ernie and another cook were frying eggs and flipping pancakes. Ernie's wife Evelyn wrote down orders, delivered them to the booths, refilled coffee, and manned the register. All in all, it was a very efficient operation, with good, reasonably-priced food. Customers were constant. The IHOP out on the bypass hadn't put a dent in Ernie's business with the residents of Narrow Creek.

Elizabeth and I ordered at the counter and grabbed a booth at the very back just as it became available. After Evelyn brought us our coffee, I leaned across the table. "I've been meaning to tell you. I talked to Scarlett a couple of weeks ago, and she explained that she was just flirting with that book salesman. She has this little game she plays with men, making them think they're going to get somewhere with her. In other words, she's just a big tease."

Elizabeth rolled her eyes and huffed. "I don't know if I buy that explanation, but I've started speaking to her again at school. It's hard for me to stay mad at anybody for too long. Scarlett seems oblivious to my disapproval anyway. It's just easier to ignore whatever she's up to and be civil to her.

"But I didn't invite you to breakfast this morning to talk about the naughty Scarlett." Two spots of color rose in Elizabeth's plump cheeks. "I've got some big news, and I've been about to die to tell someone."

I'd wondered about this Saturday morning breakfast. With the Christmas season just beginning, I had a lot to do on weekends when Joe was home to help me. Decorating the apartment, buying gifts, sending out Christmas cards—I really had no business going out for breakfast. But Elizabeth had insisted on meeting, and Joe had told me to go and he'd get the tree in the stand if Heather wasn't too much to handle.

"Is it about the adoption?" I asked, unable to wait.

"Yes! Listen, Benjamin has a second cousin who lives in Florida. This cousin's daughter is seventeen, unmarried, and five months pregnant. She's just told her parents she's expecting, but she's also told them she's not ready to be a mother. She has plans to go to college, so she and her parents think it's best for her to give the baby up for adoption. Still, they don't like the idea of the child going outside the family. Then they thought of Benjamin and me."

Elizabeth's voice had risen an octave. "We see these people maybe once every three years at a family reunion, and they know we don't have a child but want one. Two nights ago, Benjamin's cousin called to see if we'd be interested in adopting his daughter's baby. Oh, Dee Ann, she's due in April. I could be a mother by Easter." Elizabeth was practically bouncing in her seat.

"I just keep pinching myself. We've barely moved up that adoption waiting list. In fact, we've been told it will probably be another three years. And now, this wonderful blessing has come along. Thanks be to God."

As we were both dabbing our eyes with thin paper napkins from the table dispenser, Evelyn showed up with our food. "Cheer up, girls," she said, popping her gum. "Ernie's cooking ain't that bad." I smiled weakly, and Elizabeth and I took the minute or so of arranging plates on the table and getting a coffee refill to compose ourselves. Evelyn, bless her heart, didn't ask us what was wrong. I guess when you run a grill for forty years, you see all kinds of behavior.

"This is really good news. I'm so happy for you and Benjamin." I thought for a moment. "But before you get your hopes up too much, are you sure this girl is going to give up the baby? I hate to even ask you, but you've heard of cases where the birth mother backs out." What a heartache that would be. I felt a little mean-spirited even bringing up the subject, but Elizabeth needed to think about the worst-case scenario. Sometimes people can want something so badly they don't see a situation clearly, ignoring any possible pitfalls.

I hadn't given Elizabeth enough credit. "I've thought about that possibility a hundred times in the last two days. But I keep going over what Benjamin has been told by her father. The girl is an honor student in high school, excited about college. She's already been accepted at Florida State for next year. She's ready to be a college coed, not a mother.

"This isn't just her father talking either," Elizabeth went on. "Benjamin has quizzed his cousin's wife and the girl too. Both said they want the baby to have a good home, but they don't see how they can keep it themselves. This girl—Sarah is her name—is the youngest in the family. If her parents kept the child, it would be like starting over again. Not to mention the awkwardness of the baby being there every time Sarah came home, like a constant reminder of her mistake."

I could see Elizabeth felt confident about the adoption, but I had one more question. "Where's the father of the baby in all this?"

Elizabeth fiddled with her utensils. "He's out of the picture. He wants to go to college too. Adoption is fine with him. Benjamin's cousin says the situation has been embarrassing for both families, and he thinks the baby would grow up happier in a home where there's no question about being wanted."

"That would certainly be your home." I paused. "I hate to keep sounding like doomsday here, but be sure you and Benjamin get some legal advice to make everything official."

"Not to worry." Elizabeth beamed. "Benjamin is meeting with our attorney Monday morning. Now let's eat these eggs before they get cold. I know you probably need to get home and start decorating a tree or hanging a wreath."

*****

I was about to cross the street to my Toyota when I came face to face with Cynthia, splendidly outfitted in a red wool coat accented by a plaid scarf and matching beret. I instantly felt underdressed in my gray windbreaker and Saturday jeans. Why did this woman always make me feel dowdy? And what was she doing out of rehab? I'd hoped she'd be gone for at least a year.

"Hello there, Dee Ann," she blared in her shrill voice. "Doing some Christmas shopping this morning? I've just left the travel agency. Bill and I are going abroad for the holidays since we don't have children to tie us down with all that Santa Claus business. Besides, I need a trip after that two-month ordeal at my mother's bedside. I guess you heard how terribly sick she was. Quite a scare, but she's better now, and I'm free to head to Monte Carlo for Christmas."

"Joe told me your mother was seriously ill. What exactly was wrong?" Normally I wouldn't have asked such a personal question, but I couldn't resist trying to poke a hole in Cynthia's story.

I was immediately foiled. "Heart problems," Cynthia recited. "But she's on medication now and pretty much her old self again." She gave a sly smile, shifting a Three Sisters Dress Shop bag from one daintily gloved hand to the other.

"I'm happy to hear that," I had no choice but to reply. "How long will you be gone on your trip?" I asked. Years wouldn't be long enough for me.

"Ten days. We'll be flying to Paris first, where we'll stay for a couple of nights. I love Paris—I plan to do some shopping there—but it's been my experience that most Parisian hotels aren't as luxurious as those in Monte Carlo. You wouldn't believe how small Parisian bathrooms are."

Do tell. It was all I could do not to roll my eyes.

"And French food isn't as wonderful as people say. I had the worst crepes in Paris once. Nothing like what we're used to in French restaurants here in the States. Though I'm not sure what I had was crepes. The menu was all in French, and the waiter spoke very poor English."

Imagine that, a menu in France printed in French, not English, to accommodate Cynthia.

Cynthia misjudged my snicker, as she kept on with her critique. "And the French are so stingy with ice. You'd think it was gold. Beverages at room temperature! Please!"

What hardships. Oh, the horror.

"But once we get to Monte Carlo, everything will be first class, and we'll be treated the way Americans expect to be treated. No disgusting foreign food, plenty of ice in our drinks, large hotel rooms with luxurious bathrooms, and waiters who speak English."

Sure beats a prison cell, which is where you should be, I so wanted to say. Before I could think of a clever but snide way to imply I knew all about her part in the Narrow Creek drug bust, she nailed me.

"Oh, is that your *little* Toyota over there parked behind my car?" she said, pointing. "I'm driving that new black Mercedes. We traded in my '76 model, the silver one."

"I heard that you were no longer driving that car," was all I managed to say. Why didn't I have the nerve to add I'd also heard Bill had taken it away from her as punishment for embezzling from the Ladies' Society and had forced her to drive the bank's old company car?

Where was that old car anyway? Why was she gallivanting around in a new black Mercedes? This woman had stolen money from a civic club, cheated on her husband with a man who'd been murdered, and spent time in drug rehab to avoid going to prison. Evidently Bill had forgiven all, and she was back to her old flamboyant lifestyle.

She'd obviously recovered nicely, drat it all. And as much as I wanted to lay her low, she was married to my husband's boss, and it seemed Bill was under her spell. I didn't want firing Joe because I'd insulted her to be one of her wishes.

Cynthia and I crossed the street together, she on her way to Christmas in Europe and I on my way to Santa Claus in a Narrow Creek apartment.

My *little* Toyota let out a high-pitched squeal as I cranked it. Some kind of belt needed to be tightened or loosened. Cynthia looked in her rearview mirror, no doubt noting the racket.

I thought of my sweet Heather and tried to feel sorry for the childless Cynthia instead of jealous of her European trip. After all, envy is one of the seven deadly sins. Surely enjoying Heather's first Christmas was going to be better than any trip to a fabulous resort. Monte Carlo, indeed!

Chapter 29

Joe not only had the tree in the stand, but he'd also strung the lights. He and Heather sat in front of the three-dollar cedar we'd selected from the Optimist Club Christmas tree lot. The guy manning the lot had told us not many people like to decorate a cedar tree since the foliage can make a person itch. Somehow a few had come in by mistake with the shipment of Fraser Firs and Virginia Pines. We were certainly welcome to pay a fourth of what the other trees were selling for, he'd said, if we didn't mind wearing gloves to decorate.

Joe's heavy work gloves lay to one side of the tree. I'd need my gardening gloves to add the ornaments. We'd learned from our past two Christmases together that Joe didn't need to do any decorating beyond the lights. He had no patience and would sling tinsel by the handful instead of carefully placing each silver strand on a branch to create the illusion of icicles. He also had no sense of what ornaments needed to go where. I eyed a line of red satin balls hung only an inch or so apart circling the bottom branches.

"That's Heather's contribution," Joe said, grinning. "That's as high as she could reach. Are you saying you don't like her decorating either?"

"Very funny." I rolled my eyes. "I seriously doubt an eleven-month-old knows how to hang ornaments." Joe laughed as he took the balls off and carefully laid them in their box.

"Yes, ma'am. I know better than to go beyond the lights. This tree is waiting for Decorator Dee Ann."

"Entertain Heather, then, and I'll finish." I pulled on my old, ratty garden gloves. "Let's listen to some Christmas music to get in the spirit of the season. I've got some great news from Elizabeth."

Joe fiddled with the radio knob until he found a station playing continuous Christmas carols. The apartment filled with "Away in a Manger" as I told Joe about the Tuckers' adoption.

I began hanging a collection of crocheted snowflakes that Joe's grandmother had made for us. Looking at our three-dollar tree, I thought of Cynthia's upcoming European vacation and felt a stab of jealousy.

"Guess who I saw downtown driving a new Mercedes and talking about a trip to Monte Carlo that she and her husband are taking over the holidays? Cynthia Ford," I said, without giving Joe a chance to answer. "I didn't know she was already back from rehab. It seems Bill has rewarded her for kicking cocaine instead of punishing her for embezzling from the Ladies' Society and buying street drugs."

I could have added infidelity to the list of Cynthia's sins but remembered Joe didn't know anything about her affair with Gary Whitt.

"Yeah, she got home this week. Did I forget to tell you?" Joe asked, frowning as he sat on the floor while Heather crawled around him. "I hadn't heard about the holiday vacation, but I do know that Bill has leased another Mercedes for her. This year's model, a '79. I think she threatened to leave him if she had to keep driving the bank's old Buick. Frankly, I'd have told her goodbye and good riddance.

"It's sad the way she manipulates Bill," Joe continued. "He's caught between a rock and a hard place being married to that woman. Either he spends way beyond their means to try to keep her happy, or he tries to follow some sort of budget only to have to listen to her complain and threaten to walk out. He says she claims as a banker's wife, she needs plenty of money to keep up appearances. She sure wasn't too worried about appearances when she was buying cocaine, though, was she?"

"No indeed," I chimed in.

She hadn't cared about appearances either when she was stepping out with Gary Whitt. Evidently, the conniving Cynthia didn't think she'd get caught.

"The problem is that Bill doesn't make the kind of money she says she needs," Joe went on. "Even with her salary, he says they live in big-time credit card debt that is only getting worse. I guess she's quit buying cocaine, but Bill had to pay an arm and a leg for that treatment program." Heather crawled out of Joe's lap and over to the dining area, where she picked up a few stray Cheerios off the floor and put them in her mouth. Joe emptied a bag of ornament hooks and started separating them.

"How do you know all this, Joe?"

"Bill breaks down every so often and talks about how his life is a living hell of trying to figure out how to stay afloat financially. I'll probably hear about the big holiday vacation sometime next week." Joe retrieved Heather, replacing stale Cheerios with her teething ring. "I trust this conversation won't go any further than this room. Bill has enough problems without everybody in town knowing his business."

"Mum's the word," I said, pretending to zip my mouth.

I did feel a little guilty that Joe was confiding in me while I was not revealing Cynthia's affair with Gary Whitt. If I told him what I'd overheard months ago in the kitchen of First Baptist, I was afraid I'd wind up recounting my whole investigation, and then Joe would scold me for going behind his back after he'd told me to leave Gary Whitt's case to the professionals. "Oh, what a tangled web we weave, when first we practice to deceive." A lot of people think Shakespeare wrote this bit of wisdom, but actually Sir Walter Scott came up with it.

Oblivious to my musings, Joe talked on as he tried to separate the jumbled hooks. "A man can work hard his whole life and make good money, but if he has a wife who spends foolishly, he'll have nothing but financial problems. One thing I've learned from being at the bank is that people can always spend more than they make, no matter their income level."

It wasn't like Joe to be so philosophical. He felt sorry for Bill Ford and didn't even know the whole story. I unboxed the oyster shell ornaments Mama had given me the first Christmas I was married.

"I appreciate the fact that you're frugal," Joe said. "We don't have much right now, but we aren't in debt either. Well, other than the three hundred dollars we owe my dad for the Jeep. I'm proud of us, though, for paying him two hundred on that bill so far in just three months." I studied Joe's good-natured face, his blue eyes unusually serious.

"Too much debt can be a terrible thing. I couldn't enjoy a trip to Europe if it was paid for with money I shouldn't be spending. And you know what? Even if I could afford to go to Europe, there's nowhere I'd rather be than right here with you and Heather in this apartment. I'm excited about our little Christmas."

"Joe Bulluck, don't use that word *little* with me. Our Christmas is nothing to be ashamed of."

"Who's ashamed of our Christmas?" Joe said, confused. "And what's wrong with the word 'little'? We're celebrating Christmas exactly the way we should, the way most people do. Put up a tree, have Santa Claus, swap gifts, and go visit relatives."

"And go to church, too." Sometimes Joe has to be reminded about religion. He doesn't talk about the Lord the way I do. He says his faith is a private thing, between God and him. He believes in walking the walk, he says, rather than talking the talk.

Joe ignored my comment. "I'm sure Bill wishes he could stay home for Christmas instead of being dragged off to Europe to throw away money he doesn't have. Cynthia is going to spend him into bankruptcy, first and last."

Despite the soothing Christmas music coming from the radio and the tree's twinkling lights, I felt anything but peaceful. The more I thought about how selfish and unfeeling Cynthia Ford was, the more I wondered whether, despite the alibi she'd given to the police, she'd had something to do with Gary Whitt's murder. Had Bill, finding out about her affair, reached his breaking point and confronted her lover? Maybe Bill catered to Cynthia because she knew the truth and would expose him, the truth being he'd gone to Gary Whitt's house in a jealous rage and shot the man dead.

I wondered what alibis these two had given to Chief McSwain. How could I find out?

Chapter 30

Several times during the next week, I picked up the phone, ready to have another chat with Chief McSwain. But it was Christmas, the season of peace and love, and I couldn't bring myself to deal with the sordid business of the Fords' possible involvement in the Gary Whitt murder. Besides, even if I did convince the bumbling Chief to question them further, the two were heading off to Europe, and if they thought their alibi was falling apart, they might not come back from Paris or Monte Carlo or wherever the heck they were going. Better to take a holiday from sleuthing and deal with the situation once 1980 rolled around, and the Fords were back in town.

I was too busy to think much about murder suspects anyway. I'd shopped carefully for just the right dress to wear to the annual Ladies' Society Christmas party and was quite pleased with the Diane Von Furstenberg-inspired slinky black wrap I'd found at Three Sisters. Since I was making a little bit of money, I'd decided to indulge myself, buying something at the pricey ladies' boutique, but I still felt guilty about what I'd spent, even with the dress being twenty-five percent off.

"Don't give me anything for Christmas," I told Joe on Saturday evening as I got ready for the party. "I've already bought my own present."

"Now Dee Ann, you know I'm going to get you something," Joe said, knotting his red tie. "We can afford for you to have a new dress and a Christmas present too."

"I'll consider this little black dress an investment then." I admired myself in the full-length mirror I'd bought at Kress Five and Dime and nailed to the back of the bedroom closet door. "This dress is a classic. I can use it for years."

"You look very nice in it, too. I look forward to seeing you wear it for the next decade." Joe wiggled his eyebrows as he came up behind me and kissed the back of my neck. I knew he was making fun of me, but I smiled at our reflection. My blonde curls, swept back with a couple of sparkly gold hair combs I'd found in a thrift shop, contrasted nicely with Joe's dark head of hair. We made a handsome couple, if I do say so myself.

This party was my reward for sticking it out in the Ladies' Society. All fall I'd attended those boring meetings. To earn hours, I'd played Bingo at the Shady Oaks Retirement Village, sold raffle tickets for the Narrow Creek Arts Center, and just recently, rung the Salvation Army bell and manned the donation kettle at the Winn-Dixie.

I'd earned this party but hated that despite my efforts to be as nice as I could to all the members, I hadn't made any real friends in the club. Scarlett and Elizabeth were both ex-members, each with her own story of why she'd quit. According to Scarlett, the club was just a bunch of righteous do-gooders who didn't know how to have any fun. Elizabeth left after two years of feeling snubbed because she didn't dress as well as the other members and had a job instead of being a stay-at-home mom.

My strategy was to give the club one year, my pledge period. If I still felt like a social pariah, I'd leave before becoming a full-fledged member.

Perhaps this Christmas party would be the night when I finally found my niche in the club. Joe is good with people, I thought; he'll help me charm some of these women into being warm and friendly. With Joe by my side, maybe I'd get more conversation out of them than "hello, Dee Ann, how are you" before they moved on to someone else.

The cocktail party was being held at the Narrow Creek Country Club. Unlike me, most of the women in the Ladies' Society were also country club members. Joe and I couldn't afford country club dues, and his position at the bank hadn't come with a membership as a perk.

So I'd never seen the club, hidden from the road as it was by a thick grove of pine trees. Joe had been twice for business lunches, but all I could get out of him was that people said the clubhouse was built in the Tudor style and that it was big.

As Joe and I drove into the parking lot, the bare branches of crepe myrtles sparkled with small white lights. Being an English major, I knew a little about Tudor architecture and could make out the half-timbered façade of the three-story structure and the diamond-patterned windows. Sand candles illuminated the walkway to the double-door entrance. I felt as though I were entering a castle in Shakespeare's England.

"Nice," Joe said. He was looking around at the well-lit, immaculate grounds fading into a shadowy golf course.

My castle illusion vanished as soon as we opened the door and were greeted by Barbara Highland, who gave a face-splitting grin the minute she saw Joe.

"Your husband is simply the sweetest man on earth, Dee Ann," she simpered, grabbing Joe by the arm. "He's been such a big help to me these last few months. I just love him to death."

Joe gave a tight little smile and patted the woman's hand squeezing his arm. "The bank appreciates your business, Barbara."

"Y'all go in and get yourselves a drink. Joe, I'll see you sometime this week, I'm sure." She winked as Joe and I escaped.

"What was that all about?" Suddenly I felt as though Joe had a secret life.

"The biggest overdraft headache in town," he whispered. "That's your club president? It's a good thing she's not your treasurer."

"Well, what do you know," I muttered. "All this time I've been thinking these women had plenty of money." I also remembered the story of how Barbara had been so indignant about Cynthia's mishandling of the club's funds. Like the pot calling the kettle black, as my grandma used to say.

I felt positively cheerful with this new piece of information, though I knew it was unchristian to delight in evil as well as the misfortune of others. I ordered a glass of red wine while Joe got a bourbon and Coke. We'd started circulating the ballroom when I saw my dress—on someone else.

"Good grief!" I could feel my cheeks beginning to burn.

"What's wrong?" Joe asked.

"That woman has on my dress. I can't believe it. I didn't think about the possibility that someone else would buy it."

"Where?" Joe was scanning the room with a perplexed look on his face.

"Look right in front of you. How can you not see that woman ten feet away from us in the same black dress that I have on?"

"That's the same dress? It looks different on her."

"Yeah, it looks better. I'm so mortified I could die."

"Don't you think you're overreacting? I doubt anyone will notice."

At that moment, Cynthia came slithering up with Bill two steps behind. "Hi there, Dee Ann. Having fun? I see you got the black wrap dress from Three Sisters. I tried it on myself, but I was afraid to buy it since the shop had it in several sizes. In a small town, you might meet your double at a party. Enjoy your evening." She was practically cackling as she sashayed away, dragging her husband by the arm before he could say anything more than hello.

I gave Joe a told-you-so look. "No, no one will notice. What do you think that little conversation was all about? Cynthia has already matched me up with my double."

In my embarrassment, I'd momentarily forgotten that Cynthia, who was now a former member, wasn't supposed to be at the club's party. Had she crashed? Or had someone allowed her to come? Wasn't the party supposed to be for only permanent and probationary members in good standing and their spouses? Why had I done all that civic work when Miss Priss, who stole money from the club, could just waltz right in?

And why hadn't I called Chief McSwain and urged him to take another look at the Fords? Forget the season of peace and love. If I'd picked up the phone, Cynthia could be sitting in a jail cell now instead of mocking me at a party she had no right to attend. And I would be ten-grand reward-money richer and could've bought a designer original to wear to tonight's party and not have to meet my double.

I drained my glass of wine. "There is no justice in this world, Joe. Let's get another drink."

A three-man band began playing a song with the distinctive beat of beach music. People filled the dance floor, and I noticed, with considerable disappointment, that all the couples were dancing the same shuffle step of the shag. Probably the official dance of the Narrow Creek Ladies' Society.

Joe and I'd never learned to shag. In college, our dancing had been the kind that worked with rock and roll. We were Woodstock dancers, not beach pavilion shaggers.

Though I'd never tell Joe, he wasn't particularly good at any type of dancing. When we were first married, I suggested taking shag lessons. Joe had informed me that taking dance lessons was on his list of things to do, all right, number eight thousand. Right after learning to knit. I didn't pursue the matter.

Suddenly, I resented Joe, and when the music changed to a slow dance and he led me to the dance floor, I went with a grudge that he didn't even suspect.

"Have you calmed down about your dress?" he asked, sweeping me around. For a man as relaxed as Joe, he tackles a slow dance at a surprisingly fast pace.

"I'll live. I'll try to stay as far away as possible from my twin." Joe didn't seem to notice the clip in my voice. We whisked around until the final chords of "Unchained Melody" died away. "I want to find out how Cynthia Ford has been allowed to show her face here tonight," I complained.

"Bill said she's being reinstated in the club. She's somehow convinced your board that the missing money was all a misunderstanding. I think Bill made a generous donation to the club to help offset tonight's expenses and guarantee they'd get an invitation."

"In other words, she's bought her way back in. If that doesn't take the cake. I'm going to get another glass of wine."

"Don't you think you ought to slow down a little?" Joe gave me a concerned look.

"I'm trying to numb the pain. Why bother with being a good person when evil seems to be rewarded?"

Joe shook his head. "It's hardly the end of the world if Cynthia's at this party." He glanced through the open doors of the adjacent dining room. "Let's at least get some food before you start crying in your beer. The buffet is open."

I decided to let the Cynthia issue go as well as the identical dress debacle. Joe and I joined the line, filling our plates with steamed shrimp, oysters on the half shell, miniature quiches, and sliced fruits and raw vegetables. I found an empty table, and Joe sat beside me after getting a serving of rare London broil at the carving station.

"May I join you?"

I turned my head and looked straight into the innocent brown eyes of the wearer of the matching black wrap dress.

"Sure," I gulped, stifling the impulse to jump up and run. "Have a seat."

"I'm Janet Stokes. I was new at the October meeting." Her Dorothy Hamill haircut bounced as she sat down.

"I remember. You moved here from Richmond to work at the hospital. You're a physical therapist, right? This is my husband, Joe Bulluck."

She and Joe exchanged pleasantries. "My husband is waiting in line at the buffet for another tray of oysters to come out, but I had to sit down. My heels are killing me."

She gave me a tentative smile. "At least we don't have on the same shoes, right? I checked out your footwear after I realized we had on identical dresses. I hope you're not upset. I rushed out during my lunch hour yesterday to Three Sisters and grabbed the first thing that fit."

She lowered her voice and leaned toward me. "Most of these women would be mortified in our situation, but I think it's a hoot. Something about both of us matching makes me feel as though I've pulled a prank on the Narrow Creek Ladies' Society."

I considered Janet Stokes, the physical therapist with the Dorothy Hamill haircut, with new interest. "I hadn't thought of the situation that way, but we are bucking the status quo of designer originals, aren't we?"

A rebel from Richmond. Maybe this was the Ladies' Society friend I'd been looking for.

Chapter 31

First thing Monday afternoon, I dialed the Police Department hotline, which I suspected was actually the department's only number. Again, Chief McSwain himself answered. Didn't the man have a secretary or some kind of deputy to monitor the phone? Shouldn't he have more important business to tend to than catching every call? Apparently not.

"Chief, this is Dee Ann Bulluck. I don't know if you remember me, but I called a few weeks ago concerning the Gary Whitt case with a tip about Cynthia Ford."

"Yes, ma'am, I recall." The Chief switched on his friendly cop voice. "You're the little lady who lives behind the Powells on the top floor of that fancy storage building Floyd built. Never seen anything like it in Narrow Creek. Some folks got more money than sense, I guess. How's that husband of yours doing down at the bank? I've been meaning to stop in and say hello."

Oh, my word! I almost dropped the phone. Would the Chief's meeting Joe involve divulging his acquaintance with me? An acquaintance that consisted of my ratting out Cynthia and possibly Bill Ford? There would be a second murder in Narrow Creek if Joe found out I was still trying to solve the Whitt case, especially since one of my primary suspects was his boss.

"I'm sure he'd enjoy meeting you," I said tentatively. "But I trust you'll keep our conversations between us. I want to talk to you again about the Gary Whitt murder, and Joe doesn't want me to get involved. Please don't tell him I've called with any information."

"Oh sure, sure. All tips are anonymous." The Chief chuckled. "Not that we've had anything worth our time. We've chased more bad leads than Carter has liver pills. You wouldn't believe some of the cockamamie stories I've heard. I could write a book."

"Chief McSwain," I interrupted before he used up all my Heather nap time yammering away, "I think you ought to take another look at Cynthia and Bill Ford. I know you said they had an alibi for the night Gary was murdered, but how strong is it, if you don't mind my asking?" I held my breath, waiting to see whether he'd divulge whatever story the Fords had told him about their whereabouts on the night of the murder.

"They were in Wilmington that night. Gone over there to eat supper," the Chief replied without hesitating. "They showed me a receipt from the Chowder House. Ever been there? They got some of the best softshell crab sandwiches I ever ate."

"Uh, no, I haven't. The receipt, though, Chief McSwain, did it have a date and time on it?"

"I'm sure it did. I can't recall right now. You know, little Missy, you're beginning to sound just like those SBI boys. Check this, check that, they're always saying. They don't trust nobody to tell the truth. Me, I like to think people are being straight with me when I ask 'em something, especially your professional type folks. It's been my experience they ain't the lawbreakers." A slurp on the line made me suspect the Chief had taken a swig of coffee or Pepsi and having a second to speak, I gave it another try.

"I thought the investigation was focusing on ex-girlfriends and possibly the husbands they'd cheated on with Gary. Most of those people are 'professional type folks.' Cynthia Ford also had her drug problem to hide," I added, conveniently forgetting for the moment that piece of information was something Joe had told me in confidence. "She might've thought Gary was going to expose her, being her dealer as well as her boyfriend."

"The SBI decided the love angle was the one to pursue," Chief McSwain said as though he hadn't heard the part about Cynthia possibly killing Gary to hide her drug use. "Personally, I think they're barking up the wrong tree. Since you already know Gary was dealing drugs, I'll let you in on my theory: some drug lord killed him or had him killed. I'll bet the killer ain't even from around here. Gary should've known better than to get mixed up with drug hoodlums. It cost him his life. I do feel sorry for ol' Miz Adams. After all she done for that boy, to have him turn out like that."

I gave up. The SBI was going to solve this crime. I was barking up the wrong tree myself, trying to motivate this man to investigate the Fords. Heck, Gary Whitt had been a known drug dealer, and Chief McSwain had never bothered to gather enough evidence to arrest him.

Besides, I had Christmas to celebrate. "I hope you enjoy the holiday season, Chief. And again, please don't share my calls with anyone, especially my husband."

*****

An Advent Sunday at St. James did a lot to take my mind off the frustrating conversation. Joe sat to my left, and as usual, Elizabeth was on my right. It'd been two weeks since the breakfast at Ernie's Grill. As the organ music swelled, Elizabeth leaned over and whispered, "Our attorney says

Sarah and the baby's father have signed the adoption papers. I think I'm going to be a mother come April."

The last notes of the prelude faded away, and the minister stepped to the pulpit. "This morning, Elizabeth and Benjamin Tucker will come forward to light our Advent candles." Elizabeth smiled at me as she and Benjamin stood up.

Next Christmas, Reverend Shaw will call for the Tucker family, and there'll be a baby with them at the Advent wreath, I thought as Elizabeth began to read the liturgy.

*****

"I've decided to start on the baby's nursery," Elizabeth said as we walked out into the bright winter sunshine after the service. "I want to use lots of blue. I adore blue. We might get a girl, but if I use pale shades, do you suppose that would work for either a boy or a girl?"

I'd picked green and yellow for my layette and baby linens, thinking those colors would work for a Joe Junior as well as a Heather. I really didn't like the idea of a blue room for a girl, but I wasn't going to tell Elizabeth that and rain on her baby room parade.

"Anything you do will be lovely," I said diplomatically.

"I've already written a poem that I'm going to cross-stitch and frame to hang next to the crib. You know how I love to write poetry."

I was only too aware of Elizabeth's poetic nature, having been asked to read several of her heartfelt if somewhat overly sentimental rhymes.

"I'm thinking blue gingham curtains and a dust ruffle and bumper pad to match." Elizabeth grabbed my arm. "And a rocking chair, a changing table, and a small chest of drawers.

I think I can find them at the used furniture store on Baker Street, and Benjamin can paint them white.

"I'm talking your ear off, but I can't help myself. Benjamin can't quit smiling either. Don't tell him I told you, but he goes around the house singing 'Itsy Bitsy Spider' and reciting nursery rhymes. He'll grab me and start waltzing. We feel like newlyweds again." Elizabeth blushed.

Indeed, there's nothing like the prospect of a much-wanted baby to add a big dose of joy to a marriage.

"Here's the verse I've come up with for my cross-stitch project. Looking up at the steeple, she recited, "O child of mine, God's gift to me, Forever in my heart you'll be."

To my knowledge, it was the best poem Elizabeth had ever written.

Chapter 32

The hoopla of Christmas was over, and spring semester 1980 began at Narrow Creek Technical College. Spring semester, my foot, I thought when a rush of cold wind swept my hair in every direction as I was getting out of the car. It might be spring when we finish this term, but it certainly begins in the dead of winter.

I was in a foul mood. I think the toughest day for any teacher is the first day back to school after that extended Christmas vacation. Everyone, students and instructors alike, has the post-holiday blues. In the fall, people are excited about school starting, but after New Year's, the novelty has worn off and it's tough getting back in the routine.

It was certainly hard for me to leave Heather. I'd gotten used to being home with her all the time. With the fun of celebrating her first Christmas and the hustle and bustle of the holidays in general, I hadn't been bored or felt deprived of adult interaction.

Truth be told, I hadn't missed working. Did I really want that full-time position Dr. Adams had mentioned would be available one day? Here I was, gloomy and depressed about leaving Heather three mornings a week. I might want to shoot myself if I had to go to work all day every day.

I put these thoughts out of my mind and went to my eight o'clock class. I'm always a little nervous calling the roll on the first day, trying to match up students with their names. For some reason, people's names just don't stick with me, an occupational handicap for a teacher.

Maybe I needed to use those memory tricks where you associate people's names with something about the way they look or act. A lean girl named Lena, for example, or a guy who blows his nose all the time named Hank, similar to handkerchief.

One name I did learn that day was Jermaine Battle. A slender young black man with a serious expression and a close-cropped haircut, he sat ramrod straight at his desk, his notebook open and his pen poised. I love a student who takes lots of notes when I teach. I could tell by looking at him that he wouldn't be dragging into class late, wanting to borrow a pencil and telling me he'd lost his homework.

I decided to have the students write a page about anything they thought I needed to know about them. The idea was to find out something about their backgrounds and goals and also to get a sample of their writing skills without making a big deal about it.

That night after Heather had gone to sleep and while Joe was watching an old episode of *Dragnet*, I read the eighteen writing samples I'd gathered from Jermaine's class. Some were from recent 1979 high school graduates who were enrolled in the college-transfer program. At the technical college, they could finish their first two years of general college courses while living at home. This saved them a lot of money, along with the tech's tuition being considerably less than it was at a four-year school.

Several middle-aged students had written about how they'd lost their jobs when the fertilizer plant outside of town had closed. I felt sorry for these displaced workers in their forties or fifties who'd labored there for twenty-five or more years but had no retirement benefits and now needed to retrain.

Two Vietnam veterans wrote about coming to school using their GI benefits to advance in their jobs. Neither wrote anything about his war experience, but both stated they'd served in "Nam" back in the late sixties. I remembered Veronica telling me about her Vietnam vet husband when I got my first curly perm at the Kut and Kurl and wondered if these students knew him.

In the middle of the stack, I found Jermaine's paper. He began by saying that he was eighteen years old and lived with his parents. He hoped to be the first in his family to graduate from college, setting a good example for his two younger sisters. His father was a guard on the night shift at the correctional center out on the bypass, and his mother worked in the cafeteria at Narrow Creek High School. Jermaine wrote that he hoped to be a science teacher one day at that same school.

And then there was this: "*I know my parents want a better life for me and my sisters. My grandparents wanted a better life for my parents. That's the way it work in families that loves each other. My granddaddy don't know how to read or write. He work for a man and his wife sorta as their servant, I guess you could say. All he does is what they asks him to do all day. Like take out trash and cut there grass.*

"*I love my granddaddy but I don't want to end up like him. I don't want to be somebodies yard boy. I know I need an education so I can be somebody. I want to be called Mr. Battle at work. My granddaddy has never been called that. The people he work for, they call him Willie.*"

My word, I thought, is Jermaine Willie's grandson? Willie, the handyman at the Powells' house?

We're going to fix that spelling and subject-verb agreement, Mr. Jermaine Battle. And one day, you're going to walk into Narrow Creek High School as the new science teacher. I would remember Jermaine's name all right, without needing any memory trick.

I debated as to what I should write on his paper. Maybe he'd be embarrassed that I knew Willie. Or maybe he'd be pleased that he had a personal connection with his new teacher. In the end, I jotted in the margin, "I think I know your grandfather. I live in the apartment behind the Powells' house."

I returned the writing assignment the next time the class met. At dismissal, Jermaine shyly approached my desk. "Ms. Bulluck, I hope you don't think I'm ashamed of my granddaddy. I was mean, calling him a yard boy. Please don't tell him."

"Jermaine, anything you write for me is confidential," I reassured him. "Unless it's a plot to overthrow the government," I teased.

Jermaine smiled. What a pleasant face he had. Bright, intelligent eyes and a sincere look. He could definitely win over a class of high school students—or anyone. And unlike his grandfather, who'd no doubt been beaten down all his life, Jermaine looked me straight in the eye. Good job, young man.

"I really do want to be a science teacher," Jermaine said. He slung his backpack over one shoulder. "And I'd like to stay right here in Narrow Creek, even though it might be easier to live somewhere up North or out West."

At my quizzical look, he added, "Somewhere I'm not asked to come down to the police station to be questioned about a murder I don't know nothing about. Just because I'm a black man." His face, which had been so pleasant a minute ago, looked like a thundercloud. "You know, Ms. Bulluck, the government of this town might need to be overthrown.

It's 1980 but the folks who run Narrow Creek act like we're still in the days of segregation. Sometimes I think the Civil Rights Movement passed by this town."

I remembered all those months ago when Hazel Hood reported that any black man over the age of twelve had been hauled in to be interrogated about the Gary Whitt murder. Evidently she hadn't been exaggerating.

"Maybe you can run for City Council one day, Jermaine," I replied in my diplomatic teacher voice. "That might be a more moderate approach, don't you think?"

"Yes, ma'am." He paused for a moment, fiddling with the strap of his backpack. "Mama preaches the same thing. 'Be like Dr. King,' she says, 'not Malcolm X.' Dr. King was Baptist, like Mama, and Malcolm X was a Muslim, which Mama thinks is a foreign religion.

"Daddy says I need to be careful about what I say around white people. He's still afraid of the Klan, though they haven't been around Narrow Creek since I've been born. But you have a kind face, Ms. Bulluck, and I'm going to trust you with my truth."

He stood perfectly still, studying my 'kind face,' and I nodded. "I'll be listening. Better yet, write. The power of the pen, you know. And it's my job to inspire you to put words on paper," I added with a smile.

He grinned. "I'll do that. I'm going to take this assignment home and study all the corrections. I want to learn to speak and write good."

"Speak and write well," I corrected.

"Yes, ma'am, speak and write well." Jermaine frowned a little. "English wasn't my best subject in high school," he confessed. "I'm a math and science man. But if I'm going to be a teacher, I got to talk and write correct. You can count on me to do my best."

"And you can count on me to do my best to help you," I declared. How could I not? I felt sure I was looking at the future mayor of Narrow Creek. Or a congressman, maybe a senator. My post-holiday blues lifted and the excitement of teaching returned.

Chapter 33

It was news I didn't need when I went to pick up Heather: Bertha announced she was moving.

"Moving? Where?" I asked, stunned.

"Me and Buddy and the young'uns are going to live close to my mama and daddy in the Brook Valley Trailer Park on the other side of town," said Bertha, clearly distressed. "We can't afford this house no more.

"It's just bills, bills, bills," she added, twisting a tissue. "The young'uns are costing us a fortune, specially Tiffany. That child ain't never seen a pair of shoes she didn't want. And the clothes! She won't wear nothin' unless it's name brand." Bertha glanced at her own dirty Keds with holes in the sides.

"I didn't have nice things when I was growing up, and I've spoilt my two. I was hoping with Bertha's Babies, I could make enough money to stay in this house and buy all that stuff Tiffany and Jimmy want, too. It ain't much, but me and Buddy have always been proud that we was able to own a brick home." Bertha looked around her living room.

"I told the young'uns, they could have their expensive clothes or the house, and do you know, they picked the clothes. I got a real estate lady comin' here tomorrow to tell me what I can git for it." At my stricken expression, she rushed to add, "I still want to keep Heather no matter where I live. Me and Buddy just love that baby to death."

I knew they did indeed love my Heather. After my initial misgivings, I'd been pleased with Bertha's babysitting skills. She'd proved to be very attentive even though, as Joe put it, she was no rocket scientist. And Buddy seemed fond of Heather too, after he got over the shock of Bertha deciding to keep children in their home without even consulting him beforehand.

"I come home from work one Monday," he'd told me, "and there was Tiffany's old baby swing and Jimmy's old crib set up in the living room. I couldn't hardly git to my recliner. What in the world is that woman up to now? I asked myself.

"But it's okay. I'm used to Bertha's big plans. That woman's got an idea a minute. And you know, your Heather puts me in mind of my Tiffany when she was a baby."

Tiffany was thirteen now and, according to Bertha, spent all her time talking on the phone and hanging out at the strip mall. Bertha said the child hardly said hello to Buddy anymore.

Buddy saw Heather when she came on Fridays, the weekday he was home. He put in his forty hours Monday through Thursday working ten-hour days as a flagger for the State Department of Transportation. He liked his job, making people stop for highway work and then waving them on when it was their turn to go. I suspected there was very little else in his life he felt he controlled.

Buddy got paid every Thursday, and then on Friday he and Bertha would load up Heather and go pay bills. I'd said it was okay for them to take Heather with them around town. Buddy didn't drive over thirty-five miles per hour. He said he'd seen too much crazy driving while working on the roads, and thirty-five was plenty fast to go anywhere in Narrow Creek.

Bertha told me they went to the utility company or the telephone company or the bank, wherever a bill was due. She kept up with it all, she said. Buddy didn't have a head for figures. He would sit in the old white Impala with Heather while Bertha dashed in somewhere and settled up.

Buddy once said he could keep Heather from fussing while Bertha was gone if he talked to her. "I told her all about that road work out on Highway 43 South, Dee Ann, and how some young fella in a fast pickup truck 'bout run me down when I turnt the sign from slow to stop. I don't reckon he could read or didn't care none for rules.

"Heather listens good. She looks at me with them big blue eyes—that young'un's got some purty eyes—and I declare, I think she knows just what I'm carryin' on about. I believe she understands how dangerous it is working out there every livelong day for the state. I don't think Bertha does. She don't listen to me like that baby does."

When all the bill paying was finished, the Friday treat was to go to Hardee's for lunch. Buddy said he and Bertha each got a double cheeseburger, a large order of fries, and a chocolate milkshake. Heather was supposed to eat her jar of baby food I'd packed in her diaper bag. Buddy confessed to me, though, that when Bertha went to the bathroom, he'd sometimes feed Heather a spoonful of his milkshake. I told him I didn't mind.

And now they were moving. Just when I'd given up all hope of ever getting my hands on that ten thousand dollar reward for solving the Gary Whitt case, I realized how badly I needed the money. Not so I could quit teaching and stay home with Heather. I liked my job, even with the early mornings and the piles of essays. I was doing important work. My students needed me.

With the reward money, though, I could afford to pay Bertha a little more so she could stay in her house. Or heck, I could just give her a couple of thousand. That ought to keep Tiffany in name-brand clothes long enough for Heather to reach kindergarten age. But that reward money was as far away as the moon.

"Bertha, this is a shock," I said picturing my Heather across town all day in a trailer park. Suddenly, I had an idea that didn't involve the reward money. "I don't mean to pry into your business, but if you found another baby to keep, would you be able to stay in your house?"

"I'd have to sit down and add up my figures before I knowed for sure," Bertha said, "but maybe. Mama and Daddy are real excited about us comin' to live in their mobile home park, but to tell you the truth, I ain't big on the idea." Bertha began to cry a little. "Don't get me wrong; I love 'em and all that, but they can be a lot of work. They don't have no car, so I have to take 'em everywhere they go, and I figure the closer I am, the more they'll want me to drive 'em around."

Bertha dabbed at her eyes with her twisted tissue. "I hate to talk about my own mama and daddy, but they've always been a little mean to poor ol' Buddy. They don't think he's good enough for me. Lord have mercy, they have a fifth-grade education theirselves; neither one of 'em even knows how to write out a check, and they want to talk about Buddy.

"I don't want to live at Brook Valley, but Mama's found this trailer close to her, and if I move anywhere I feel like I got to go there or it would hurt her feelings. But if I figured out my money so's I could stay here, she'd understand that. Even Mama knows that a brick house is better than a trailer."

I agreed with Bertha's mama. "Then we've just got to find you another baby. And I have an idea of who that baby could be."

Chapter 34

It was a bitterly cold January afternoon, and after our Sunday lunch Joe had added more logs to the small flames in our fireplace. Not many apartments come with a real brick fireplace, and I'd enjoyed this feature since winter set in. The hiss and crackle kept me company while I graded essays at the kitchen table. Joe dozed in front of a basketball game on television, and Heather slept sitting in the crook of his arm. When the telephone rang, I jumped to get it.

"Thank God you're home. I don't know what I'm going to do," wailed a female voice.

"Scarlett? What's wrong?" I suspected it was the end of my peaceful afternoon.

"J.T.'s gone crazy, and I had to leave the house." The words came through the receiver so loudly I covered the mouthpiece.

"Where are you?" I tried to speak quietly, thinking maybe Scarlett would too.

"I just checked in at the Holiday Inn out on the bypass," Scarlett managed between sobs. "I didn't even have time to pack a bag. I've never seen J.T. in such a state. He was possessed by something awful. What am I going to do? Where am I going to go?" The questions were followed by hysterical weeping.

I had no idea. "Scarlett, listen to me. Try to settle down. Do you want to come over and talk?"

"Is Joe there?" Scarlett hiccupped between loud sniffles.

On the couch, Joe was now wide awake and studying me with a serious expression. "Yes, he's watching television." I rolled my eyes to let him know no one had died.

"I don't want to see anyone else right now, Dee Ann." Scarlett sounded desperate. "Can you come to the Holiday Inn? I'm in Room 210."

Going out on a cold afternoon to find Room 210 at the Holiday Inn was about the last thing in the world I wanted to do, but Scarlett had turned to me for help. "Okay. Give me a few minutes."

"What's wrong?" Joe whispered the minute I hung up. He eased up from the couch with the still-sleeping Heather on his shoulder. "Who was that?"

"Scarlett. She's been kicked out of the house. My bet is J.T. has finally heard some of the gossip that's always out there. It sounds like the day of reckoning has arrived."

*****

A puffy-eyed Scarlett answered Door 210 at the Holiday Inn. "You're finally here," she cried. "I'm going out of my mind sitting in this room by myself."

She lay back on a double bed made up with a green and yellow floral comforter and stared at the gray ceiling tiles. I sat in the room's black faux leather chair. "Okay, I'm ready to hear it when you're ready to talk about it."

Scarlett turned on her side and closed her eyes. "The argument actually started this morning. J.T. decided to skip church, for once, and then he remembered he hadn't checked the mailbox on Saturday. He went out, came in with Saturday's mail, and went in the library with it. A few minutes later he came storming into the bedroom, where I was going through my closet and pulling out old clothes to give to Ida.

Out of the blue, J.T. started accusing me of having an affair with this guy who built our pool house last spring."

"Scarlett, sit up and look at me," I said rather sternly. "Is it true?"

She scooted up against the bed's headboard and met my eyes. "No, I swear." Her gaze returned to the ceiling tiles. "You and I've been over this before. Yes, I flirted with the guy. I couldn't help myself. He was a young, good-looking contractor, lean and tanned. But you know my policy; flirting is it."

An alarm went off in my head. "Who was the man?"

"Why does that matter? I told you, nothing happened."

"Then why is J.T. suddenly upset about a guy who worked for y'all last spring? Exactly what did he say?" I was trying hard not to sound like a prosecutor grilling a defendant on the witness stand. But I really did want the truth, the whole truth, and nothing but the truth.

Scarlett shifted her eyes from the ceiling to the one window of the motel room, which framed a mostly empty parking lot. "I don't know why J.T. got such a bee in his bonnet all of a sudden. The entire morning, he hammered away at me with questions. How could I have done such a thing? Did I think he was a fool? Didn't I care about our marriage? Didn't I care about John Thomas? By noon he'd worked himself into such a rage, I was afraid to stay in the house any longer. He was throwing my clothes out of the closet and screaming at me to get out. I was so unnerved I didn't even pack a thing. I just grabbed my purse and left." Scarlett's eyes filled with tears as she hugged the motel room pillow.

"Where is John Thomas?" I asked, on the verge of tears myself. Had the child witnessed this ugly scene?

Scarlett reached for a wad of toilet paper and blotted her eyes. "He's spending the weekend with J.T.'s mother. She has this big sleepover ever so often where all the cousins get together. He'll be coming home this afternoon, though, and wondering where his mama is." Her voice was strangled. "J.T. said he'd make sure he got full custody of John Thomas, and I'd see as little of my child as possible." She flung the toilet paper aside and began weeping hysterically.

I couldn't imagine too much worse in this world than having Heather taken away. "What can I do?" I was shivering, and one of my legs was jumping up and down in a nervous rhythm.

Scarlett suddenly quit sobbing, scooted to the bottom of the bed, and took both my hands in hers. "Could you get Joe to go talk some sense into J.T.? He respects Joe. He's so angry with me right now he won't listen to anything I have to say. Maybe Joe can find out what set him off this morning."

I withdrew my hands. "I doubt Joe wants to get involved," I said firmly. "He wasn't too crazy about my coming over here to see you."

It was the truth. Although Joe had encouraged me to continue being Scarlett's friend and have that frank discussion with her about cleaning up her cheating act, he'd told me before I left for the Holiday Inn that I was stepping into something I shouldn't. "If the cat's finally out of the bag," he'd said, "Scarlett and J.T. need to be the ones dealing with it."

Seeing her stricken expression, though, I softened. "Let me work on Joe. I'll try to get him to talk to J.T. this afternoon. Maybe we can get you home by the time John Thomas gets back. And Scarlett," I added with a no-nonsense expression, "I hope you've learned a lesson from this mess. You need to save the flirting for just J.T."

*****

When I got home, Joe and Heather were on the living room floor, stacking plastic blocks. As I'd expected, Joe's sunny face clouded over the minute I asked him to intercede.

"Guys are different from women," he said, nervously juggling a block from one hand to the other. "Men don't like to spill their guts about their personal lives. What's going on between Scarlett and J.T. is none of my business. I'd feel uncomfortable asking him why he thinks his wife is cheating on him."

The pile of stacked blocks crashed to the floor and Heather squealed, looking at me to see if I thought tumbling blocks were funny. I picked her up and hugged her.

"Normally I'd agree with you, but we've been asked to interfere. Scarlett is sitting in a motel room this minute without so much as a toothbrush. J.T. was in such a rage she left home with only the clothes on her back."

Joe stood and began bouncing on the balls of his feet, a sure sign of anxiety, but I had no choice but to push him to help. "She's waiting for you to find out what's wrong with J.T. Her son is coming home from his grandmother's house this afternoon, and Scarlett wants to be there."

Heather started squirming in my arms, and I put her on the floor. "Can't you at least call him? Despite what you say about men keeping their problems to themselves, he may need a friend right now."

Joe sighed in resignation. "This isn't a conversation for the telephone. I'll go see him, but only because you've asked me to and because I consider him a friend. I'm not going for that crazy Scarlett's sake, and I'm not asking him any nosy questions either. He can just tell me what he wants to.

"And you, Miss Busybody, are going too," Joe said, pointing at me. "He may not let his wife come home today, and if that's the situation, you can pack her a suitcase so we don't have to make another trip out there tonight."

I didn't want to go see J.T. either, but I knew better than to say so. "Maybe Miss Josie can keep Heather for a couple of hours. I'd rather she stay here than be a part of all this.

And Joe, thank you for going. I really think we're doing the Christian thing here."

I hoped we were doing the Christian thing even though right offhand, I couldn't think of a single example from the Bible where Jesus got involved in a marital spat.

Chapter 35

The Hoods' house was dark and quiet in the late afternoon shadows. Joe and I stood shivering on the front porch as the doorbell echoed inside. "He may have gone to pick up John Thomas," I said. "I didn't think about his not being home. But I smell smoke, so maybe he's inside with the fireplace going."

Before Joe could reply, the door opened a crack and a disheveled J.T. peered around the edge. "Scarlett's not here, Dee Ann," he slurred. "Hey, buddy," he said to Joe.

"J.T., we know Scarlett's not here," Joe said. "Dee Ann talked to her this afternoon. She asked that I come see you. It's up to you, man, whether you want to talk."

J.T. opened the door wider and stood back for us to enter. I smelled sweat and bourbon. Day-old stubble covered his face. He wore wrinkled khakis and an undershirt with what appeared to be a soot stain on the front. He was still a handsome man but looked as if he'd aged ten years since I'd last seen him.

"It's bad, Joe. It's really bad." He ran his hands through his dark hair and squinted at Joe with bloodshot eyes. "People warned me for years that she was running around, but I never believed 'em. Didn't wanna believe 'em. Then I saw it for myself. And took care of it, or thought I did." J.T.'s slurred voice was growing louder and louder.

"But it won't go away." J.T. was close to wailing. "I did it for her. I thought she'd see how much I loved her and straighten up." Giving us a desperate look, he groaned and then dug at his eyes with balled fists.

"Y'all come on in the libr'y and sit down," he said in a now eerily calm voice. "Let me show you what I got in the mail. Just let me show you what I got, and then tell me what to do."

J.T. was weaving as he led the way to the library.

"I'm here to help you, buddy," Joe said, "not to pry into your personal business. You don't have to show me anything. You don't have to tell me anything, either. We'll leave, and Scarlett can come home and talk about whatever you got in the mail."

"Hell no. I don't ever wanna see that woman again!" J.T. exploded. "I'll kill her if she comes in this house."

I gasped, and J.T. looked around as if he suddenly remembered I was there. "I'm sorry, Dee Ann. I shouldn't talk that way in front of you."

"Go pack some of Scarlett's things while I speak to J.T. alone," Joe told me. Evidently he suspected, as I did, that Scarlett wouldn't be coming home that day, if ever.

"I dunno what you'll find," J.T. mumbled. "I burned a bunch of her stuff. Made a big fire in the backyard and threw all her clothes and shoes on it. Even burned those new clothes she brought home on Friday. Still had tags on 'em." J.T. collapsed onto his massive leather chair at the desk.

"Go on, Dee Ann. See what you can find to pack," Joe said, not taking his eyes off J.T. "I'll call for you when we're through talking." Joe eased himself down in the chair on the other side of J.T.'s desk.

I closed the door behind me and put my ear to it.

"J.T., I know you're in pain, but you're not the first man to have a wife step out on him. It probably seems like the end of the world right now, but you'll pull through," I heard Joe say.

"I wish you were right, Joe. But you don't know the whole story." A drawer opened, paper rustled, and then J.T. said in a choking voice, "I'm being blackmailed. The sonna of a bitch says if I don't pay him fifty thousand dollars, he's gonna tell Roger McSwain."

"Adultery is bad, J.T., but it's not against the law. Why does somebody think you'll pay him off not to contact the Chief?"

"He's not gonna report Scarlett; he's gonna turn me in. Somebody knows what I did." There was a long minute where no one said a thing, and then J.T. confessed.

"I killed Gary Whitt. I went to his apartment and shot him five times, right in his pretty boy face. Used that Colt 38 Special I showed you the time you and Dee Ann came for dinner.

"I knew he was having an affair with Scarlett. I saw her flirting with him when he built our pool house. When she started coming up with reasons for staying out late, I followed her one night. I won't ever forget what I saw through an open blind. I should have gone in right then and there and killed both of 'em." J.T.'s hysterical voice softened a little. "But she's the mother of my son."

My knees buckled, and I slid to the floor on my side of the library door. I wasn't on the road to Damascus, but the scales fell from my eyes and like Saul, I was no longer blind. Of course. Why had I not suspected J.T. Hood, a man who had an arsenal right there in the very room where he was confessing to my husband?

Suddenly, I feared for Joe. J.T. was drunk and unhinged. Suppose he regretted telling Joe and decided to kill him too? And then come for me? I needed to get to a phone fast.

Before I could pull myself together, though, Joe's calm, steady voice reassured J.T. "You don't have to be blackmailed. Call Chief McSwain yourself and explain what happened. Don't you think that's the best thing to do?"

I heard loud sobs and then J.T.'s choked answer, "Can you place the call for me, Joe? You getting that ten thousand dollar reward is about the only good thing that would come out of this whole sorry mess."

"Dial the Chief, Joe!" I wanted to shout. "I agree with J.T.!" I forgot all about our being J.T.'s next victims as I sent Joe mental telepathy.

"I'll dial the number, J.T., but you're man enough to talk to the Chief yourself," Joe replied. "We'll let Gary's grandmother keep her ten thousand dollars."

Speak for yourself, Joe. I started to open the door and dive for the phone but heard Joe ask an operator for the number of the Narrow Creek Police Department, a number I had called on two fruitless occasions. Joe must have handed the phone to J.T., who said in a robotic voice, "Roger, you'd better come out and get me. I'm the one who killed Gary Whitt." There was a silence and then J.T. added, "I'll tell you more when you get here. Yeah, my house. Don't bust down the door or bring the SBI. I won't give you any trouble."

Ten thousand dollars vanished. Why was I married to the most moral man on earth? How could Joe let that reward money slip away?

Because he was walking the walk, I reminded myself. Joe was doing the Christian thing by not taking advantage of the situation and collecting what now was beginning to feel like blood money.

I tiptoed away from the door. As is often the case in times of tragedy, the business of life continued. Joe had told me to pack Scarlett some clothes. In the master bedroom closet, one side was completely empty. In an antique chifforobe, I found

Scarlett's underclothes, nightgowns, jeans, and sweaters. I grabbed what I could and stuffed everything in a laundry basket.

I flew to the adjoining bathroom for a toothbrush and makeup. Searching in a drawer, I uncovered Scarlett's engraved lipstick case, the one with the hearts and the initials "TB" and "S."

Something clicked. What was Mrs. Adams' nickname for her precious grandson? Teddy Bear. Evidently he'd shared that pet name with his lover. "TB" and "S." Teddy Bear and Scarlett.

I heard Joe calling me.

"I've got what I could find," I said, meeting him at the library door. J.T. was slumped forward in the chair, his face planted on the desk, fingers laced on the back of his head. I was glad to see those hands weren't holding a gun.

Joe looked as shell-shocked as I felt. "We're going to stay with J.T. until Chief McSwain arrives," he said quietly. "I'll explain everything later."

"I know," I whispered back. "I was listening at the door."

The Chief must have driven those 15.2 miles from town to the Hoods' house at record speed as he arrived in under thirteen minutes. I was never so relieved to see law enforcement: a skinny Barney Fife sergeant and Chief McSwain himself, an overweight fiftyish fellow sporting a salt and pepper Burt Reynolds mustache.

We might've had a drunk murderer in the room, but J.T. still had manners. He lifted his head and struggled to his feet. "Joe, Dee Ann, this is Chief Roger McSwain and Sergeant Andy Jones. Roger and Andy, this is Joe Bulluck and his wife, Dee Ann. Scarlett asked them to come out and check on me today." He spoke as calmly as if he had the flu and we'd brought chicken soup.

His social duties fulfilled, J.T. fell back into his chair while everybody else shook hands. "Sorry to meet you under such circumstances," the Chief said. "You're the new man down at the bank, aren't you? Nice to meet you too, Miz Bulluck."

I thought I saw a twinkle in the Chief's eye as he pretended we'd never talked on the phone. Or maybe the man really had forgotten my two crazy calls with bogus leads. Or maybe he didn't count phone conversations as having officially met someone. In any event, he hadn't ratted me out to Joe. More pressing matters were at hand.

"So, J.T., what the hell?" the Chief said, sitting in the chair in front of the desk. Looking ill at ease, Sergeant Jones stood behind him.

"It's like I said on the phone, Roger. I did it. I'm the one who shot Gary Whitt. I found out he was running around with Scarlett."

The Chief cleared his throat and sat up straighter in his chair. "Don't say no more, J.T. I need to read you your rights, and then you'll want to call your lawyer to meet you down at the station. I'm gonna have to take you in. You know I hate to do it." The Chief glanced at Joe and me. "You folks can go on home now. I'll be in touch if I need to ask you any questions."

Joe and I eased out the door as the Chief began to recite: "You have the right to remain silent. Anything you say can and will be used against you in a court of law...." I walked past the basket of clothes and toiletries I'd collected for Scarlett. Since J.T. was under arrest, she could come home. I dreaded the phone call I would need to make informing her of J.T.'s confession. But maybe she already knew, or at least suspected, that her husband had killed her lover.

Outside, the weak afternoon sun was setting as Joe pointed out a thin plume of smoke rising from the backyard. "That's the smoke we smelled."

I nodded. Scarlett's clothes going up in smoke was the least of it.

Chapter 36

The forsythia was beginning to bloom, and the first daffodils of the season had burst forth in a happy riot of bright yellow. The blue jays and mourning doves were flitting around Miss Josie's bird feeders, back from their winter in Florida. I stood ironing and occasionally gazed out the window at the fine day unfolding.

Joe came around the corner holding Heather's chubby finger as she took tiny, wobbly steps. My baby girl had started walking. "We're going to Ace Hardware, Mommy," he said. "Anything you need while we're out?"

"Nothing at all," I replied, smiling at my two favorite people. Joe picked up Heather at the door, and I heard his steps on the stairs.

It'd been almost a year since we'd moved to Narrow Creek. "God's in His heaven and all's right with the world," I murmured.

Actually, all was not right, but I'd reconciled myself to matters I couldn't change. J.T. was out of jail on a two hundred thousand dollar bail, living at home and preparing with Ray Williams for his trial, the date of which had yet to be announced.

"If there's any attorney in town who can get a man out of a murder charge, it's Ray Williams," Joe'd said. Remembering how the lawyer had helped Cynthia with her drug bust problem, I agreed.

In fact, in more than one late night drunken phone call to Joe, J.T. blabbed that Ray Williams was going to have him plead temporary insanity combined with the North Carolina Alienation of Affection Law.

"The North Carolina Alienation of Affection Law? How does that work?" I'd asked Joe.

Apparently the law allows someone to sue an individual who's caused a married person to lose the love, or affection, of his or her spouse.

"Suing is one thing, Joe. J.T. blew the man away."

"I agree it's a stretch," Joe'd responded, "but we live in a conservative small town, and J.T. is a prominent local landowner with a crackerjack attorney. Temporary insanity plus this law might be the trick. I wouldn't be surprised if he at least got a reduced charge of manslaughter. Heck, he may not even see jail time."

Joe thought the blackmailer, who turned out to be, of all people, an SBI agent, was probably in more trouble than J.T. "He claims he was setting up a sting operation to see if J.T. would pay the money, and in doing so, prove his guilt," Joe said, "but the problem is the agent failed to inform any of his colleagues of his plan. Sounds like he discovered J.T. killed Gary Whitt and decided to pad his salary with a blackmail bonus."

Yep, people hate a crooked cop, a lot more than a deceived husband who reached his breaking point.

Once J.T. was released on bail, a scant twenty-four hours after being arrested, and returned home, Scarlett moved out. She was in an apartment, living off her teacher salary with partial custody of John Thomas and a generous allowance J.T. gave her for child support.

"He always paid for everything," she'd told me, "even the house, so my name was never on anything we owned. He said I didn't need to worry, that it was a man's job to take care of his wife. Now I don't own a thing, and J.T. won't give me any money other than what he says is for John Thomas. He's punishing me, I guess. Oh well, I'll skim off that child support and wait for J.T. to come to his senses. He'll want me back. If nothing else, he misses having his son around all the time."

In a rare moment of truthfulness about her extramarital behavior, Scarlett had admitted her part in causing Gary Whitt's death. "I didn't know J.T. could be violent, Dee Ann. I never saw that side of him. I didn't think he even cared enough about me to be upset if I saw other men. I guess I was wrong."

Boy, was she ever.

She'd apologized for lying to me about her infidelities— yes, there had been other men over the years, she finally confessed, including the book salesman at the conference. "I'm not proud of what I've done," she said, "and I realize the pain I've caused. Even though he annoyed me a lot of the time, I did love J.T. in my own way. But I guess I loved the thrill of meeting new men more."

When I considered the Hoods' situation, I thought of Tom and Daisy Buchanan, the wealthy couple in Fitzgerald's *The Great Gatsby*, who carelessly wrought havoc in people's lives and then blithely went on their way, leaving others to clean up their mess.

I, for one, was through being involved in the disaster J.T. and Scarlett had brought on themselves. I'd started distancing myself from her since that Sunday afternoon when Joe and I had gone to see J.T. and learned the truth. I realized then I'd never really known the woman I'd considered a good friend.

But if I'd lost one friend in Narrow Creek, I'd gained another. I liked Janet Stokes, my Christmas party twin. Since our matching dresses episode, we'd gabbed on the phone and gone to the movies. She liked to read as much as I did, and we'd formed a two-woman book club, swapping novels.

Janet had talked me into reading Stephen King's *The Shining* and though I was thoroughly creeped out by it, I did plan on seeing the movie with her just as soon as it came to Narrow Creek. I've always loved anything starring Jack Nicholson. In return, I'd encouraged her to read *Sophie's Choice*, which had me in tears several times before I finished. She said if that book was ever made into a movie, we definitely should go.

In true Narrow Creek fashion, I'd invited her to church, but she politely declined. She and her husband Roger were Episcopalians and had already joined the small congregation of St. Andrews. Still, Joe became better acquainted with Roger through Rotary Club, and finding out he enjoyed hunting and fishing, added Roger to his list of sports buddies.

Janet had confided that she and Roger wanted to start a family as soon as they felt settled in Narrow Creek, and they both adored my Heather, which, of course, made me like them even more.

My thoughts this morning turned to Elizabeth. In just a week or so, she and Benjamin would bring home their baby. Benjamin's cousin's daughter was due any day. The telephone rang, and I put down the iron.

"Elizabeth," I said, recognizing her voice, "I was just thinking about you. Are you excited?"

"You don't know the half of it, honey," a breathless Elizabeth said. "Can I drop by for a minute? I've got big news."

I felt a stab of anxiety. "Is everything all right?"

"Nothing's wrong, you worrywart. In fact, everything is absolutely, positively terrific. Are you going to be home for the next half hour? I want to tell you in person."

"Sure. Come on by. Joe and Heather have gone to Ace Hardware, and I'm just ironing and listening to the birds sing."

"I'll be there in ten minutes. Don't move," Elizabeth said.

That baby's been born and she wants to see my face when she tells me. I was hanging up Joe's last dress shirt and preparing to put away the ironing board when I heard Elizabeth's car in the driveway.

I waved her into the living room. "So what's the big news?" I asked, expecting to hear about the birth of a baby. Elizabeth was flushed with excitement, a huge smile creasing her chubby cheeks.

"You're not going to believe this. When it rains, it pours, and sometimes that's a good thing. I haven't been feeling the best in the world for the last couple of weeks, so I went to see Dr. Whitaker."

"You're pregnant!" I squealed.

"I'm pregnant." She squealed back. Elizabeth grabbed my arms and jumped up and down in excitement. "I'll have two babies within a year, one this month and another in December. An Easter baby and a Christmas baby. It's an absolute miracle. God has answered my prayers in abundance."

"Bertha's Babies will have not just one, but two new customers," I said, laughing.

"You know, Dee Ann, I'm absolutely the happiest woman in the world."

And so am I, I realized. And so am I.

Note to Readers

I hope you enjoyed *Ms. Dee Ann Meets Murder*. If so, please do one or both of the following:

- Tell your friends to read the book (but let them buy their own copy!).
- Post a review on Amazon.com. It's easy. Simply find *Ms. Dee Ann Meets Murder*, click on the title, click on customer reviews, and then click *Write a customer review* to add your two cents' worth.

Pending positive response, I'll release my sequel, *Life and Death in Narrow Creek*, which picks up the story of Dee Ann and her cast of friends, neighbors, and nemeses three years later when there is yet another death that Dee Ann feels compelled to investigate.

Discussion Questions

1. The story takes place from spring of 1979 to spring of 1980. What cultural and political references indicative of this time are sprinkled throughout the novel?

2. Discuss the significance of the juxtaposition of two very different quotes in the preface, one from Proverbs and one from Gloria Steinem.

3. Although Dee Ann is college-educated, she still retains her down-to-earth Southern voice. Why do you think the author portrays her this way?

4. Dee Ann is caught in a struggle between being a stay-at-home mother to her baby daughter and pursuing a career. What mixed messages does she get from society about these two roles?

5. Dee Ann encounters sexism in the workplace in her relationship with her dean of instruction. How does she deal with this? How does her friend Scarlett handle Dr. Adams' chauvinistic behavior?

6. Why does Cynthia Ford, the wife of Joe's boss, belittle Dee Ann? What does her behavior say about the way women often treat one another?

7. How does Dee Ann's first impression of Miss Josie change? Of Scarlett?

8. Are Bertha and Buddy Joyner in the novel purely for comic relief, or are there lessons to be learned from these characters?

9. How do the black characters in the novel portray the complexity of race relations in the South in 1979?

10. Were you surprised to learn the murderer's identity, or were you fooled by the "red herrings" in the story?

About the Author

Patsy Pridgen is a lifelong resident of Eastern North Carolina, where she has absorbed the culture and dialects of this distinct part of the state. Married to her high school sweetheart since the Carter administration, she is a mother of three and grandmother of five. Patsy taught English in the community college for 27 years, handing in her red pen the semester she turned 60, the magical age when state employees with her time served qualify for a retirement check.

Patsy blogs at *www.patsypridgen.com*, where she comments on everything from being stuck in an Italian parking garage to planting cucumbers and squash in her shrub beds. *Ms. Dee Ann Meets Murder* is her debut novel.